The Panhandle Picasso

Kendra Hoey

Kendra Hoey Novels, LLC

Publisher: Kendra Hoey Novels, LLC

Editor: Elizabeth A. White

Cover Design: Brailey Hoey

Brailey Elisha Designs, LLC (Instagram @artbybrailey) (TikTok @brailey55)

Follow on Instagram @panhandlemysteryseries

www.kendrahoeynovels.com

30A Retail Locations and Book Signings Events

Author Book Club Requests

Praise for

The Panhandle Picasso

"Retired businesswoman turned citizen detective, Trina Scotsdale finds herself investigating the death of a well-known local artist everyone had a reason to want dead. Following her gut instincts and keen attention to detail, Trina works to unravel the mystery. It's a whodunit with twists that keeps you guessing from the first chapter to the very end. If you enjoyed *The Panhandle Predicament*, you will not be disappointed in *The Panhandle Picasso*." ~ LR

"I was hooked from the first chapter. Trina once again magically blends in with the locals to get to the bottom of an untimely death. The captivating story delivered exactly what I was looking for: lost love, interesting plot twists, and familiar places on or near 30A. This book will not disappoint." ~ CW

"Brushstrokes of romance and mystery collide in this beachside page turner. The Panhandle Picasso takes you on an adventure through the 30A art world and 30A lives and quaint seaside villages." ~ AW

For those touched, inspired, and hugged by art.

Content Advisory

Though the names of some businesses, organizations, events, and individuals have been incorporated to enhance the fictional plot, none of the storylines, characterizations, conversations, or actions are meant to represent the beliefs of those businesses, organizations, events, or individuals.

This book includes scenes involving alcohol addiction, domestic abuse, and homelessness.

My Partners in "Crime"

Thank you for supporting me on my writing journey.

My readers – A warm prideful embrace that pushed me forward

30A Community – Unwavering support for a debut author

Lynn, Colleen, & Allison – An eye for missing ingredients

Emerald Coast Storytellers – Inclusion and Inspiration

My artistic collaborator, Brailey – Creative branding dedication

My cover model, Cori – Perfect tattoos

My family – Belief, pride, and love

Thank you for believing in me.
Until next time .....

Table of Contents

A Joy Ride

Chapter One

Present Day

Her instincts were stirring. A well-known artist from the coveted 30A Panhandle of Florida was dead. As soon as she'd heard, that rumbling in her gut started. Maybe she was simply letting her ego take the driver's seat after Detective Trent's compliment earlier that day. At least she thought it had been a compliment. The reality was she was blatantly guessing, but Trina didn't think the sculptor had died accidentally. Something didn't feel right, and that's why Detective Trent had asked her to come to the crime scene.

Maybe it was the incessant chatter from the standing-room only mob of gawkers. Or the lack of true sadness floating above the group like a rain cloud waiting to burst. Silently observing the crowd, Trina felt like she was witnessing a casting call of actors practicing emotional devastation. The tears drowning the hodgepodge of artists seemed legitimate, but were they crying over his death or the cancellation of today's art installation?

No, that wasn't it. It was something she'd heard when she first walked in. She didn't know who amongst the crowd of forty or so had said it, but she'd heard it clear as day:

"Killed by his own creation. If that's not genius, I don't know what is. His art is going to be worth millions."

She knew absolutely nothing, yet she knew something was off. Someone had killed Ian Scott.

Today was the day Ian's sculpture and three other handpicked artists' pieces were scheduled to be carried on a barge from Destin to the beautiful, clear waters of Grayton Beach to be purposefully placed in the Gulf of Mexico's Underwater Museum of Art (UMA). The Cultural Arts Alliance, in conjunction with the South Walton Artificial Reef Association, created the UMA in 2018. The sixth annual installation of one-of-a-kind sculptures to support and stabilize marine habitat with eco-friendly artwork was scheduled for 11:00 a.m. Unfortunately, the devasting discovery of Ian's untimely death had indefinitely postponed the event.

Trina stood on the gravel driveway in front of the Artists Warehouse of South Walton on Route 393 behind the growing cluster of police cars, television vans, yellow police tape and patrol officers. Wearing a light-blue T-shirt, an athletic skirt, and a pair of walking sneakers, she stood silently and effortlessly blended in. While others wrapped their arms around one another and tissues miraculously materialized, Trina was in Sherlock Holmes mode. She was assessing body language that didn't match communication. Skittish eye contact. Exaggerated levels of sorrow. Masked signs of anger. Hidden signs of satisfaction. As her eyes darted from person to person, she eavesdropped and observed.

She knew she looked like the rest of the nosy neighbors, and once that realization hit her, she understood. Her methods of discovery were simple. Immersion. As a resident in the serene vacation town of Blue Mountain Beach, Florida, part of the nationally recognized 30A communities, Trina simply lived her life as a Local. Conversations happened. Tidbits of seemingly meaningless information slipped through the cracks. Being in the right place at the right time had its benefits. Over the last few months, she had successfully uncovered evidence that helped the local police close a case. And now, though Detective Trent had not come out and said it to her directly, she didn't think he'd asked her to come along to give her a joy ride.

He knew she had the potential to be useful in this investigation. She had effortlessly bonded with "OG" 30A locals who lived on the twenty-six-mile stretch of pristine beach and proven she had the ability to camouflage herself amongst them. As a retired businesswoman, she had generated rapport working alongside an endless stream of volunteers at monthly cultural events and charitable organizations. As a part-time employee at a local gift shop, she interacted with visitors from all over the country, while also developing loyal relationships with local shoppers. Her secret weapon was literally the best source of information in any community—other women. Trina could learn things the police couldn't by simply hanging out with friends and her community.

Trina wasn't naive, though. There were hundreds of local residents who could say the same thing, and Trina was not a detective. Her only claim to sleuthing was that she possessed quirky, obsessive-compulsive behaviors like the character on the show *Monk*. In particular, her compulsion to not leave evidence of her own presence made her keenly aware of outliers—the Waldo in a room of red, blue, and white. She had an eye for seeing what others didn't. What did Detective Trenton Oliver hope she observed today?

A piece of art obviously could not be guilty of murder, so who in this crowd could be? Ignoring the reporters and the police, Trina quickly categorized the crowd:

Pry-ers — Serving a five-course meal to their own selfish curiosity.

Criers — Sharing sorrow with others but thankful it didn't happen to them.

Storm chasers — Creating (versus collecting) facts to capture social media worthy pictures.

Connivers — Planning ways to replace Ian Scott in the art community.

Show Must Go Oners — Analyzing obstacles and identifying opportunities.

Who had a motive? Opportunity? Was anyone jealous of Ian's new-found fame? Or maybe it was an accident. Trina's mind was spinning.

She really had no business being here, but that feeling in her gut told her she should.

The Girl with the Dolphin Tattoos

Chapter Two

Present Day

A hush settled over the crowd as a tall, striking woman stepped out of the driver's seat of a beat-up Land Rover. Her dark-black hair was accentuated by a streak of vibrant blue. She wore a basic black tank top that accentuated the fact she was in her final trimester and revealed tattoos canvassing her arms and neck. Silver jewelry decorated her wrists and fingers, and hand-drawn inked images popped off the fabric of her elaborate jeans. She walked to the back of the car, popped the trunk covered in car decals and reached in. As she stretched to grab a well-aged leather messenger bag, her top rode up revealing the massive tattoos decorating her torso—two dolphins. The dolphin inked on her chest met the dolphin on her back by curving around her shoulders and neck, meeting at the edge of her hairline. Even a quick glimpse of her tattoos revealed the quality of the incredible craftmanship. A slow murmur from the crowd began to spread.

"It's Rachel Fairfield."

"It's the Girl with the Dolphin Tattoos."

Rachel walked around to the passenger side, opening the door to let someone out. The younger man smiled and gave her a hug, then accepted the bag from her. They were greeted by a policewoman, who walked them into an art studio adjacent to Ian's. The man walked with a slight but experienced limp of someone who had learned to cope.

Santa Rosa Beach was a relatively small town. Although thousands of visitors flocked to the snow-white covered beaches every year, less than twenty-five thousand people claimed residency, of which, half spent only the off-season in Florida, avoiding the high traffic summer season. Within months of living in the intimate community, the average 30A Local would have checked out at the grocery store, sat at the bar, or attended an entertainment event next to or with at least 70% of the resident population. As with any small town, it came with both benefits and hidden secrets. Knowing there was always someone there to have your back was a comforting feeling but knowing everyone was watching your back elicited another one entirely.

Trina, like most of the community, knew Rachel because Rachel's mother, Lily, operated the Beach-N-Bagels Café in Dune Allen Beach. The café was a small diner on the west end of town that catered mostly to residents, providing quick breakfasts and grab-n-go meals. In addition, Lily and Trina were part of a small ladies group who got together once a month for "Whine Night" to drink wine and share life's challenges. Whine Night started eight years ago after Lily's only son experienced a life-altering trauma, the result of a golf cart accident. Lily was already struggling to operate the café as a divorced woman with two children, but when her son, Rodney, required months of physical and speech therapy, the community came together to become Lily's "It Takes a Village" support system. Whine Night was a fun way to provide her with one night a month of uninhabited stress relief.

Rachel had been forced to grow up quickly, as circumstances demanded she step up financially and emotionally to help support her family while still trying to find her own way. Working as a professional tattoo artist, Rachel poured herself into each design. Customers from all over the country secured appointments with her at Mercy Tattoo Studio in Miramar Beach. Lily didn't love Rachel's goth sense of style, but she understood the reason behind the dolphin tattoos. Dolphins symbolized protection, and Rachel wanted to show Rodney after his accident she would always be there to watch over him.

Trina wasn't surprised to hear the admiration from the crowd since Rachel was well known for her ink designs, but Trina had forgotten Ian Scott was Rachel's boyfriend. Another gut punch for Lily's family. Trina was motivated more than ever to dive in and help Detective Trent investigate Ian's unexpected death. With that thought, the realization dawned on her that she was standing outside an active crime scene. For the second time that year, she was standing close enough to criminal activity she could almost smell the sweat and adrenaline evaporating off the investigation team and concerned citizens. She wasn't sure what was transpiring inside, but outside, the nervous energy between spectators was seamlessly transferring like the tap of an Apple iPhone sharing pictures.

If his death seemed suspicious, the police would be looking for a suspect. Was there an undercover officer mingling in the crowd making observations? Instinctively, she calculated what she had done, where she had walked, and who she had talked to since arriving. Was she being recorded right now? Would they review the videos to see who showed up at the crime scene to relish in the attention the death had generated?

How many of her hair follicles had drifted off her shoulder toward the entrance to the bloody studio?

Concentrate, Trina. You did not murder Ian. The detectives are not monitoring your actions. You should not—cannot—let your over-obsessive tendencies distract you from helping Lily and supporting Rachel. Don't worry that you touched the inside of Detective Trent's government-issued vehicle. Who cares if you forgot to wipe the rim of the Bloody Mary glass at lunch. Nobody is going to see the skin you scratched off after the mosquito bit you. Ian's family needs you to focus. Even if Trent doesn't end up relying on you for information, you can still become a strong support system for the Fairfields. Poor Lily doesn't have time in her busy life to figure this out.

Imagining the crime scene, Trina refocused. Ian was killed, somehow, by his own art. What would the inside of the art studio look like after a crime had been committed? Trina visualized neon green and blue painted handprints marking the path of a potential murderer. Instead of red blood dripping from Ian's throat, Trina was picturing thick red paint oozing down onto a sharply pointed paintbrush. An elaborate collage hung on the wall with two knife slashes through the center.

Oh Trina, you have definitely been watching too many TV shows. Murder is never that colorful. If someone wanted an artist dead, they would have been smart enough to wear blue booties on their shoes so they wouldn't track painted footprints to their getaway vehicle. Think simpler. Think accidental. How could someone make his death look like Ian was a fumbling idiot?

Realizing she is missing an opportunity to pry, Trina searched her bag for a clean tissue and walked up to a group of artists standing together at the entrance to another nearby studio.

"It looks like you could use a fresh tissue." Trina handed the most emotional one a tissue and rested a hand gently on her wrist. "My name is Trina Scotsdale. I am sorry to hear you've lost one of your own. Have you heard any updates from the police? Details have been a little murky so far."

"Hi, Trina, I'm Felicia. We don't know very much. We keep thinking this was a prank. It can't be real, can it? A death is shocking enough, but one right here in our cozy, community-oriented art center? It's making me question the safety and serenity we were accustomed to. I wish we could turn back time and go back to being blissfully unaware." Felicia blew her nose and looked depleted.

"It does feel like we're extras in a *Dateline* documentary. I'm very sorry you feel less safe in your safe place. Could his death possibly have been accidental? I heard that a portion of his sculpture broke and fell on him. Is that true?" Trina said, turning to a tall woman with dried clay stuck to her apron who looked like she was built for a volleyball court not a pottery kiln.

"Hi. I'm Zee. They aren't telling us much. We've been trying to figure it out ourselves, but we can't understand how a professionally welded metal sculpture could break so easily, so abruptly. Ian has been working on this design for months. His main cement sculpture had already been shipped to Orange Beach to be cured in its six-inch thick concrete base by the Reefmaker. He was only finalizing the metal flourish, which was going to be adhered to the cured design before deployment. There has been an endless parade of artists visiting him over the last several months providing him welding advice to ensure stability. The design should have been stronger than an ox."

The third member of the group stood ramrod straight with her back against the wall. She kept peeking at her cell phone and repeatedly licking her lips. She was about the same height as Trina, and her brown, shoulder-length hair was tucked behind her ears, displaying two gold spiral earrings that were so long they touched her shoulders. If she was an artist, she was a very meticulous one because her white T-Shirt was covered with a spotless white apron, and she wore ironed denim jeans and squeaky clean sneakers resembling a Martha Stewart impersonator more than a potter or painter.

"It doesn't make sense. When we stopped in to check on him yesterday, he said he was done. Although to be honest, he has said he was done for several weeks. He was always putting the finishing touches on the piece. It sort of seemed like he didn't quite have a vision. Most artists complete their art independently, but Ian was not shy about asking for help. What he lacked in skill he made up for in arrogance. He actually paid other artists to help him complete his clients' commissioned artwork, and he never gave credit where credit was due. I think his truth finally caught up with him. Sorry, I shouldn't be sharing gossip and speaking ill of the dead, especially since he's only been dead less than a day." The Martha Stewart look-alike tucked her eyes down as she obviously finished sharing and brought her cell phone back up to hide behind.

Zee jumped back into the conversation. "Samantha is being way too kind. It sucks Ian died today, but he was a prick. He didn't know the difference between a paintbrush or a welding gun. How he got selected as one of the underwater sculptors is a mystery. There were so many other more talented and experienced artists who submitted applications. Like everything else in this town, it's who you know, not what you know. Luckily, his assistant, Victor, knew enough to help Ian design the main concrete structure, but Ian has had too many other hands touching the steel accents. He was supposed to finalize the fusion with marine-grade safe sealant over a month ago, but somehow his family connection opened the exception gate wider than artistically feasible. Once I heard he was planning on attaching his metal sculpture, or flourish as we artists call it, the day of installation with concrete slurry, I predicted structural failure. However, I didn't think it would fail before it was even sunk in the Gulf." She glanced at her companions. "I've had enough of this circus, ladies. I'm going back to my studio. Maybe today's calamity will give me inspiration."

The three retreated back inside their studios.

Trina was left standing near a male artist, who had been picking dried paint off his hands while the others talked. "You'll have to excuse Zee, she's a little rough around the edges," he said. "Nice to meet you, Trina. I hope you're not a friend or family member of Ian's. He could rub people the wrong way, though, so I hope she didn't offend you. My name is Johnni." He wiped his hands one more time on his wrinkled and paint splashed T-shirt, then reached out to shake Trina's hand. Trina's OCD subconsciously kicked in, and she wished she had kept the tissue to wipe her hands after shaking his.

"No excuses needed. I'm a friend of Ian's girlfriend's mother, but no family relation. I've heard similar grumblings before so don't feel like you have to hold back," Trina said, hoping to dispel his fears of sharing, "What was Ian's sculpture supposed to be? I hate to admit it, but I'm not up-to-date on this year's installations."

"*Unflappable*. That's what he called it. I don't really know what the meaning behind it was, but I'm sure it will be all over the news. He should have sculpted a big bottle of bourbon. Emptying a bottle was his only recognizable talent. When he moved into his studio, he was so obnoxious and blatantly overconfident, I decided pretty quickly to steer clear. I do feel bad for Rachel. She seems so kind and genuine. I don't know what she saw in Ian, but it's none of my business. The only thing I'm curious about is whether Victor will be asked to finish Ian's piece or if they'll put Ian's work aside and let Samantha step in. I guess it doesn't matter either way—once again, Ian will steal everyone's else's thunder with his death overshadowing this year's installation."

"Well, I hope things get back to normal soon. It was nice to meet you, Johnni." Trina nodded as he walked away, then stood watching the crowd. If Ian lacked the skills to be a qualified metal sculpturer, maybe his death was simply a horrible accident caused by faulty construction. But Johnni had highlighted a good point. If someone could have benefited from the notoriety and publicity of Ian's death, maybe someone made sure his sculpture was faulty.

There were way too many 'what-ifs,' 'hows' and 'whys' to dig into. How precisely did he die? How many artists worked with Ian? Who would have access at the time the death occurred? Why would Samantha be asked to step in? How important was Ian's work now that he was dead? Would the Cultural Arts Alliance install one less sculpture, or would a replacement artist be granted Ian's spot? What impact did delaying the ceremony have? Was his death related to today's events or was it coincidental? Was Ian even the intended target? So many questions.

Trina saw Detective Trent walk out of Ian's studio with Detective Jenifer. Trina had become acquainted with the two detectives after discovering a skeleton in Point Washington State Park a couple of months ago. Although Trina had no sleuthing experience, she had uncovered facts that brought clarity to the identity of the victim and had played a part in the resolution of the case. She knew the detectives would be too busy to chat with her now, but she also knew they would bump into each other sooner rather than later, as Trina had become close friends with Detective Trent's wife, JoAnn.

She walked close enough to make eye contact with Detective Trent. They gave each other a subtle nod, and Trina turned to leave. As she walked down the narrow driveway overpopulated with police cars and investigation vans, she recognized the woman who was running up the sidewalk toward the art studios.

"Lily, you look frazzled. I saw Rachel and Rodney when they arrived about fifteen minutes ago. I didn't get to talk to them, but Rachel seemed like she was holding it together. Are you okay? Is someone watching the café for you?"

"Oh, Trina, I am so glad to see you. Rachel texted me and I got over here as soon as I could. I can't believe Ian's dead. The night before last, he stopped by the house to grab some clean clothes before heading back to the studio. I was so focused on household chores; I didn't wish him well on the installation. Once Ian started guilting Rachel for not spending the day with him before his big day, I went upstairs to escape the drama. Rachel works so hard and bends over backward for Ian. No matter how many times he pops her bubble, she smiles and gives in. I don't understand it. When will Rachel ever put herself first? Well, I guess now she can. I know I shouldn't be complaining about Ian, but between you and me, I'm not sorry to see him go. I wish it didn't happen this way, though."

"As a mother to a mother, I empathize. We can't protect our children from life's challenges, but we can be there when they fall and prop them back up. Go on up. I think they're both still inside the studio. Please call me if you need anything. I only work a couple days a week at Grayton Loft & Gifts, so if you need me to help with Rodney, the café or funeral planning, please don't be shy." Trina gave Lily a long hug. She pulled away and wiped a tear from Lily's cheek.

"You're going to be fine. Rachel's going to be fine. You have dealt with much harder blows in your lifetime, Lily. Go be there for your daughter."

Lily adjusted her shirt, straightened her hair, and walked up the slight incline toward the continuing commotion.

Trina opted to walk the mile and half to the corner of 30A and texted David, her husband, to meet her at Shunk Gulley Oyster Bar—famous for its panoramic views—so he could drive her back to her car outside of the Red Bar. Detective Trent and Trina had driven over to the crime scene together after their lunch was cut short by news of Ian's death. As she turned south heading toward the Gulf, Trina processed the events of the day.

Detective Trent had requested they meet for lunch to finalize his investigation report on the human remains Trina had discovered. Although she'd been able to help him with the identification of the skeleton in the woods, there were still unanswered questions about the other girls who disappeared from the area during the time she had spent summers on the panhandle with her family decades ago. Not being able to help find Jasmine, one of the girls who had gone missing when Trina was a teenager, weighed on Trina personally. She knew Detective Trent would do everything in his power to fill in the blanks for the families, but so much time had passed.

After he dotted his "i's" and crossed his "t's on the police report, Detective Trent had surprised her. He had hovered around the subtle insinuation he trusted her investigatory instincts. She got the feeling he would like to use Trina's community relationships to help him sleuth out details the police couldn't. She knew her compulsive habits after years of reading fiction novels compelled her to hyperfocus on tiny but valuable details of daily life, but she was a little startled to think he appreciated that quality enough to consider future collaborations. She would never be as qualified at investigations as Detectives Trent or Jenifer, but if she could deliver a dose of whipped cream on an expertly crafted dessert of underlying crime details, she was ready to sweeten the serving.

Trina retrieved a plastic bag from her purse so she could pick up litter as she strolled toward the restaurant. Within minutes, she had filled her small bag. She knew there was a trash can inside the Historic Gulf Cemetery on 393. Trina walked through the quiet, historic graveyard and took a moment to honor the dead. As she turned, she saw a woman bent over a trash can dropping packages on the ground. As Trina approached, she recognized the woman.

"Hey there, Jen, how are you doing today? Did you lose something? Can I help you find it?" Trina gently offered assistance to the relatively well-known homeless woman.

Being without a permanent residence in Blue Mountain Beach, Jen stood out. Their beach town was overpopulated with elaborate vacation rental homes, and many full-time residents were retired professionals in the middle to upper-middle class. Not everyone had vast wealth, but any casual observer could quickly assess that the heavy majority of both the Santa Rosa Beach residents and annual visitors were not struggling to get by.

Jen's family used to live in Grayton, and when she fell on hard times up north, she decided to come back to the sun and the sand. Unfortunately, she lost her family's home and access to any financial support. But Jen wanted to listen to the waves and breathe in the warmth of her hometown. The locals were well aware Jen sought shelter in the high dunes along the beaches, and she had been known to travel from store to store to use the facilities.

Trina was continually impressed with Jen, who always looked well put together considering her circumstances. Trina enjoyed listening to her recount memories of growing up in a small cottage in Grayton. Jen was a very friendly woman, and Trina did her best to make her feel welcome and valuable.

"I didn't steal this," Jen said, pointing to the button-down, long-sleeved shirt. "I only kept the shirt and dumped the rest. Green is my favorite color, so I'm going to keep it," she explained as she pointed to the top of the trash bin.

"You look fabulous in green, Jen. It matches your sunny complexion." Trina noticed the shirt was covered in small paint splatters.

"It fits me perfectly. It's mine now," Jen said as she took off the shirt and stuffed it into a dilapidated shipping box.

"I agree Jen. Finders keepers!" Trina dropped the contents of her plastic bag into the bin before using the plastic to pick up the trash on the ground, including an empty bottle of liquor, a couple of cups, and a to-go container. She reached down again when she noticed a white container lying nearby on the ground. She read the label: *Gabapentin 100 mg- 500 capsules.* The bottle looked to be the size of that a pharmacist would use to dispense individual prescriptions from. Trina picked it up and unscrewed the cover. Although the inner seal inside had been broken, the bottle seemed full.

"Jen, does this belong to you?" Trina asked.

"No. No. That's not mine. I have all my stuff. You can have the rest." Jen grabbed her box and walked deeper into the cemetery.

Trina noticed a small smear of blood on the container. Her curiosity was piqued.

How did a seemingly full inventory-sized bottle of prescription medicine end up in a cemetery?

Home for the Holidays

Chapter Three

2014

A *ahhhhh. Finally.* After driving five hours from Atlanta, Rachel could see the approaching Philips Inlet Bridge as she drove through Panama City Beach, Florida, on her way home from college for the holidays. She had completed her first semester at the Atlanta campus of Savannah College of Art and Design (SCAD), and she craved the calming, magical feeling of crossing over the bridge. The peak provided an unrestricted 360-degree view of one of the many storybook Walton County beaches and surrounding landscape. The vast forest of pine trees, surrounded by sparsely inhabited land to the north, was complimented by the breathtaking views of the Gulf to the south. The water glistened as if it were populated with dancing fireflies as the bright sun spotlighted the beauty of her hometown.

She was counting down the minutes before she would turn left on Scenic Highway 30A, a quintessential two-lane road that paralleled twenty-six miles of pristine beaches. Her shoulders relaxed and her smile widened after she made the turn, maintaining the twenty-five miles per hour speed limit. Her entire demeanor transformed as she glanced up through the sunroof at the beautiful oak trees bordering the cobblestone streets. Adorable immaculate homes and stretches of green parks lined the entrance of Rosemary Beach. The walking path was over-flowing with couples with small children and numerous bike riders. Even though it was mid-December, T-shirts and flip-flops were worn by many, and shoppers were decked out in fancy sunglasses. Eighteen years of fond memories filled her mind as she breathed in the fresh air and carefree vibe.

Only fifteen more miles before she would be home hugging her ten-year old brother, whom she hadn't seen since August. Rachel and Rodney had strong bonds with each other and their mother, who raised them single-handedly after divorcing shortly after Rod-ney was born. Once Lily had opened a café, the three of them worked side by side on a daily basis. Rachel had spent as much time wiping tables and processing take-out orders as she had doing homework.

Being accepted on a scholarship to SCAD was a dream come true. The scholarship paid for tuition, and Rachel took out a student loan for housing and incidentals. Although she hated to leave the nest, she knew studying alongside the best would catapult her ca-reer. Her confidence was squashed, however, after only one week on campus. All the students possessed stellar talent, be it painting, sculpture, photography, media, or literary prose. The reality of her new competition was debilitating. Every student who walked in the doors with a big head quickly shrunk down in stature upon sharing workspace with so many vibrant, unconventional, and impressive artists. Although the competition motivated Rachel to push herself, she was constantly questioning her skills, second-guessing her style, and redefining who she wanted to be as an artist.

She hoped spending four weeks back at home would regenerate her energy and guide her on the right path for the second semester. Plus, she missed Rodney dearly. He FaceTimed Rachel almost every day, sharing stories about fifth grade and his most recent surfing accomplishments. With the onslaught of social media influences, she was happy Rodney stayed busy away from his phone. He had the surfer boy enthusiasm for simple things like swimming with the stingrays or catching a wave. He was as eager to find a sand dollar today as he was when he was two. Rachel knew her departure put compounding pressure on her mother; keeping the café operational was stressful enough. Thankfully, neighbors and friends took turns with school drop-offs and beach-side pickups, making Lily's daily schedule less burdensome.

Rachel pulled into her driveway and had barely put the car in park before Charlie, their doodle, came bounding out to greet her. After getting tackled like a football player and licked like an ice cream cone, Rachel stood up and gave Rodney a tight hug. Her brother was tall for his age, and his height was equally adorned by lean muscles sculpted by years of swimming. His gray eyes matched his permanent grin and youthful energy, and his blond, wavy hair hung slightly past his shoulders in an earnest attempt to look like John John Florence, the prior year's runner-up in the World Surf League Championship.

"Rachel, I'm so glad you're home. Do you want to go surfing? I could show you this new spot we found. We still have time to catch a wave," Rodney said as he opened her trunk and grabbed a duffel bag. "Or maybe we can go to It's Heavenly in Seaside. I think they're staying open for the holidays, and I know Mom will let me have an ice cream treat now that you're home. I can show you my new favorite fishing spot. I caught an eight pound redfish last week."

"Rodney, all those things sound amazing. I'm so tired, though. Could we order a pizza tonight and maybe you can show me tomorrow?" she suggested as they entered the house.

"Mom cooked your favorite—shrimp and grits—but let's ask her if we can order pizza tomorrow night. Do you want to see my history project? I got an A," Rodney said as he pulled her free hand down the hall and directly into his bedroom.

"Hi, Rachel, come give me a hug when you're done," Lily called out from the kitchen.

"Okay. I love you. The food smells delicious. I'm starving. I'll be right there."

Rachel spent the rest of the evening relishing in the tranquility of home. No project deadlines, no peer pressure. Just the simplicity of hearing fifth-grade stories, filling her belly with homemade cooking, and listening to the waves crashing as she rocked on the porch swing overlooking the beach. She needed this. She needed this so bad. First semester had been tough.

She had always struggled with personal demons when it came to confidence, but she had the added burden of inheriting red and yellow color blindness from her mom. She had devised everyday solutions to compensate for her disability over the years, but sometimes the pressure to perform in class thwarted her ability to rely on them. She survived through her mom's confidence-boosting emails reinforcing how incredibly powerful Rachel's digital designs were. Her mom knew how to focus her attention and reestablish the reasons why she was there.

The next night, Rachel headed out to meet friends in the parking lot of the locals' hang out spot, an Irish pub called Johnny McTighe's. All the legal drinking-aged college students grabbed drinks at the bar, while the rest milled outside reuniting with friends home for the holidays. Rachel had no desire to drink, even though several coolers were scattered in open trunks because the reconnection with her friends was already bolstering her sense of self and she wanted to remember the feeling.

Catching up with her two best friends, Jennie and Cameron, provided Rachel with an hours' worth of entertainment. However, Rachel was completely distracted by the five-month transformation of one particular high school classmate, Tony Miller. Standing tall and broad, his pale-blue, button-down, long-sleeve flannel shirt, weather-worn jeans and scuffed up boots brought a spotlight to his complexion. Tony was not audaciously handsome—he didn't have glistening white teeth or chiseled cheek bones, and his nose was a little crooked from a baseball accident when he was younger—but he had the most striking dark-brown, almost charcoal eyes. They were so magnificent, when he made eye contact, Rachel felt bewitched.

When he saw Rachel, his smile widened; instantaneously making her feel as if she'd been wrapped a warm blanket on a cold night. She could feel her heart rate thump as if she was witnessing the finale of a fourth of July fireworks show.

Tony had always been in a relationship in high school but had returned last summer at the end of his freshman year of college as a single man. Tony had been Rodney's surfing coach, which conveniently provided Rachel with access. Tony was always polite and respectful, treating Rachel slightly more friendly than the average customer. They'd shared many hours sitting on the beach, watching dolphins dip in the sunset, and playing competitive games of beach tic-tac-toe.

One night they had come cripplingly close to kissing before Rodney had surprised them by showing up for an unexpected night swim. Tony had produced a believable excuse as to why he was standing so close to Rachel—something about extracting a spider from her hair. The excuse wasn't needed, as Rodney had dropped his towel and run into the water before Tony and Rachel could separate.

They'd stayed connected over the semester, and she was looking forward to finishing what they'd started. After politely regurgitating the last four months of her life to her girlfriends, she created an excuse to step away. As she sauntered over to Tony, whose feet dangled off the back of his pickup truck, the front door of McTighe's slammed open and two men shoved someone down on the front porch.

"Don't come back! That was your last warning."

The door slammed shut, and the blatantly drunk college student could be heard laughing as he lay on his back. The intoxicated student had dark-brown hair cut in a short, feathered style, offset by two distinct eyebrows that communicated his confusion without words. His striking blue eyes were semi-hidden beneath heavy eyelids. Although dressed in high-quality clothes—a button-down Peter Millar performance polo and crisp khaki shorts—his penny loafers where showing signs of the evening's festivities. A couple of the local boys rallied around, picking him up and supporting him as he swayed to a nearby vehicle. Once the commotion died down, Rachel continued on and plopped up next to Tony.

"Good to see you, Tony." Rachel said as she bumped shoulders with him.

"Good to see you, Rach. As usual, you're looking cuter than a puppy in a Christmas gift box." Tony turned, leaning his back against the side of the truck's bed so he could face Rachel.

Although the parking lot had no lights, Rachel's stomach began the slow melt as soon as she peered into his eyes. "Thanks, Tony. Who doesn't like to look cuter than a puppy." She laughed, as she knew what he was implying.

Tony smiled. "How's Rodney? Is he happy you're back?"

"It feels great to be home. I know what every fifth grader ate for lunch this past semester, how many times he got bonus points on his science tests, and all thirty-seven days the surf on Grayton Beach was perfect for catching a wave. I see not much has changed around here. So, what's the story with Ian now? What's he done to be permanently kicked out of McTighe's? That's a pretty tough thing to do given the business caters to locals. Getting banned permanently means Ian's leaving a new kind of legacy in our quaint hometown."

"Surprise, surprise. He hasn't changed since the last time we saw him. Ian tried three different fake IDs, drank so much in the parking lot he passed out in the back of the owner's truck, and now he's been caught after sneaking in the back kitchen entrance. His dad has bailed him out of so many incidents; the guy doesn't comprehend personal repercussions. If he graduates from the University of Florida, I'll be shocked. He couldn't pass any of his freshman classes and spent all his time at his frat house. This semester, he was suspended for hazing and plagiarism. My dad told me Ian's dad is running on a short fuse. Ian's going to burn every bridge he's got. Enough about Ian. How did your final semester project turn out? I bet your Media teacher loved it."

"I'm too scared to look at my grade. During the final presentations, all I could think about was the things I did wrong or could have done better. There were so many amazing submissions. The class was tough, so I'm really looking forward to taking the Visual Effects class next semester. The professor's world renowned and supposedly an amazing mentor. Speaking of visual effects, I would love to show you my—"

The sound of metal hitting metal silenced the ongoing chatter. The rear of Ian's red Ford Mustang was now combined into an intricate puzzle with a white Chevrolet SUV, shattering glass all over the pavement. Several of Ian's friends, obviously scared of being linked to the crash, ran off across the parking lot, jumped in their cars and took off. Ian opened his door, resting one hand on his car for balance and his other hand on his head. Several patrons exited the restaurant to satisfy their curiosity. A group of construction workers formed a semicircle close to Tony's truck to analyze the situation.

"Damn. Scott kid strikes again. He's like a blender stirring up shit on turbo."

"You'd think his buddies would be smart enough to take his keys away. The kid's a menace."

"If my father was Pierce Scott, I'd be drowning in a damn bottle every day too. But at least he was born into the right family. We can guarantee his daddy's going to make sure Ian gets off "Scott" free, once again."

"If his dad treats his son as bad as he treats his construction crews, the kid probably has more bruises than a rotten apple."

Rachel winced. Did Ian's dad abuse him? She had witnessed his father giving him a verbal whipping over the years, but she'd never seen or heard that he lived in a physically abusive home, although living in a verbally abusive one was no better.

Still, everyone in town knew Ian was a walking disaster. He had been to the local police station more times than the postman. But if Ian was dealing with repeated abuse, though it didn't excuse his repeated stupidity and inexcusable actions, it sure did explain it. She'd assumed he was just a stereotypical kid experimenting with alcohol, but the thought he may be drowning himself in a bottle to escape made her sad. She hoped these guys were just making assumptions to badmouth their boss.

The crowd eventually simmered down. Rachel and Tony waited until the police arrived and then parted ways. Over the next couple of days, rumors focused on the predictability of Ian's lack of punishment since his dad, a major home developer in Walton County, knew everyone and their secrets. The rumors became a reality, as Ian only had to complete a few hours of community service, and his father, once again, paid for all vehicle damage.

The last weekend of holiday break came quicker than expected. Rachel, Tony, and the rest of their friends met on the beach for one more sunset. Tony and Rachel took a quick dip in the cold January Gulf water, then sat by a fire watching dolphins as they gracefully swam by.

Ian's last day of community service required him to paint a storage gazebo near Western Lake. Somehow, he manipulated everyone into helping him on Sunday.

After walking along wooden trails to the west of the Watercolor community, Rachel, Jennie, and Cameron reached the spot where the group had congregated. Several open paint cans and wet brushes were scattered on the ground amongst as many open six-packs and empty beer bottles. Ian was making a spectacle of himself, painting the gazebo with his hands, and wiping more paint on his clothes than on the gazebo. Rachel could see zigzagged paint strokes on the side of the building. She walked around the circumference, confirming three sides were painted relatively normally with a few inconsistent coverage spots.

At least Ian had attempted to do the right thing. As she found her way back to the unfinished side, she saw Tony crouched down with a dripping paint brush in his hands.

"Tony, are you the only one here actually coloring in the lines?"

"Hey, Rach. An hour ago, Ian, Mike and I were all pretty focused, but as the beer tabs started piling up, Ian lost his way. I'm not sure this side is going to be finished by the end of the day. Hey, I could use a swig of water. Let me go put this somewhere, and I'll meet you over by the tree stump," Tony said as he wiped excess paint off his brush.

Rachel and Tony sat watching the continued decline of Ian and a couple of his close friends. By three o'clock, the entertainment of slathering paint on each other had waned, and Ian was two sips away from being plastered. Tony, the only sober guy remaining, picked up the debris and rinsed paintbrushes at the faucet. Rachel, Jennie, and Cameron hung back, ensuring they didn't get caught by random paint sprays.

The group had dwindled, but enough hands remained to carry the almost empty paint cans and miscellaneous supplies to Ian's truck. Walking along the backside of Western Lake on the cool January afternoon, Rachel was contemplating her return to SCAD. She'd enjoyed her holiday break but was apprehensive about her personal artistic growth and ability to master a singular skill. She frequently overanalyzed things, self-critiquing and doubting. She poured herself into every assignment and sometimes forgot to let the artistic process lead her to a natural conclusion. Painting and drawing always made her nervous since she wasn't seeing what everyone else saw due to her color blindness.

She found comfort in digital art. She could create masterpieces and knew she had the right combination of colors because the software told her so. But could she make a career out of digital art? Could she become financially independent and relieve the stress on her mother? She kept mulling these thoughts as she reached the opening of the trail onto 30A and took a right toward the bridge over Western Lake.

By the time she got there, Ian had stripped off his shirt and was dipping his hands in the remaining paint. He began painting his body, slurring threats he was going to paint a picture in the water. His two lapdog friends cheered him on, and before anyone could stop him, he jumped over the railing into the lake, black and white paint swirling off his skin. Since the water was colder than he expected, he quickly swam to the rocky base under the bridge, calling out for a towel. After a couple minutes, Ian demanded someone bring him a paint can. The rest of the group scrambled to the railing, peering over to see what Ian was going to do next.

"He's painting under the bridge with his hands. This is going to be a shit show."

"Let's hope there are no security cameras down there."

"I guess we can add graffiti artist to his list of offences."

On and on the comments came. Eventually, some of the kids climbed down to join him, and she couldn't help but discern the bewilderment and astonishment in the tone of their voices when they viewed his handiwork.

Although she didn't want to get caught up in vandalism, curiosity was a powerful force, and the artist in Rachel had to fill in the imagination gap. Tony advised her against it but agreed to help support her as she climbed down the big boulders under the bridge.

As she walked around and under, she saw Ian standing proudly in front of his handiwork. Spread across the cement under the overpass was a messy but strong and powerful image. A silhouette of a young boy with one arm constricted by a large snake. The apparent venom dripping from the snake's mouth was composed of dollar signs. The boy's shadow stretched out long on the opposite side, locked behind the bars of a jail cell.

The image was sloppy—Ian obviously was still under the influence—but the underlying message was explicit. Ian was definitely carrying personal baggage.

Rachel's heart broke, as she couldn't help but feel the pain the image projected. Her mind was in a tug-of-war. Ian was a pompous, egotistical, punk kid; there was no doubt. But no matter how irritating he was, he'd whipped out a compelling piece of art, with his hands, no less.

His insanely powerful image would have taken Rachel hours, even days. Did she have what it took to be a successful artist? Ian's spontaneous creativity hit her like a rock hitting a windshield. The crack was small now but would grow exponentially.

Welcome home, Rachel. Welcome home.

Talent Runs in The Family

Chapter Four

Present Day

*L*ean left. A little more to the right. Balance yourself. You got this. Trina was moving gracefully on a paddleboard in the early morning hours. Her sunglasses slipped down her nose as she navigated the water in search of marine life. The light blue, almost translucent color surrounding her made her feel like she was floating on the sky. To the east, she saw an object poke out of the water and hoped it was a dolphin. *Wait, there's another one. Oh my gosh, there are three.*

The fins approached her, quickly encircling her board creating a predatory boundary. Those fins didn't belong to dolphins; those were sharks! Her instinctual reaction was to escape, but helplessness overwhelmed her strength and stability. Her calves shook as she began to lose her balance. She felt the front of the board go up and something in the rear weighing her down. A sinking feeling rose heavy in the pit of her stomach.

The light in the sky grew brighter, more intense. Shining down on her like a flashlight, as if she were standing on a stage with a spotlight pointed directly at her. The sharks became more aggressive, circling 360 degrees around the board. Her heart hammered against her life jacket.

The waves rocked as she stuck the paddle in the water to push away. One of the sharks jumped out of the water, biting the end of her paddle. But the shark's face was not a shark. It was a person from her long-forgotten past. The person who had ignited her OCD compulsions many moons ago.

Trina's eyes shot open as she sat up in bed. She grasped her face with both hands, closed her eyes, and pushed a long shaky breath out. Just a dream. It was only a dream. But so realistic. She could almost feel the shake in her legs and the dampness of the Gulf. Her husband grumbled something, rolled over and started snoring.

Weird. So weird. She thought she had buried the image—deep. Her mind was playing tricks on her subconscious. Ian's death and the uncertainty surrounding his passing must have intermingled into her thoughts last night. She wiped the perspiration off her brow, pushed her blanket off and swung her legs over the side of the bed.

What did such a vivid dream mean and how did it relate to her present life? The sinking feeling that came with inescapable fear. The loss of control. The hunter instinct. Did the sharks represent Ian? From everything she heard recently, he didn't seem like a stand-up guy. Maybe she was feeling this way because someone close to the case was feeling trapped, cornered.

As she splashed water on her face and looked into the mirror, rays from the morning sun reflected back at her reminding her of the beam of light from her dream, which stirred too many fragile memories from her youth. Searching the dunes in the darkness so many years ago for her missing friend Jasmine. The frustration of focusing her eyes in the deep, dark night for any sign abandoned on the beach. The hopelessness of so many flashlight beams swaying back and forth across the sand. She closed her eyes and rubbed her temples. She couldn't change her past. She had learned that the hard way.

She let their two dogs outside and put the coffee machine on, returning to the bedroom to jump in the shower before David woke up. A simpleton when it came to getting ready, Trina combed her brown, straight hair, brushed her teeth, and threw on a blue Athleta skirt, a light-brown T-shirt, and silver hoop earrings. *What do I need to do today and what do I want to do today?* She wasn't scheduled to work, so how could she be useful?

Priority one. Connecting with Lily. She'd send her a text to see if she needed anything. After drinking her coffee and taking their energetic dog Freckles for a walk, she sat at the kitchen counter while David made himself a piece of sourdough almond butter toast.

"David, you're a whiz when it comes to anything mechanical. I'm curious what your thoughts are. Why do you think Ian Scott's sculpture collapsed? You own every tool known to mankind, including the gadget you use to stick two pieces of metal together. What do you call it again? I remember you and Hunter used it to fix his circuit board, and Trevor borrowed it to fix a broken tailpipe on his first car. What could go wrong with two pieces of metal soldered together?"

"Trina, Trina, Trina. Is Detective Trent short staffed or something? You don't really think he's going to start asking you to officially investigate crimes, do you?" David said as he sat down at the counter with his toast and coffee. "Providing him with some old newspapers and telling him about Sean's Jeep doesn't turn you into a detective. The only reason he took you to the crime scene the other day was so you could help comfort Lily when she showed up. I know you like to pick Trent's brain and pretend you're a small-town investigator, but I really don't think they need you digging into Ian's death."

"You know me, always at the right place at the wrong time. Luckily, we don't have a lot of crime here. Normally, the biggest 30A mystery is how to find a parking spot in Seaside. I think Detective Trent likes to pick my brain because I'm not on the police force, but I'm fascinated with the process of solving a crime. Plus, you know he's very protective of JoAnn. You're jealous because I got a free lunch at The Red Bar."

David chuckled and nodded.

"Plus, I'm not the only one fascinated with why people do crazy things. Crime is a billion dollar industry. Podcasts, TV series, true crime documentaries," Trina said, proving her point.

"You got me there. Who could have predicted shows like *Ozark* would become so popular. If I'd only kept my Netflix stock back in '18, I'd have my dream garage by now."

"Now that you're done interrogating me, Mr. Sleuth, can you answer my original question?"

"Why would a piece of metal break from another piece of metal? That's a loaded question. A soldering gun, like the one the boys and I use to fix small problems, produces a relatively weak weld. Soldering melts solder, or flux paste, to join metal. It's strong enough to fix a lead or copper break, but you wouldn't use it to build a structure meant to withstand the test of time. Remember, you're talking about an eight-foot tall by ten-foot wide piece of intricate, metal art. The news report online described his design as a huge sun with twenty rays bursting out all around it. The steel piece was scheduled to be mounted on the concrete, sun-shaped structure. The final metal design would have had to be sturdy on its own prior to being affixed using concrete slurry. I would have to assume he used a Metal Inert Gas, or MIG, welding gun to attach each ray to the circular sphere center. The process of welding melts the metal to metal versus using solder as glue to hold an object together.

"In addition to the sun itself, he had constructed an elongated shadow, also made from cylindrical shaped metal, which came to a narrow point directed at a globe of the earth engraved with an outline of the United States. The cone was directly focused on the state of Florida, and the shape was intended to provide a safe haven for fish and invertebrates like sea urchins and starfish, while providing more surface area for the algae to grow."

David pointed to the laptop. "His vision for *Unflappable* was that the state of Florida represents a continuous symbol of strength, not only surviving but thriving during calamities like COVID, hurricanes, and the last several years of political fearmongering. But to get back to your question, without seeing the material, methods and quality of workmanship, there are a thousand ways a piece of metal could have destabilized and broken. Because there are so many possibilities, the investigation will be tricky. Based on the initial report, one of the sun's rays broke off the main structure and punctured Ian in an artery causing him to bleed out. Horrible way to die. The broken piece landed accidently, or dare I say, perfectly in the right spot. Which makes me curious about why Ian was underneath the sculpture when it broke."

"Yikes. Not a pleasant image. I would hate to have witnessed his last few moments, and I'm glad I'm not privileged enough to have seen the crime scene. Thanks for putting it in layman's terms. What's on your agenda today?" Trina said as she pulled the laptop closer and examined the art design.

"I've got a conference call from ten to two and then I need to work on client pricing. I hope to be finished by four so I can meet up with Sean for a bike ride. What about you?"

"I want to see if Lily needs any help before I make too many plans. She's probably knee-deep in helping Ian's family with the funeral arrangement. I texted her a little while ago, and she said Rodney is at the café today and she would love it if I could swing by and grab him and then drop him off at her house. I guess Rachel's at home going through Ian's things. I'm going to swing by 3 Sons Bar-B-Q and grab some brisket. I know how much Rodney loves barbecue." Trina stood up and opened the refrigerator, grabbing herself a drink for the ride.

"Alright. Can you pick up a to-go order of ribs for dinner tonight? And tell Lily hey for me. I've got to prepare for my call." He bent over and kissed her, then walked to his office with the two dogs following behind.

Trina drove down 30A toward the west end of town, arriving at the restaurant before the lunch crowd. She stood in the short line, chatting with a sweet couple visiting from Alabama. The owner stood at the register ready to check her out.

"Ribs and brisket today, Trina? Are you hosting an event or stocking up?"

Trina used her tap-to-pay application, eliminating the need to touch any public surfaces. She used to pay cash for everything to eliminate any financial trail of her purchases—a bad evidence-hiding habit she was slowly breaking—but technology and convenience had forced her to mend her ways. At least tapping to pay meant one less fingerprint left behind, although her digital trail would be there forever.

"I'm headed over to the café to see if Lily needs any help, so I thought I would grab some extra for Rodney. You know how much he loves your brisket. Will you be able to break away and go to Ian's ceremony? I heard there's going to be a gathering for the art community at the Watersound Pavilion, and a private ceremony for the families later next week," Trina said as she accepted the two bags.

"I wish I could. We're working with a skeleton crew this week. Send my best to Lily. Tell her I'd be happy to help in any way I can, especially with Rachel's due date approaching. Nice to see you as always, Trina." She gave Trina a small embrace, then returned behind the counter to help the next customer.

Trina climbed into her car, and the smokey, sweet smells wafted through her nostrils making her stomach growl. She arrived at the café a couple minutes later and found an open spot to park in the shade. She cracked open the windows so the car would not smell like a *BBQ Pitmasters* competition by the time she returned.

Trina entered the adorable little café and was immediately filled with a feeling of contentment. Lily had put so much effort into making her restaurant feel like a comfortable and welcoming place. Homemade wooden squares decorated the walls in an orchestrated pattern winding around the four large windows that let the sunshine in. Each box captured one thing unique about each of the sixteen 30A communities. A charming miniature European home reminiscent of Rosemary Beach; a piece of green turf with a small white stucco ball similar to the Alys Beach vacation homes; and a toy-sized aluminum food truck with an extended canopy, tiny table, and umbrella like those that populate Seaside. The windows were adorned with delicate cream drapes, blocking the heat of the sun but allowing patrons to feel like the outside was in. In addition to a full offering of freshly baked pastries and creatively crafted sandwiches, the café sold handmade jewelry, a variety of local artists' beach prints and novels based on 30A.

Half the tables were occupied by locals, and the checkout line replenished itself with a constant stream of workers who were grabbing a quick bite on their lunch hour. Rodney worked behind the counter, greeting each customer by saying, "Thank you for supporting local, what can we do for you today?" However, since Rodney's post-accident speech impediment resulted in frequent mispronunciations, it sounded like he said, 'Ank eww faa supping Local, what can we do faa eww tay?'

Regulars always answered him politely and with legitimate respect, looking him right in the eyes. Some even shook his hand before placing their order. Vacationers were sometimes a little thrown off but quickly adjusted their reactions.

Trina approached the register, waving at Lily, who was in the kitchen. "Hello, Rodney, how are you today? Did your mom tell you I was on my way to pick you up? Are you finished working and ready to head home? Lily said Rachel's at home waiting for you."

"Yes, ma'am. Eed to uzz bathm," Rodney said as he took off his apron and hung it on a hook behind him. He asked a coworker to take over the register and walked to the bathroom.

Lily came out and pulled Trina aside. As petite as Lily was, she exuded confidence, warmth, and character. She had long, straight, auburn hair, with wispy bangs she tucked behind her ears. She wore no makeup, but her gray-blue eyes sparkled when she laughed. Donning a custom café navy apron under a pair of work jeans and a white T-shirt, she looked like a Napa Valley Airbnb proprietor who was eager to serve you breakfast and hear all about your plans for the day.

"Thank you so much for taking him home. He has been a lifesaver today. We've been going non-stop all day. I hate to keep him here while I finish my inventory, and his sister's supposed to be working on a project at home today. If not, Rodney's fine by himself. I'll be home soon. He can usually handle most things by himself."

"Don't you worry. I would love to sit with him for a while. I'll see you soon." Trina gave Lily a hug as Rodney met her at the front with his bag.

Rodney had graduated high school but would most likely remain working at the café. His physical limitations had improved immensely after years of physical therapy following the accident. He continued to have a slight limp, and in addition to an uncontrollable tremble, his left hand was incapable of grasping objects; thankfully, he was right handed. Overall, he had recovered physically, but it had been a long and dedicated road to recovery. The real trauma was in reduced mental capacity. He had suffered a major blow to his head, which severely impacted his ability to not only speak but also process thoughts. His communication, written and verbal, had progressed but patience was required.

As they drove to Lily's house, Trina asked him questions and focused intently on his answers. She had learned sometimes it was easier to have him write his answers, usually spelled phonetically, because his pronunciations were difficult to interpret if you weren't used to it. Luckily, the drive was short, so no major miscommunications occurred. When they got out of the car, Trina noticed Rachel's car was not there.

"Rodney, do you know where your mom hides her key? It looks like Rachel must have run out on an errand." Trina could hear their dog barking and saw his face plastered against the door's adjacent window glass.

"Unda the mussroom," he said as he motioned to the garden mushroom decoration while holding his leather messenger bag in one hand and the bag with brisket in the other.

Trina grabbed the spare key and unlocked the front door. The dog came bounding out, greeting Rodney, but was quickly distracted by the smell of barbecue. They went inside, and Trina made a plate of brisket, coleslaw, and baked beans for Rodney. While he ate at the kitchen counter, she walked around the dining room looking at the family photos on the wall. She turned and scanned the enormous pile of papers scattered all over the dining room table. All were filled with incredible graphite-drawn artwork, extremely detailed and inescapably accurate. Each was signed "Crummey" on the bottom, with a small picture of a hand over a heart.

"Did Rachel draw all of these? They are amazing. So lifelike, almost like photographs."

"No. Rach uses puter. I draw." His answer was even harder to understand because he had a mouthful of brisket.

"You drew all of these? Wow, Rodney, I had no idea you were so talented. These are incredible. So, you draw, and Rachel works on the computer to create her tattoo designs. You come from a very talented family."

Trina continued asking Rodney questions about his art, and he proudly showed her many pieces. About ten minutes later, Rachel walked in the door.

"So sorry I'm late. I had to run a quick errand. Rodney, is everything okay? I smell brisket. Did Miss Trina spoil you today?" Rachel asked as she walked over and gave him a hug.

"Not spoiled. Jss ungree." Rodney sat at the table and opened up his leather bag, pulling out a bunch of pencils. He pushed all the drawings to the side and started sketching.

"Thank you for helping. The last couple of days have been a little chaotic."

"I can't even imagine. Your mom said you were going through some of Ian's things. Are you responsible for cleaning out his art studio?"

"The studio is still under police restriction. I'll have to tackle it later since his family wants nothing to do with it. I was boxing up some of his art supplies. Want to come see? He was using our garage as another workspace. I'm going to turn it into my tattoo parlor. Luckily, my clients will follow me anywhere. If I turn the garage into my studio, I can meet my clients here and focus on my digital art during downtime. I'm actually super excited to renovate and turn it into my own space. With the baby coming, my mother thought this would be the best of both worlds. I can keep the baby here while I work, and I can be here for Rodney. I'm actually jazzed about the idea."

Rachel checked on Rodney and then directed Trina out the side door to an enclosed double-car garage. As Trina followed Rachel, she was impressed again by the brilliance of her dolphin tattoos. The extremely realistic, colorful images popped off her skin so vividly, Trina felt like she was wearing 3D glasses. In addition to the dolphins on her torso, Rachel's arms were a complex museum of art, concluding with an intricate flower design encapsulating her wrists.

The garage had been converted into a brilliant creative space. A large, brown paint-sloshed canvas lay in the center of the room like a rug on the gray-painted cement floors. A chalkboard filled with random sketches stretched across an entire wall. The opposite wall was covered with art supplies spilling over five-foot-tall shelves. A huge desk covered in drawings and prints sat in the center of the room. There were several boxes marked "Used Art Supplies" stacked up near the rear exit, topped off with one open box full of paint-caked brushes and tubes of half-empty acrylics. Trina noticed a huge stack of painted canvases propped up against the wall, and a plastic tub overflowing with what appeared to be rolled up painted images on canvases of all sizes.

"I've been organizing all day. I packed up most of the used art supplies and need to organize the unopened supplies next. I don't know what I am going to do with it all. I can paint, but I am not a painter. My passion and creative processes all take place behind a screen," Rachel said as she took another framed canvas and stacked it in the pile. Trina was a little taken aback. Ian had only died three days ago, and it seemed like Rachel had already moved on. Although she had to agree, converting the garage into a baby's room and an inspirational place for Rachel would be the best of both worlds.

"What are you going to do with all of Ian's work?"

"He usually worked here for inspiration and completed his commissioned pieces at the studio. The vultures started reaching out almost immediately, so I'll sell his pieces to the highest bidder. The price for his work has already sky rocketed. As of right now, anything he touched is fetching $8,000 to $20,000 apiece. Absolutely crazy if you ask me. His dad has been forwarding all the messages to me. He wants nothing to do with it. He was never proud of Ian being an artist. He also doesn't need the money. I will cipher through the offers eventually. Right now, I want to finish the renovation so I can turn in my notice at work."

"If you really don't think you would eventually use the supplies, I would be happy to drop them off at the Bayou Arts Center once you're done packing up. I'm sure they could use them for the Prison Art Program or Art for All program, which provides supplies and classes to local school children."

"Oh, yes! I love the idea. Thank you so much for offering to help," Rachel said as she walked around the room repositioning things on various shelves.

"How long had Ian been living with you and your family?" Trina asked as she examined some sketches still on display on the table.

"He moved in a several years ago. Once his dad cut him off financially, this was the best way for us to make ends meet after he signed the lease for the art studio." The sound of a car door closing echoed in the thinly insulated garage. A couple minutes later, Lily walked in.

"I'm home, finally. Wow, the space looks bigger already. Great job, Rachel, you've been busy. Don't overdo it, though, you have a little one to look out for now. Trina, thank you so much for bringing Rodney home and treating him. Come on in the kitchen while I get situated."

Trina and Lily walked back into the house, where Rodney was cranking out one piece of art after another. Trina sat down next to him while Lily unpacked some bags.

"It's been a crazy couple of days. Rachel seems to be dealing with everything way better than I expected. The house seems much calmer and stress free without Ian," Lily said as she released a sigh.

"I didn't realize Ian lived with you. How did it all come about?"

"It was a difficult choice. I've lived without a man in the house for almost twenty years. When Rachel begged me to let Ian move in, I talked it over with Declan, my ex. Ian had borrowed money from him after she begged him to help Ian. And, well, without getting into details, things didn't end well. Ian needed a place to live because his father kicked him out. The Scott family has a plethora of demons, and Ian inherited a few. Needless to say, as parents our disdain for Ian grew, but we had to do what we thought was best for Rachel.

"I was never pleased with the arrangement. I don't agree with Declan very often, but I would agree Ian was not the best choice for our daughter. He was a conniving son of a gun. I'm sure living under his dad's roof all those years wasn't easy, but his dad spoiled him by solving all his problems. Declan and I believe in tough love. Watching your kids make mistakes is not easy, but they learn much faster when they fail and have to figure it out on their own. Mr. Scott was too worried about his own reputation. He smothered money over Ian's endless mistakes, and Ian took advantage of the open treasure chest until the gold coins ran out."

Trina picked up a piece of Rodney's art and walked to the kitchen. "Well, you have your house back now, and it sounds like you'll be seeing more of Rachel once her studio renovation is complete. By the way, you have very gifted children. I had no idea artistic talent extended to Rodney. I've only seen a few but his style is unique. The images pull you in. I'm curious, though, why does he sign everything Crummey?" Trina asked as she pointed to the hand over the heart design and the signature, making sure not to smudge his work in the process.

"Ever since the accident, Rodney's thoughts have been blurred, sort of like a mixed up taco. Sometimes, the taco is perfectly layered and delicately balanced. Other times, it's messy and complicated. It still tastes good either way. We've adjusted. When he was younger, surfing was his passion. After the bump on the head, the power of the left side of his brain exploded. He whips out museum-quality pieces faster than we can buy reams of paper. He started signing them Crummey almost immediately. We always thought it's his way of trying to phonetically spell out Rodney. Over the years, we've asked and asked, but he just repeated the word 'Crummey.' With limited time on my hands, I've learned to pick my battles.

"The hand over the heart is a special thing between Rachel and Rodney. Makes each one of his pieces much more sentimental to me. Believe me, I have boxes of his art stored away. I've never tried to sell them. It wouldn't feel right. I don't want to disturb his freedom of expression. If he decides he wants to sell them, I will support him. But right now, I love being surprised every day. However, I will 100% support Rachel's efforts in reaping some benefits from selling Ian's. I don't want any reminders of him left when she's done. Although honestly, Rachel should be getting all the recognition and fame for work Ian signed. If there was a way to distinguish Rachel's brush strokes and creativity on Ian's work, you'd think you were looking at a butterfly on a chest X-ray—bold and beautiful in contrast with black, white, and boring. Ian's ego and self-righteousness was the only thing he contributed to his art."

Trina was a little taken aback. Lily's reputation in town was one of the highest moral and ethical personas one could craft of oneself. She was the person folks went to when they needed a shoulder to cry on, the one you bounced ideas off of to get a supportive reply. To hear Lily talk about Ian with such ferocity was distressing. Trina chalked up the uncharacteristic behavior as most likely the result of a stressful week.

"I'm no art critic, but I think Rodney's work is incredible. Just my humble opinion, but the world deserves to see it. Now Rachel's clients will be coming here for tattoo services, maybe Rodney's work can be used to decorate the walls. He can decide whether he wants to sell them once he hears what others have to say. Sorry, I have no right to stick my nose in where it doesn't belong. I'm simply blown away by the few pieces I have had the honor to examine," Trina respectfully stated as she returned to the dining room table.

Picking up a couple of finished drawings from the large selection spread over the table, Trina wondered where his inspirations came from. Rodney dropped his colored pencil and handed her the drawing he had been concentrating on; an incredible graphite drawing of a beautiful, tattooed woman with black hair standing with both arms splayed outward, her head tilted up to a bold streak of blue thunder flashing in the sky. The contrast of the black drawing with the splash of blue color was striking. She stood on top of a large mountain made of hundreds of broken chains.

The mind was a magical and mystical thing. Rodney may have difficulties communicating verbally, but his ability to send a message with his art was visceral. Ian's death had obviously freed Rachel from relationship subjugation and, from the sound of it, artistic servitude.

If Detective Trent was seeking a motive, Trina stepped on a huge pile of it. She wanted to stick her shoes in a washing machine to wash it all off because she didn't like where her thoughts were leading. Trina knew Detective Trent was hoping she could gain some insight, but right now she felt like she was standing on the dance floor trying to figure out the moves while still acting like she knew what she was doing.

Rodney smiled as he held his hand over his heart and said, "All bettah now."

Priorities

Chapter Five

2017

"You know, Rachel, just because you're my daughter doesn't mean you automatically get the money. You have to work as hard as everyone else. When we select the top four graduating seniors to receive the annual $50,000 artistic entrepreneurial start-up fund, it's because those seniors have proven to the Board their future holds the most potential. Their theses must be compelling, spellbinding and conversation sparking. When I was elected to SCAD's Board of Trustees, I didn't accept my duties lightly. I have to remain independent to ensure the Board supports the school's mission. I cannot give you any advantage. I love you, but your art has to speak for itself. This is your third year. By now, you should know who you are as an artist. The junior year pre-thesis presentation is vital to finding your way to the top. You need to dig deeper. If you want to become the next Meredith Pardue or Lavar Munroe, you need to refine your talent before you can showcase it."

Rachel blinked and wiped her eyes. She was driving home from SCAD on her spring break and was rehashing her last conversation with her father. *Ugh. Why did he have to be so...so...right? Darn it.*

She didn't know who she was. Even after almost three years at college, she was still swimming in garbage soup, all her leftover ideas thrown in a pot, hoping some flavor would burst out by the time she was done. In reality, she was holding on to the nearest piece of pasta for dear life. Any idea with staying power. If she thought the competition had been tough freshman year, it had only increased ten-fold as students who couldn't hang on, dropped out. She was so close to the finish line, but she still didn't know what she wanted when she crossed.

Right now, she could be sitting front row in a theater on Broadway, strolling through Central Park, eating lunch in SoHo, or visiting the Noguchi Museum with her college friends. Instead, she was driving home to finalize her thesis. She'd been drifting from one extreme idea to another. Bright and bold neon displays of power and principle to black and white vague shadows of despair. Digital abstract designs that rotate, swell, and explode. Realism. 3D. Lifelike. Personable. Relatable. Living. She wanted her art to breathe, but she didn't know yet how to give it oxygen.

She always became more centered when she was home. Although she really would have enjoyed a week in New York City, she knew eight days back in Florida would set her straight. She was ready to trade her subconscious gray skies with blue. She was also ecstatic Tony decided to come home for spring break. They had started dating last summer and had spent hours on the phone with each other over the last couple of months. Tony was going to school for business but had started exploring singing as a way to make extra cash. She'd heard him sing a couple of times over the winter break and was lucky enough to hear him sing nightly before she went to sleep. He had a soulful voice, and he was surprisingly talented at writing lyrics too. She had created some of her best work while listening to him practice.

After stopping at her house to catch up with her family, she drove to North Beach Social on the Bay. Her inner battles were quickly forgotten as she turned left into the parking lot across the street from the restaurant. The gravel lot was lush with huge oak trees with long and majestic branches curved in unique patterns and decorated with Spanish moss which made the trees look like they'd dressed up to see her. She loved staring up and twirling in a circle, feeling like a little girl protected by Mother Nature reaching out to secure her passage.

She crossed the street and separated from two other groups of customers, who veered right to head upstairs to Farm & Fire. She loved the redfish and rice dish at Farm & Fire, but her number one priority was to see Tony. She walked over the short, planked boardwalk to the back of the building, which brought her directly to the stage next to the bar. Eighty percent of the round, wooden picnic tables stationed along the beachfront were already occupied by families. The bar was completely full of college kids, and the sounds of Florida relaxation and joy filled the night air.

The stage was empty except for a stool, a guitar, and a microphone, and she figured Tony must be in the back getting ready. She grabbed a chair at a table for two and ordered herself the famous "The Carson" chicken sandwich and a Spicy Paloma cocktail. She could taste home by placing the order.

Rachel looked around at the Friday night crowd. North Beach Social sat on a corner lot looking out directly into the Choctawhatchee Bay. The shallow water was filled with young children even though the temperatures in March were too cold for most Floridians. A long line of dolled up college girls pranced down the quaint pier to take selfies at the end of the dock, as the beautiful soft colors of the sun dipping in the sky made the perfect backdrop for social media worthy pictures.

She couldn't see the bartenders behind the L-shaped bar since there was a line of patrons three people deep waiting to place orders. A group of girls with cowboy boots, short skirts and tank tops flirted with a group of guys all wearing their college T-shirts. The girls looked like a special boxed set of Barbie dolls, glistening with plastic smiles.

Already feeling the effects of specialty cocktails, the young men were zeroing in on their targets for the night.

"Call fire and rescue, I've got a five-alarm fire burning in my heart for you."

"You're so hot, you making me thirsty."

"You're as thin as a baby sand dollar."

Rachel chuckled as she overheard the dorky pick-up lines she had heard a million times before. She was so happy she had Tony and didn't have to weed through false flattery and pretentious competition.

"Baby, your legs are as long as the strings of the singer's guitar." Rachel winced at the pick-up line but swiveled quickly back to the stage when she heard the word guitar.

Her breath slowed and her eyes focused on Tony's slightly crooked smile and backward baseball cap surrounded by thick brown curls. His head was down, hands fiddling with the guitar. He cleared his voice and straightened the microphone, then scanned the crowd. Stopping, focusing on her; he grinned. He held his fist up to his mouth for a moment, hiding his grin, then moved it over his heart, beat it two times and blew her a kiss.

"Happy Friday, everyone. It's an absolute stunner of a day here at North Beach Social. Thanks for coming. Are you ready to give your dancing shoes a workout? Fair warning, y'all are going to leave tonight with no voice after singing all your favorite songs. Let's get this show started."

Tony began strumming his guitar. He loved to play the chords of recognizable songs, teasing the crowd for a couple beats until they started singing the lyrics before he did. His smile and penetrating stares quickly engaged the audience, as did his blue-collar clothes—worn T-shirt, rugged jeans, scuffed boots. He had the innocent look of a high school athlete, with the broad shoulders of a farmhand. His calloused, dry, cracked knuckles gave the impression he worked hard for a living.

He had the crowd entranced before the end of the first song and played for forty-five minutes to a loud, rambunctious reception. The small standing room only dance floor resembled a Gershwin pickle jar as his positive energy filtered its way into the entire restaurant. Rachel was so spellbound, she almost forgot to eat her food. Her foot was unconsciously bouncing to the beat, and her shoulders swayed from side to side. She mouthed the words to several songs, enjoying his performance as much as the crowd. She was eager to hear his final song because he had hinted to her earlier in the week he had a surprise for her.

The chair opposite her was yanked back abruptly, and to Rachel's dismay, Ian Scott sat down.

"Racheeeeeeeeeeellll, you're back. How you been? Looking fine, girl. Mighty fine. Did you get kicked out of college too? I thought only my dumb ass could screw that up. When did you get home?" Ian asked as he flagged the waitress and ordered another drink, not bothering to ask her if she needed anything.

"Ian. Nice to see you. Sorry to hear you were kicked out. What happened this time?"

"I paid some kid to write an essay. I mean, who's stupid enough to write their own essays? I'm never going to have to write an essay in the real world. Stupid college crap."

"Ah, I see. So, are you working now?"

"My dad got me a job at a bar in PCB, but they fired me today. The jackass bartender working with me turned me in for bumping up the tips on credit card receipts. I don't see what the big deal is. Most of these vacationers have so much money, what's a few extra dollars? They're not going to miss it." Ian let out an obnoxious burp as he accepted a fresh beer from the waitress. Rachel really hoped Ian was not going to stick around. She wanted to hear Tonys' last song.

"What's your father going to find for you next?"

"He flipped a gasket today when he found out. Said he was done bailing me out, but he eventually comes around. He owes me. I've taken his verbal blows for years, and I can hit him back where it hurts—his wallet and his pride. I love knocking his reputation down a few notches."

Rachel felt sorry for the guy. She was disappointed in most of Ian's life choices, but it sounded like he hadn't had the best upbringing. Having wealth didn't automatically translate into happiness.

"I can't wait to tell him what I plan to do next. He always wanted me to follow in his footsteps, become a successful businessman. But fuck that. I'm going to be an artist. That should give him a heart attack for sure," Ian said, then burst out laughing.

In the background, Rachel could hear Tony introducing his next, special song. This must be the surprise. But Ian's plan had her startled. "An artist? What do you mean?" Rachel darted her eyes to Tony and back to Ian, trying to listen to the song and Ian's answer.

"Some guy called me up last week. He found out I painted a crappy picture under the bridge, and he wants to pay me to do a piece of art for him. Can you believe it? Like I have any idea how to paint. This just fell into my lap. But it's the perfect way to get back at my old man. Oh hey, I see Mike over there. I'll see you later. Good to see you. Let me know if you ever want to hook up." As fast as he had appeared, he was gone.

Rachel felt a little angry, but mostly disappointed. Ian Scott, an artist. A commissioned artist. What the hell? She had been impressed with his bridge artwork, but had he spent three years at SCAD? He didn't even want to be an artist. How come he was getting recognized? As these thoughts swirled in the back of her mind, Tony's lyrics came into focus.

Her heart beats with my kind of magic
She's the only caffeine I need
Our thoughts are weaved into a specialty fabric
Quilted with care, forever ours, guaranteed

Rachel forgot Ian. Forgot her jealousy and angst and melted into her seat. The little kids running around on the beach behind her were invisible. The rowdy patrons clamoring for another round were tuned out. She was alone, sitting in a room watching her man sing directly to her. She had a beam of focus on his quirky smile and soothing voice. *He wrote a song, a song about me.* It was beautiful.

Tony finished, thanked the audience, and turned his microphone off. She burst out of her chair so fast; she tripped on the corner of the table and fell flat on the floor. Ian saw it happen and burst out laughing. Tony dropped everything and ran over to help.

"I think I am falling for you, Tony Jackson Miller," Rachel whispered as Tony pulled her up.

"Are you okay? How much have you had to drink, silly girl? I'm falling for you too. Watching you watch me made me want to go home and write ten more songs. You look—no, you ARE—my beautiful Rachel." He picked her up, wrapping her legs around his waist and kissed her. Several patrons who were sitting close by said "Awwwww" in unison.

"You wrote me a song. I can't believe it. Wait, it was about me, right?" she said, blushing, realizing she could be making a bad assumption.

"Yes, of course it was about you, you dork! Did you like it? I've been working on it for the last couple of weeks. I was worried it wasn't going to be good enough to sing in public, but I feel pretty good about the final result. I call it 'Dolphin Magic.'"

"Oh my gosh, Tony. I love it. I can't wait for Rodney to hear it. And my mother, of course. Thank you. Thank you so much. I'm going to need a little dolphin magic this week for some artistic inspiration."

"You don't need me. Your work is incredible. You're too hard on yourself. I can't wait to see what you come up with. Unfortunately, I'm singing almost every night during spring break, but I can help inspire you all day as long as Rodney doesn't pull me away surfing every day."

Tony was so endearing. The warmth in his grin; the way he tapped on his jeans when he was crafting lyrics; the subtle way he valued her family because they were important to her; stopping in to see her brother as soon as he made it back in town; texting her 'You Got This' memes;

stocking her favorite A&W root beer in his car. She adored Tony and all his quirkiness.

She was disappointed she'd let Ian distract her from listening to the whole song, but she didn't have to hear all the lyrics. The act of writing a song for her was gift enough. They sat down together, and Rachel chatted with Tony while he ate. They packed up his equipment and headed home around ten.

She wished all her high school friends were back home for break. They were an eclectic group, each one harnessing a unique personality like the characters from the Netflix show *Sense8*. They had nothing in common but were magnetically forced together and couldn't seem to separate. Thankfully, the week flew by regardless. Rachel spent hours on her computer devising an endless stream of thesis ideas. She homed in on a concept by Thursday and put her head down to work through the details. Tony stopped by several times during the week, but when he saw her full blown concentration mode, he silently slipped away to give her space.

Saturday was her last chance to enjoy the bliss of the sand and sun. In the morning, she met Tony at the beach with Rodney in tow. The water was as smooth as glass, so the boys were not going to catch any waves, but the three of them enjoyed a couple games of TidalBall and frisbee. Later, Tony threw the football with Rodney while Rachel read a book. By the afternoon, they headed back to Rachel's house to grab a late lunch. Tony had brought his guitar, and he sang a couple of his favorite songs—"Somewhere on a Beach" by Dierks Bentley and "American Country Love Song" by Jake Owen. Rodney eventually disappeared into his room, and Tony and Rachel sat outside together.

"Now it's my turn."

"What do you mean? You want to sing a song?" Tony said, stretching one hand out with the guitar still held tightly.

"No, silly. Unless you want to hear "Ring around the Rosy." I want to hear my song."

"Were you too distracted by Ian's charm to hear the whole thing last week?" he said, bringing the instrument back under his command. He pulled her next to him with his free hand and starting thumping a soft beat on the front of the guitar.

"The only charm bedazzling me was your country western foot stomping and seductive and sexy eye contact. I'm ready for it this time. I'm closing my eyes, and I'm going to memorize the lyrics." Rachel sat on the porch swing with her hands wrapped around her bent knees. Her tan toes rested on his thigh.

"Okay, get ready to be bedazzled." Tony began humming the beat of the chorus. He sang "Dolphin Magic" with the conviction of a soldier saying his last goodbye at the airport. A deep, emotional, and heart-wrenching performance. The hair on her arms were electrified and wet drops streamed down her face. The song. Those words. His soul and his intentions had been woven into a dream unexpectedly becoming a reality. Even the melody was rich and imaginative. He had a gift, and she felt so lucky he had shared it on her.

Rachel's eyes remained closed after he finished the song. He bent over and kissed her accepting lips which were slightly salty from the tears. She could hear him move the guitar, but she remained in her spot, her mouth begging for more. Gracefully, he picked her up and held her in a tight embrace, allowing his tongue to communicate. They found a spot to enjoy a private moment, until Rachel heard Rodney yelling it was time to go from inside the house. They separated reluctantly and agreed to call each other after his night gig at Old Florida Fish House.

Rachel dropped Rodney off at his surfing lesson, then returned home and grabbed her computer. Her mother was attending a book club, her one night a month off, so Rachel needed to use the couple of hours left Saturday night to finish her concept.

Around seven o'clock, she received Rodney's text he was ready to be picked up. Rachel was in the zone and didn't want to lose her momentum. The critical final touch to her digital design was flowing freely through her fingertips. She didn't want to bother her mother on her night out, Tony was working, and her two closest friends had left to go back to college. She hated to do it, but she texted Ian.

He responded and said he was close by, and that he would swing by and pick up Rodney if Rachel agreed to grab dinner with him. Rachel told him she didn't have time for dinner, but he was welcome to pick up some tacos on the way. She knew it was a bad idea giving Ian wrong signals, but she was so close to finishing and Rodney was literally less than five miles away; it shouldn't be a big ask. She never put herself first, and asking Ian for help would be a one-time thing. How often did her mom tell her she needed to make herself a priority.

After Ian said yes, she texted Rodney and told him she would be at home waiting for him. She was soon lost in thought finishing up her design concept.

Ten minutes later, her cell phone beeped with a text.

It was Ian.

Headed to the hospital. Rodney's hurt. Golf cart accident. Deer crossed the road. Rodney hit a tree.

Don't
Forget-Me-Nots

Chapter Six

Present Day

"Not a problem, Jane. I would be happy to help. I can borrow David's truck. I'll be there in fifteen minutes. See you soon." Trina ended the call and walked down the hall to her bedroom. She opened her vanity drawer and reached for an eyebrow pencil and eyeliner. She had planned to clean out the refrigerator, change bed sheets and then shower before heading over to Lily's house to prepare for the post funeral community gathering. Now, she was giving herself a five minute makeover to help a friend in a pinch.

The local flower shop owner, Jane from Beachy Blooms, had called her in a panic. She had one wedding, two private dinners and a bachelorette party to deliver flowers to, and she wasn't sure she would get to the church in time with the five remaining condolence bouquets. Trina and David had become friends with Jane and her husband when they met at a Point Washington Medical Clinic fundraiser. Since then, Trina had relied on Jane more times than she could count to deliver a last-minute bouquet to cheer up their home for spontaneous gatherings. The least she could do was help her with a scheduling conflict. She would have to go without a shower since the arrangements were supposed to be dropped off before the funeral guests arrived.

She texted JoAnn and told her she was going to swing by early to pick her up and explained why. She brushed her hair and found a black pantsuit in the closet. Grabbing the pasta salad she had made last night from the refrigerator, a cooler from the garage and David's key fob, she knocked on his office door. He was working on his computer and lifted his head up.

"Headed out early? I thought we didn't have to be there until twelve?"

"Jane called. She's in a pinch. I'm going to borrow your truck to pick up the last five bouquets and drop them off at the church. Luckily, she already dropped off the large arrangements so JoAnn and I should be able to manage the small ones without you. I left my keys on the counter. I'll see you over there." She patted both dogs, made sure they had water and headed out the door, texting JoAnn that she was ten minutes out.

As she drove down 30A to prepare for a funeral, it felt like a juxta-position to see numerous families with beach wagons overflowing with rafts, towels, and coolers. Mothers with little kids squeezed on their hips and a toddler, clothed in bathing suit trunks, grasped in their spare hand. Dads towing the line behind with umbrellas, Tommy Bahama chairs, and see-through bags filled with sand toys.

As Trina waited at the traffic light adjacent to Blue Mountain Beach Creamery, she glanced at the gathering of customers standing in line waiting to get their cone of ice cream, which would melt in the summer heat before they had a chance to eat it. The simple pleasures of being on vacation, treating yourself, saying yes when normally one would say no.

The exhaustion of working so hard to squeeze out every hour of a sunny day in Florida when you'd soon be headed home.

Trina turned right onto Route 83, reminding herself to be thankful. She was alive and well. Her family was healthy and happy. Definitely not perfect. Her children had challenging work deadlines, complex relationship issues and unexpected financial challenges, but overall, they had a great life. Lily, on the other hand, had been hit with life's bowling ball several times. Divorced at a young age. Juggling the financial strains of starting a business while managing two children on her own. Then having all ten pins knocked down when Rodney had his accident. So many hours driving to various hospitals to find the right doctors and therapists. Helping him walk again. Hiring speech therapists and cognitive specialists to teach him how to function semi-normally again. Having Rachel's not so pleasant boyfriend move in with her. Rachel's pregnancy out of wedlock. Now Ian's death. Trina had so many reasons to be thankful. She pulled into JoAnn's driveway and beeped. JoAnn climbed in the truck with her hands occupied with two casserole dishes in warming sleeves. She leaned back to place them on the rear seat and buckled in.

"Thank goodness I'm wearing flats. I'm not sure I could have climbed into this truck with heels. How are you, Trina? All the bouquets ready for pickup?" JoAnn asked as she opened her purse and applied lip balm.

"Yes. Jane said her staff would help load them, so we'll only have to get them into the building. How are you? Is Trent going to come today?"

"Yes, and a couple members from his team. The turnout at the Watersound ceremony was huge. There were a couple of amazing speakers, and a really lovely musician playing music in the background. Today should be much more intimate."

"I'm surprised to hear so many people turned out. The general consensus is Ian was not very well liked in the art community."

"I had heard the same undertones, but the speeches were more... how shall I say, generic? Not really recognizing Ian's accomplishments per se, more acknowledging how important the art community is as a whole to this area. It was very tastefully done."

"Dare I ask? Has any new information about his death been uncovered?"

"Of course this is confidential, but I trust you. Initial assessment on scene was accidental death, but Trent told me Ian's blood alcohol levels were off the charts. Which, come to find out, was not alarming. I guess he had become a serious alcoholic over the years and had been in an out of rehab. But the interesting twist is the lab found traces of a tranquilizer in his blood stream. That, along with the placement and alignment of the metal rod, has raised suspicion. Trent's team is interviewing all the artists at the warehouses, and they are compiling a list of other potential persons of interest.

"I never realized how much structural evaluation and validation was required to coordinate each individual piece of art for deployment. The Underwater Art Museum website provides a cursory overview, but Trent has learned so much about the hundreds of people behind the scenes who make this unique experience come to life. It makes me appreciate the arts so much more now that I understand how much effort goes into bringing these art installations to fruition."

"I can only imagine. Think about how much planning it takes to pull off a decent dinner party. I cannot even fathom the logistics it takes to haul massive art structures into the Gulf. So, given the lab results, do they think Ian was drugged by someone else, or do they think he was self-dosing?" Trina was trying to concentrate on the road, but this revelation was setting off alarms in her head remembering the tranquilizer container she'd found at the cemetery.

"I try not to ask too many questions. I know he does his best to keep me protected from details of ongoing investigations." Trina decided not to reveal her cemetery discovery until she dug a little further.

They arrived at Beachy Blooms, and Jane's helpers quickly loaded the rear of the truck. Jane was busy finishing up arrangements but graciously thanked Trina for the help. About ten minutes later, Trina pulled into the circular driveway in front of the church and parked the truck. Trina climbed up into the bed of the truck to gently move each bouquet to the end. It took them ten minutes to retrieve and place all five bouquets at the altar. Trina walked around to read the notecards on the bouquets already positioned on the platform, while JoAnn visited the restroom to wash dirt off her shirt. Trina used a tissue from her purse to touch each card, ensuring she didn't leave a dirty fingerprint behind.

She recognized some of the names of local artists and business owners in the area who were sending their condolences to support the Scott and Fairfield families. There were ten large arrangements written specifically to Mr. Scott from various people who benefited from befriending the largest Walton County developer. Reading the cards, she realized influence ran deep, even at a funeral.

There were several names Trina didn't recognize, and one message was unique enough Trina stopped and read it twice.

Sometimes death can be beautiful, and it can also be a hidden thief. May Ian's death bring solace to those around you. – inspired by Lacey Sturm

The card was signed EDAD.

She wasn't sure how to interpret the message. Who was EDAD? Was it signed by an artist insinuating Ian's death was a form of art? Or was Ian a thief and deserved death? How would his demise bring solace? The card was not addressed to anyone specifically, either. She could tell the bouquet was not delivered by Beachy Blooms because their signature card and envelope were not used. Trina would have to try to figure out the source another way. She snapped a photo of the card so she could google Lacey Sturm and EDAD later.

Trina spoke with the funeral director and ensured the placements of the flowers were appropriate before she and JoAnn went outside. They sat on a park bench to wait for the families and guests to arrive.

Trina had never met the Scott family, but she could make an educated guess when several high-end vehicles pulled up front and parked that the prestigious family had arrived. While the family appeared polished and reserved, Trina couldn't help but evaluate and characterize their body language. Certain couples were holding hands, while others walked side by side like soldiers. Certain guests' tissues were damp from wiping tears, while others used theirs as a form of a fidget spinner held in their fists. Many lingered outside in small groups reading text messages or surfing social media platforms, while others were checking the attendees for the who's who of Santa Rosa Beach.

Eventually, Lily, Rachel, and Rodney arrived together and joined Trina and JoAnn before walking through the front door. David joined them soon after. It was a little awkward in the church during the ceremony; no one seemed devastated or in despair and there were few tears. Rachel released the most, but Trina was surprised by the overall lack of emotion in the room. Ian's mother gave a short speech providing accolades for his recent successes in the art world, but it was apparent she'd scraped together positive attributes. Mr. Scott didn't hide his paternal disappointment and was rude enough to accept a phone call in the middle of his wife's speech. Interesting family dynamics for sure.

The ceremony was over quickly, and Lily asked Trina to drive Rachel and Rodney home because she had to meet someone for a quick exchange before guests starting arriving at her house. Detective Trent had showed up toward the end to show his respects, so JoAnn joined him in the drive over to Lily's house. David returned home to get back to work.

Rachel sat in the passenger seat, with Rodney in the back seat listening to music on his AirPods. Rachel sat quietly, contemplating, while she rolled a small piece of paper in her hands. Round and round her palms rotated as the paper slowly disintegrated. The flower tattoos decorating her wrists seem to glisten off the rays of sun through the windshield.

Trina didn't want to waste the opportunity to talk with Rachel. "Rachel, you showed so much strength today. You're an extremely mature woman, and your constant resilience proves to me you are going to be a strong, caring mother."

"Thank you so much. I think I'm sort of numb to tell you the truth. One day he was sharing my bedroom with me and the next... " Rachel stared out the passenger window.

65

"I assume you met each other in the art world?"

Rachel sighed. "Heh. Well, art sort of fell in Ian's lap. Ian is one of those artists who— well, whatever, it doesn't matter now. Ian and I were thrown together, sort of magnetically pushed together. Our paths crossed, and I couldn't untangle them. Ian didn't travel down the same road as me, but we ended up at the same intersection."

"It seemed like Ian's family wasn't super proud of his decision to become an artist. Do you feel like you have a good support system?"

"Oh definitely. My mother has never questioned my abilities and was ecstatic when I was accepted into SCAD. But she really needed me when Rodney got injured. She would never have wanted me to change my career path, but the needs of my family came first. I sort of had to put my dream of becoming an artist on hold," Rachel said as she began squeezing her left wrist with right hand.

"Every once in a while, I think about trying to get back in. Re-exploring. Tapping the recesses of my buried ideas. My dad was never a fan of Ian, and therefore as long as Ian was in my life, he refused to financially fund any plans I had to become a commissioned artist. He didn't understand why I stayed with Ian, so I had to move on and find another way to make it. Honestly, it's been tough, but it feels great to say I've paved my way with no financial support. I feel more independent and capable."

"It looks like you're sharing your talent with the world one tattoo at a time. Maybe one day, I'll step out of my comfort zone and ask you to give me one. By the way, after seeing your tattoos up close the other day, I checked out your portfolio online. Your designs are phenomenal. You can see the investment, thoughtfulness and care you put in each one.

Your art isn't hanging up in a person's home or in a gallery, but it is walking around for everyone to see and appreciate. You might not be creating art the way you imagined, but you are still an incredible artist."

"Thank you. I appreciate the compliment. I do like creating tattoos, but I think I have more to give. My mom always said, '*Things happen in waves; one wave can suffocate your confidence, while the very next one can take you on the ride of your life. Waves are free. Don't waste a freebie.*' I'm not wasting this opportunity. I'm ready to tap back in and explore digital art.

I recently submitted designs for two digital art bids. An aquarium in Tennessee is seeking an interactive mural for the exterior of their renovated building and a local hospital received a grant for their children's ward. They're seeking twenty unique digital scenes to be looped in 4k resolution throughout all the ICU patient rooms. If I can secure one golden opportunity, I truly believe more will follow.

Also, my dad called me after he heard about Ian. He agreed to provide me a little extra financial support to get me going. I'm starting to feel like I'm getting my mojo back. I'm going to turn the garage into the coolest retro-tattoo parlor and digital design studio on 30A."

Trina pulled up to the mailbox at Lily's home and turned the truck's engine off. She turned to Rachel. "I've only seen a tiny glimpse of your talent, but I cannot wait to see what you unbox during the next phase of life, Rachel. I am really so sorry about Ian's death, but I'm so glad you're focusing on the positive. You haven't had it easy, and you deserve a fresh start."

"You know, Mrs. Scotsdale, I've spent my life feeling like the underdog. Always struggling with anxiety. Am I as good as? Do I have what it takes? Will my art speak? Will it communicate? I watched a documentary recently on Tim Berling, who was also known as Avicii. You probably never heard of him, but he was a worldwide recognized IDM music wizard. Basically, making record-breaking melodies using his computer. No matter how many concerts he sold out, how many famous musicians wanted to work with him, no matter how many bestselling charts he broke, he still doubted his ability to pick up a guitar and play a musical instrument. I don't want to make the same mistake by letting my self-doubt hinder my artistic dreams. I know what I'm capable of, and now I have the freedom to explore."

"I know it's a natural thing to doubt yourself, but the first step to believing in yourself is knowing you need to change your mindset. You have an unbelievable gift many would envy. I'm sure you will make your mother proud no matter what you do, and I hope you continue fostering your talent. The world deserves to see what you can imagine." Rachel gave Trina a shy grin and held one wrist with the other hand while she seemed to be pondering something.

"Hey, if you don't mind me asking, what's the meaning behind your wrist tattoos? They almost look like handcuffs, but they're delicate and beautiful at the same time. They almost look real enough to make me believe I could lean over and smell them."

Rachel looked down at her wrists and rubbed her finger along the path of the flower's stem. "I did these myself. Do you know how hard it is to tattoo your right wrist when you're right handed? Very hard. These flowers represent the constraints of a beautiful life and a sign of regret for not being able to keep a promise." Rachel rested her hand over her heart and a small tear glistened on her cheek.

Trina reached out, grabbed her hand, and squeezed it. "The flowers are stunning. Are they forget-me-nots," she asked as she tilted her head, examining Rachel's wrists.

"Yes, and I think it's time to unlock them."

The Struggle is Real

Chapter Seven

2019

Rachel sat on the hard packed sand on an empty beach, so close to the water the waves washed up and tickled her toes. She closed her eyes and let the sun soothe her soul. Waking up and sitting alone on the beach as the sun rose had become her daily habit. The sound of the water lapping back and forth. The occasional squawk of a seagull. The tall, elegant heron standing in the nearby lake while sandpipers pecked tiny disappearing holes. The beach re-centered her, put everything back into focus.

She had a good life.

She had a loving family. She had a financially secure job. So what if she never finished her college degree? It didn't matter she spent her days inking tats on strangers' bodies instead of creating pieces for a gallery. She had a roof over her head and a family that loved her.

She opened her eyes and saw a pod of dolphins about forty feet away, their fins dipping up and down in a playful dance. Rachel stood up and placed her hand to cover the glare. There were two baby dolphins and four adults. Instead of swimming away, they circled back and forth in front of her. Jumping, twisting, and playfully falling back in the water.

Rachel was mesmerized. The dolphins were sending her a message. You got this, Rachel.

She thought of Tony. Their first kiss years ago. Their summer of flirting. The long calls each night during her first semester of junior year of college. The lyrics to her song; the song that melted her heart. Memories of sitting together at bonfires, taking cold plunges in the Gulf, watching Rodney surf for hours.

Rodney. The last two years had been rough. He had sustained life-altering injuries in the golf cart accident. The night, Rachel's life sustained a life-altering turn as well. She never returned to college. She became a full-time caregiver, taxi driver and emotional cushion. Lily did as much as she could to share the burden, but the café paid the bills. Rachel and Rodney had always been close but now they were inseparable. It took months before Rodney was able to take steps, and a year before he could walk independently. His cognitive skills had been depleted, but with a dedicated team of doctors and nurses, he eventually began communicating.

The family developed their own special language to bridge the gap. Several months after the accident, a speech therapist had suggested Rodney draw his thoughts. The flood gates opened thereafter. Rodney began drawing anything and everything. He drew for hours every day, and although he had to work harder to keep the paper still with his trembling hand, he began drawing amazing illustrations. It took another two months for him to learn how to write out his messages when he was struggling to communicate verbally. He didn't remember how to spell accurately but was able to spell based on how it sounded in his head. It worked.

It had been her decision that changed the course of Rodney's life. Her decision to protect those five precious minutes, keep them for herself. Her stupid thesis. Proving herself to her dad, to her peers. Why hadn't she picked him up like she had done a thousand times before? Her selfish decision forever changed his world. She would never forget it, never forgive herself. Rachel bore the guilt like a parent who missed too many ballgames. She knew she had to silently hold on to it, couldn't let it go, or her world would fall apart. She had to be strong for Rodney.

Rachel had asked Rodney so many times—what happened when Ian picked him up? Why hadn't the lights on the golf cart given advance warning before the deer crossed the road? His response was always the same: "No idea, Rach. No idea." Eventually her mother told her she had to stop. Her interrogations were creating more anxiety than Rodney needed. She had to let the past rest and concentrate on the future.

Before the accident, Tony had become as vital to her as nutrients. He supplied her with love, compassion, and positivity. Then she had made the decision to text Ian for help. Rachel's future had crystallized in that moment and shattered soon after. Tony didn't belong to her anymore. Instead, she had Ian strapped to her like a straitjacket, squeezing the vitality out of her every day.

Ian unexplainably became an integral part of her life. He'd manipulated his way in and now they were dating. Dating. It still bugged her. Rubbed her like a poison ivy rash that wouldn't stop itching. She didn't see any way around it. Ian had guilted her into it.

"You called me to pick him up. You were too busy for your own brother. Rodney was sitting there waiting for you. I was the hero who saved the day. The deer caused the accident not me. You owe me Rachel.

I told everyone we had pre-arranged the pickup. No one knows you failed in your sisterly duties. You owe me."

Internally, she raged. One split-second decision. This one time. Ian was right. She put herself first. She let his words sink into her pores, her mind, her subconsciousness. Ian began stopping over every day. Working her. Breaking her down. She was so focused on Rodney's recovery, she eventually weakened. She gave Ian an opening, and he barged in like a *Gold Rush* bulldozer. Now she was dating Ian, not the love of her life who she deserved.

Did she deserve Tony? No, she didn't. She was too selfish. He deserved better.

Over time her self-esteem diminished, transforming her self-image. The cute, simple, adorable hometown girl, who was known for her simplistic ponytail, baby-blue tops, and light-gray eye shadow, vanished. The Rachel of today wore platform boots, corsets, bold black eyeliner, and a short pixie haircut dyed black. Her skin was the only canvas she had left to express her true self.

It was as if misery took a hold of the keys to her life, driving her down abandoned roads, tossing the luggage of her past out the windows, and leaving a trail of hope and dreams behind. She was buckled in but no longer had control over which way the wheels turned.

It didn't matter she didn't have time to explore her passion for art. It didn't matter she woke up in tears lying next to a man she despised. No one cared that Tony was the only man who could make her happy. Rodney was more important than her silly teenage love story. Plus, Tony deserved someone who could put him first, not second or third.

Who she climbed into bed with at night didn't matter.

It shouldn't matter.

Rodney's safety, his happiness, his health. It's what kick-started her every morning.

She stood up and took one more cleansing breath as the sun rose in the sky and beachgoers started to trickle around her. As she walked home, she let her fingers graze the tall stems of the sea oats populating the dunes, and her fingers were pierced by the sharpness of the palmettos near the boardwalk. Connecting with nature through touch gave her strength and stamina to keep moving. Today was going to be a good day.

When she saw a vibrant blue, almost indigo-colored plant bursting with life, she stopped and stared. The vibrant petals, stuck in the middle of generic greens and browns, were communicating with her. She knelt down and let her fingers feel the soft, fragile petals. She remembered learning about forget-me-not flowers in a history class. Something from the Medieval period; a symbol of everlasting love and devotion. As she absorbed their beauty and Zen, Rachel knew what new tattoo she was going to design today.

She walked in the front door a few minutes later as her mother was walking out. Lily tried to get to the café by ten each morning. Her baker and morning team normally managed the breakfast crowd, and Lily managed the lunch and next day preparations.

"Rodney's speech therapist will be here at eleven, and Miss Jenna will come over until I get home tonight. Have a good day at work, Rachel. Love you." Lily gave Rachel a hug as she walked into the garage with her hands full of paperwork.

Rachel didn't know how her mother managed—ordering inventory, running payroll, keeping the bakery stocked and new menu items in weekly rotations. Lily took Mondays off to attend Rodney's specialty doctor appointments, and thankfully she had several reliable employees to call on in a pinch, but the café had taken off over the last couple of years. It had been a struggle for Lily to keep up but, like many parents, when it came to doing what was needed to protect her family, Lily had superpowers and was accomplishing the unthinkable.

Rachel went into the dining room and sat down next to Rodney, who was sketching something. Based on the display of creativity spread across the table, it was his tenth one for the day. Rodney grabbed her hand and held it on his heart. He leaned his head to her shoulder and smiled.

"Hey, Rodney, how are you today? Looks like you have been very busy. This one looks amazing. Is this you on a surfboard? The magic of the sunlight combined with the layers of color in the waves is incredible."

He smiled and nodded.

"You have a gift, Rodney. You could be a famous artist someday. Although you'll have to learn to sign your name on the bottom. Remember: R–O–D–N–E–Y."

Ian walked into the house, slamming the door behind him.

"Is he drawing more silly pictures again? You're not helping him by telling him he's talented. I don't know why you lather him with lies. Even he thinks his art stinks; he signs each one Crummy," Ian grumbled. He dropped his bag on the table, ruffling some of Rodney's work in the process, then headed over to the refrigerator.

"How come your mother never has any good food in the fridge? We eat the same food all the time. Doesn't she know how to cook anything not on the café menu?" He reached in and grabbed a chicken salad sandwich on freshly baked bread, with garden-fresh arugula and grapes from the local farmers market. The sandwich was one of the top selling sandwiches at the café.

Ian shoved the sandwich in his mouth while munching on a bunch of salted chips made from scratch daily at the bakery. Rachel ignored his negativity and began to draw a sketch of forget-me-nots.

"I've got to pick up a shift tonight at the bar, so I'll be late. Can you make me chicken parmesan, so I have some food to eat when I get home? I hate eating crappy bar food. What time are you leaving for work? I could use some help washing my car. It's filthy from riding the trails with Mike yesterday."

"I'm leaving for work shortly. I don't have time to cook you chicken parmesan. And I'm sure my mother will bring us home something from work."

"Well, can you at least start washing my car? I need to jump in the shower."

"I really don't have time. I need to leave shortly myself to prepare drafts of my customer's tattoo design before they arrive."

"You don't have time to wash my car, but you have time to sit with your brother and draw stupid pictures of... flowers?" Ian said incredulously as he picked up Rachel's sketch. "Really, Rachel? Your boyfriend should be your first priority,"

"I'm working on a new tattoo; they're forget-me-nots."

"Whatever. Keep coloring with your brother. Just don't ask me for any favors." He stood up and stared at her, trying to make her feel guilty. Getting no response, he headed upstairs to the shower.

Rodney scribbled something on the paper and handed it to Rachel. *No idea, Rachel. No idea.* It was signed "Crummey."

Rachel patted his head. "I know, buddy. It's okay. Someday everything's going to be okay."

Rachel finished her drawing, folded it, and tucked it in her pocket. She talked to Rodney's speech therapist when she arrived and ensured Rodney was all set before leaving for work. When she walked into Mercy Tattoo, she was immediately greeted by a love-sick couple wanting matching tattoos. Rachel sat them down and let them look through the studio's portfolio while she set up for her first appointment, scheduled to arrive in thirty minutes.

The couple waved her over and she sat down, ready to listen. The two were holding hands and sitting so close to each other their skin blended into one. They locked eyes with each other every few seconds and wore the most endearing expressions. It was like staring at a real life version of Claire and Jamie from *Outlander*, but instead of wearing a puffy sleeved shirt and a billowy corset dress, they were wearing paint-splashed overalls and unbuttoned denim shirts.

"Thanks for letting us look through the book. We're both artists ourselves. Shelly is a watercolor artist, and I craft art out of recycled materials. We've been together for three years, and we now know alone we are nothing but together the world is infinite. Shelly is my caffeine, my daily mojo. She's like my own personal garden; I pick exactly what I need to nourish me. Not only does she make me a stronger, more versatile artist, she brings humor into my life and reminds me life is too short to worry about the little things."

"Oh, baby, you are so cute. Felix is the sweetest, most thoughtful boyfriend. We feel so lucky to have found one another. We really would like our tattoos to communicate that we are not complete without the other. Our favorite thing to do at the end of every day is stare at the moon and the stars. Could you ink half of a moon on his shoulder and the other half on mine? Then on the inside of the black and white moon, tattoo a blue and black butterfly split between us."

"I think I know exactly what to show you. Let me pull it up on my profile. I did something similar for another client. Hold on a minute." Rachel searched her database and clicked on an image, then swirled her screen toward them. "This is similar to what you are asking, but the butterfly was flying away from the moon. I could enlarge it and layer the details to enhance the contrast. How does that sound?"

"Yes," they said in unison.

"You nailed it. How long will it take?" Shelly said.

"I have an appointment on his way here, so can you come back in three hours?" They set the appointment and filled out paperwork while Rachel began prepping for her client.

She loved interpreting the lovebirds' wishes, but it did make her pine for a stronger relationship. How nice it would be to feel the safety and security of boundless love. To know if you needed a push, someone was there to propel you. If you needed a hug, someone was there to embrace you. If you needed quiet and solitude, someone was there to hold your hand. She had none of that.

If she needed a push, Ian would shove her right off the ledge. His hugs were hugs of negativity, filled with anger, stress, and condescending comments. And the only time Ian was good at giving her quiet and solitude was when he was passed out drunk every other night.

As Rachel began working on her client, her mind drifted off to sitting side by side on the beach on a wet surfboard, sharing a watermelon slushie and intertwining toes underneath the wet sand with Tony by her side.

Now that was her kind of mojo.

The Waiting Game

Chapter Eight

Present Day

"Henry, does your delivery route include the Artist Warehouses on 393?" Trina asked the UPS driver as she accepted a package.

"No. I handle everything from here down to Inlet Beach. Why, did I drop off something to the wrong address?" he asked as he rechecked the labels on the four boxes he was delivering to Grayton Loft & Gifts.

"No. There's no mix-up. I was curious if you know any of the artists. I haven't heard any updates on the Underwater Museum deployment schedule. It's been three weeks since Ian died. I know your eyes and ears are always tuned in even though most people think it's only your hands and back hard at work," Trina freely joked with Henry. They had become acquaintances over the last year, as he stopped at the shop a couple times a week.

"Don't share my secret, Trina. My wife enjoys a nightly recap of my day's observations over a glass of cabernet. It's a rare occurrence to hear the undertones of animosity amongst the creative community, but I did hear the guy burned bridges faster than a California wildfire. I'm sure you know how supportive most artists are of one another, so he must have been quite a character. I'll ask around and see if I can dig up any dirt. Gotta go; I've got a truckload to knock out. Have a good one."

Trina waved goodbye as she grabbed a box cutter to open the first box of new candles. As she unwrapped and retagged inventory, she thought about the art community. Someone would had to have been pretty brazen to purposefully damage the metal framework in hopes of injuring Ian. Even if Ian took advantage of other artists, what would be their motive for killing him? The endless stream of visitors who willingly emptied their purses at art markets, festivals and gift shops created a positive, supportive energy within the art world. They didn't need to fight for customers.

On the other hand, the valuation of Ian's art had skyrocketed since his death. If someone wanted, or more importantly, needed to make a quick buck, killing Ian might have been motive enough.

What if someone bought a couple pieces of his art before his death knowing their valuation would double or maybe triple? It was a good theory and worth digging into. She didn't think Rachel could have played a part in his death, and for Lily's sake, she hoped Rachel didn't. Especially given she would reap the biggest financial gain.

Gaining access to Ian's studio would have been a challenge for anyone who was not an artist or a paying customer. A prowler hiding behind blank canvases ready to pounce? If it wasn't someone who physically gained access, then maybe the bonding material was manipulated. Or a vindictive apprentice who mixed a gas agent into the air conditioner system.

While she worked, Trina was watching mini murder mystery scenes in her head. Her mind twisted and turned in so many directions. One minute she was thinking the family was involved, the next a jealous artist. Maybe a person from Ian's past who finally got their revenge? She was visualizing the deadly deed and then solving the crime like a local hero. If the imaginary actors didn't do a good enough job portraying her theory, the remote control in her head clicked to the next mini movie. She kept devising theories and thinking about all the ways a murderer could hide. Surely, one of these scenarios would lock her attention and keep her moving on the right path.

At the end of her shift, Trina shifted gears slightly and headed home thinking about the plans she and David had with Detective Trent and JoAnn after work for a five-course dinner and musical performance. This would be the first time she had spoken with Trent since the incident. She had hoped to learn more about the tranquilizer she had found before she spoke to him, which reminded her to make a vet appointment. She had read up on the uses of Gabapentin but remained curious as to the coincidental discovery so close to a crime scene. She might have to put on a show of ignorance in front of her vet to gain a little more insight.

After handing their keys to the valet at Old Florida Fish House a couple of hours later, David and Trina walked slowly through the gazebo-covered walkway to the hostess stand. The outside dining area was already packed. The restaurant offered many choices of food and beverages, four to five unique sitting areas, and a list of nightly talent Nashville or Los Angeles would clamor for. The variety of ways to seek entertainment on 30A were endless, and the talent never disappointed, which was one of the main reasons she loved living here.

The quarter-acre lot in front of the restaurant had been renovated over the last couple of years with beautiful flower planters, firepits and artificial turf lined with stone walkways. As the hostess walked them through the front door, she led them past the bar and the U-shaped sushi counter out to the lakeside backyard. A huge white tent covered the grass lot, with twenty tables decorated with tablecloths and elegantly paired table settings. A small pop-up bar was situated in the corner, and an artificial turf wall with a neon sign blazing across center was set up for patrons to take photos with the evening's musicians. A line of guests with wine goblets in hand and cell phones ready had already formed.

The Olivers were waiting for them by the bar. "Hey, you two. So glad you could make it," JoAnn said as she gave them both an embrace and Trent shook David's hand. "My kids get a kick out of seeing proof Trent and I are living our best life. Trina, let's go get our picture taken with tonight's singers before dinner service starts."

"Sure. It's nice having a social calendar as full as our adult children. We may go to bed before ten, but we fill our days with more activities than most."

They left the men at the bar and joined the line of mostly women waiting for their turn. Neither Trina nor JoAnn recognized the first musician, who looked like he was in his late twenties or early thirties. He had dark-chestnut wavy locks, short stubble around his chin and deep, dark, piercing eyes. He was an average height with broad shoulders. She recognized the Marshall Tucker Band logo spread across two guitars in an X shape shrouded by angel wings on his shirt. By the looks of it, the T-shirt had lived a good life and witnessed many nights of musical history.

They listened to him chat with the three older ladies who were staging themselves around him for selfies. He was funny, respectful, and polite as he complimented the women on their outfits and energy and let them take as many pictures as they wanted. When the group departed, he waved Trina and JoAnn up to the platform. Trina noticed both of his arms were decorated with tattoos, and he wore a leather bracelet on one wrist and a small silver chain around his neck. They stood on either side of him smiling for the professional camera, then asked if he could take a selfie of the three of them. He knew how to work the crowd in a Texan kind of way as he graciously agreed. They thanked him, then stood ready to get a picture with the main performer, Jared Herzog. Trina had seen Jared numerous times and joked with him she was becoming a Santa Rosa Beach groupie.

Photos accomplished, they returned to the table as a bottle of 2021 Vineyard 29 Cru Cabernet was being poured. The men chatted about recent sports scores, political announcements, and an upcoming car auction, while JoAnn and Trina caught up on the upcoming local charitable events, book recommendations, and recent stories of visiting teenagers causing havoc on 30A.

"Did you see the TikTok of the high school students on the Seaside Lyceum causing mayhem? The gathering started out small, but within fifteen minutes, it looked like a hundred kids had bombarded the stage and wrapped themselves around the upper deck ignoring the curfew in place for unaccompanied teenagers. Liquor bottles were thrown from the second floor, smashing on the platform, while other kids had liquor poured in their mouths from the second story. Luckily, the police arrived pretty quickly, but I heard the kids caused over a thousand dollars' worth of damage," JoAnn said as the men turned to listen in.

"Real shame to see kids disrespect property," David chimed in. "I remember being young and foolish, but I don't remember thinking it was okay to overrun private property and leave it in a state of disrepair."

"So much of it is driven by the desire to get more social media likes," Trent noted. "The unfortunate thing is less than 5% of visiting teenagers act out. The majority simply want to enjoy a great beach vacation, but their freedoms are being stripped away, or at least limited, by more police surveillance because a select few have made bad choices."

"Speaking of surveillance, were you able to generate any leads from cameras at or around the Artist Warehouses?" Trina asked while accepting a lump crab tower plate from the waitress that was a perfectly crafted rainbow of garden and seafood vibrancy.

"The nine, one-story buildings that make up the Artist Warehouses are easily accessible from the rear and the sides if on bike or on foot, so we requested all available video footage. Not all the artists have installed security cameras, and the property management system only has one central one pointed toward the main gate. Ian's studio doesn't have a camera, but the warehouse directly across has an active Ring camera. Unfortunately, once we obtained access to the footage, we discovered someone had blocked the camera lens prior to the incident. We collected a small, black piece of felt that had been slipped over the lens.

"The four artists who co-rent the unit claim to have turned their camera alerts off, so no one noticed the footage was blacked out. And because the felt fit perfectly over the lens, it wasn't noticeable. They told us they use the system more as a deterrent since they've never had any incidents that required them to access their footage. We finished evaluating all the videos from neighboring buildings, and we're still gathering street footage, but unfortunately the most critical camera had been manipulated in advance of the incident. My team is working on compiling a list of potential suspects to interview, but as of now nothing material has popped up."

"The blocked camera is a big clue, right? Shows premeditation," Trina added.

"We are inclined to assume there was intent. Someone wanted to hide their entry into the studio."

"Seems odd all four artists didn't notice the camera was recording a black screen. But I guess if you're not truly relying on the camera for security but merely as a deterrent, the lack of alerts wouldn't have raised concern. I have yet to learn anything worthy of your attention, but I'll let you know if I hear anything relevant."

"Thanks. As you can imagine, his death is sending nervous vibrations throughout the art community. We'll keep digging but appreciate an extra set of eyes and ears," Trent said with a brief nod to Trina.

"Ladies, you so graciously arranged tickets for this five-course dinner tonight, who are you most excited to see?" David asked, changing the subject as one waiter cleared plates and another began serving the main course of blackened grouper with lemon beurre Blanc sauce, rice pilaf and seasoned vegetables.

"To be honest, I don't recognize the opening act but always enjoy hearing Jared sing. I love that Old Florida Fish House is sponsoring this Locals Only week of musicians. Now, don't misunderstand me. I love hearing talent from Atlanta, New Orleans, and Birmingham, but there is something special about listening to talented musicians in their own hometown. It's so nice to know they can make a living while giving back to their own community," Trina said.

Trent's phone rang. He glanced at the number and excused himself.

All eyes in the restaurant turned to the stage as the first singer approached the microphone with an acoustic guitar. A black cowboy hat hung low over his eyes, and he carried a short tumbler with what appeared to be whisky. He placed the drink on an empty stool and stood in front of the microphone. Several audience members let out some hoots and hollers, and a welcome round of applause quickly spread through the crowd.

"Wow. Thank you. Thank you so very much. For those of you who don't know me, my name is Jax Miller. Some of you may recognize my one claim to fame: my song "Again," which made it to the Top 20 of country music this past year." Applause and more cheers erupted. He bowed his head, raised his hand to his mouth and gently wiped it with his thumb. He took a moment and then looked back up to the crowd. His voice was deep, and he spoke slowly and confidently, but at the same time, bashfully.

"Tonight, I want to take you on a journey back to my youth. I grew up here in Santa Rosa Beach. There weren't too many families making the white crystal sand their full-time home back then. We took advantage of the gorgeous water, Dune Lakes, and empty streets. Like any typical teen, we were always looking for something to keep us busy. When you live near the sand and sun all year round, you start to get a little restless with spending your time at the beach. I personally had a couple bouts of recklessness. Knocking over a mailbox or two, stealing bikes from beach accesses, and swiping a beer from Grandpa's cooler while catching a big marlin. But I wouldn't have called myself a rebel. However, I did have a friend or two who repeatedly made bad choices.

"As children, we were taught bad choices have repercussions. But life has taught me that's not always true. Sometimes bad people are rewarded, and good people are left with only their dreams. I would like to share with you a song I wrote called "Rewards." This song is about my dream coming true."

He adjusted the microphone and hummed a few notes. The harmony and melody was strong, warm, and relaxing. Small ballet dancers pirouetted across Trina's arms as his voice opened with a soulful, yet majestic sound. He tilted his head, allowing the audience access to the character in his eyes. His boot tapped rhythmically, and one hand strummed on the strings while another beat gently on the front of the guitar.

"My youthful choices were my own demise

Friendships flawed in their disguise

The thief who stole you from my grasp

Will no longer haunt my delightful past

A decade has blinked, stealing from us

You had your reasons, my respect and love

He had your hand; I had your heart

We will do this together, right from the start

Throw away his negativity

Unlock the chains, you are free

Swimming side by side

My dreams and yours finally collide"

Trina was mesmerized. She heard a hint of John Meyer's innocence mixed with the gruff of Santana and power of Chris Stapleton. He sang with so much purpose and heartbreak. An image of him standing on a pier holding a picture of his girl and tears rolling down his cheeks filled Trina's mind. Whoever took his girl had torn his heart out and burned a deep scar in this man's life.

When he finished, the crowd stood up. Whistles, applause, and stomping feet filled the intimate venue. He had touched everyone. Trent returned to the table with another bottle of wine, Jax sang a couple more of his songs, then finished it up with two fan favorites. There was a ten minute intermission before the next set started.

As soon as the local favorite, Jared, began to sing "Speechless," goosebumps spread across Trina's arms. He killed the next four songs, and the crowd was standing, dancing, and forgetting their desserts and wine goblets. Trent and JoAnn departed before the last song wrapped, but Trina and David decided to stay to the end. Jared settled the crowd down with the first ten chords of "Hallelujah" and finished his set with his new top hit, "Carolina Blue." A great way to end a night of delicious food, bold wine, and Grammy Award-level talent.

While David went to stand in the valet line, Trina examined the merchandise for sale at the musicians' tables. She glanced at T-shirts and logo-emblazed hats, but the cover for Jax's new CD single, "Rewards," caught her attention. She paid the clerk for the CD and Jared's new Carolina Blue hat, then met David in the parking lot.

As they drove home, she flipped through her phone and zoomed in on the selfie taken with Jax.

A delicate weave of green stems wrapped around both his wrists, popping with five-petaled flowers that matched the innocent blue of the ocean, offset with a tiny white star-shaped center. Recognizing the forget-me-nots on his wrists, Trina stared at the CD cover, which depicted two dolphins tattooed on a leather messenger bag.

She recalled the lyrics of the song. Love lost by time and youth as he waited for the reward of reuniting with his special one. *Unlock the chains, you are free.* The combination of those lyrics and the similarity of the flower tattoos around his wrists had Trina staring through an imaginary microscope.

Who exactly was Jax and how was he entwined with Rachel?

Could this handsome, innocent-looking musician have taken steps to help Rachel unlock her relationship chains?

Trina needed to find out.

A Picture is Worth A Thousand Words

Chapter Nine

2020

"Don't. Please don't say that. It is not your fault." Tony stood holding Rachel's hands in the back of the tattoo parlor.

"But it is my fault," Rachel said. "My brother should be falling in love with his high school sweetheart, getting ready for his junior prom, and surfing to the state championship. Instead, he struggles to talk, walks with a limp, and is going to spend the rest of his life with his mother and sister instead of a wife and a family of his own." Rachel sat down on a metal chair. She had her black hair wrapped in a bright-blue scarf. Her recent nose ring and fourth ear piercing were still slightly red from the punctures. She ripped a piece of paper off a notepad and began rolling it into a small ball, a habit she developed when she was a child to keep her hands busy when she was thinking about something.

"Rach, the deer would have crossed the road even if you'd been the one to pick him up. The same result, different circumstance. You need to let it go. Rodney is still the same happy-go-lucky kid. I bet he wakes up with a smile on his face every morning, ready to tackle the day."

Rachel smiled. "He does. I don't know how he does it, but he still finds joy in all the little things. The other day when we walked to the beach, he stopped me when we reached the top of the stairs as we both stared at the beauty of the Gulf. He put his fingers over my eyes and told me to listen. 'Still have this. Nobody can take it away,' he said. Breaks my heart. He's right, though. We still have each other. And he can still listen to the surf. And maybe one day, he'll ride a wave again."

"See, there's the Rachel I know and love," Tony said, grabbing her hands.

"Oh, Tony, I'm so sorry. My life choices suck! It's pathetic. We should be honeymooning in Hawaii, listening to you make patrons swoon at a bar in Honolulu. Instead, I'm... I'm..." Rachel let out an exasperated sigh.

"You're in a relationship with the wrong guy. You dating Ian is like Princess Diana dating Squidward from *SpongeBob SquarePants*. You have grace and honor and the most giving heart. He, on the other hand, is ignorant and arrogant, and his egotistical tentacles are in everybody else's business. He blames everyone else for his bad choices. Remind me, why are you with him again?" Tony smiled and leaned in, touching noses.

"Great. How am I going to get that image out of my head? I'm going to be climbing in bed with a man who has arrogant tentacles." Rachel laughed. "Tony, you have to go live your life. Not just live it, I want you to live your dream. Live our dreams."

"No matter how many times I've told you, you still don't get it. I am never going to be 100% if I'm not with you. My dreams are fuzzy and unfocused, like trying to stare through filthy sunglasses on a bright day. When I'm with you, I can see my career unfolding out like a red carpet at the Grammys. I feel stronger, bolder, and wilder. Life's moments are radically better with you." He took her arm and spun her in a halo. "You are the fizzle in my drinks, the honey in my yogurt. You are the hot sauce on wings, and the craving that feeds my sweet tooth." He gently touched her hair, her cheeks, and her lips with each statement. "You are the hydration that helps me grow, and the warmth that makes me secure."

"Oh my gosh. I can feel my heart melting as it drips down my torso. You know how to reach in and grab a woman's soul. I'm doomed."

Tony wrapped his hands around her slender waist and continued. "Let's make a bet. If Ian magically disappears from your life in the next five years, you promise to be chained to me forever."

"I'll do better than promise. Come here. I have an idea." Rachel dragged him through the curtains out to the front of the studio. Two other tattoo artists were bent over clients, working on various stages of inking. Rachel sat him down. After making sure he was clean and properly prepped for the process, Rachel pulled up an image on her computer screen.

"Do you trust me, Tony?"

"One hundred percent."

"My past choices are restraining me like kudzu vines, but the beauty of these very special flowers means I promise not to ever forget you." She pointed to an elaborate drawn image of forget-me-not flowers. "If you let me tattoo this on your wrists, as I will do mine, we will always have a small piece of each other no matter where we go."

"It's as much my fault as it is his that we're not together. I let my fears and my sympathy for your situation blur what was rightfully mine." He pulled her close, so their lips were millimeters from touching. She closed her eyes and took a deliberate breath. Her hands reached up and held his chin in a gentle embrace. His hands rested gently on her knees, which were straddled on either side of his chair.

Tony whispered to her as if the words breathed life directly into her slightly parted lips. "I don't need a reminder; I want a reminder." He leaned in an extra inch, his lips grazing hers. "Rachel, do your dolphin magic."

***

"Stand over there, Rachel. You're in the shot." Ian grunted as he fixed his hair in the hall mirror near the family room. He took a swig from a flask he kept in his pocket and smiled at his reflection. Ian continued sneaking alcohol even though he recently came back from three weeks at a rehab center.

Rachel walked away to escape the unmistakable smell of bourbon and rested her hands on the kitchen sink staring out the window. Today was going to be a proverbial slap in the face. She was the professionally trained, educated artist with so much talent bubbling at the surface she was ready to explode, yet her irritating, self-righteous boyfriend was getting his picture taken for an upcoming article in a local magazine. Photographer Jamie Rich was unpacking her camera equipment and setting up a tripod in the living room to take photographs of Ian for the feature focusing on newly discovered talent along the Emerald Coast.

His artwork on the bridge had exploded in popularity after some vacationer made a TikTok standing next to it. Now, Ian was getting requests for commissioned art left and right. It didn't make sense. Ian was not an artist. He had no spark of creativity. No visions dancing in his head. He literally typed the description of what his clients asked for into the computer and stole ideas from other artists' works. If someone paid him to draw a black square, he would beg her to help him figure out how to draw the four lines. He was as inspirational as a flower garden after an unexpected freeze.

That one day under the bridge was a unicorn experience. He was as much an artist as calling the middle school kid who cut your grass a landscape designer. She spent more time finishing his commissioned artwork than he did messing it up. Sometimes, she would stay up late at night, paint primer over his work, and redo the entire piece; Ian never even noticed. Ian thought in black and white. What made him look good? How much his career pissed his dad off. How much money he could squeeze out of a client. How quickly could he finish so he could go play golf?

As she listened to the photographer directing him into positions, she could hear him spewing lies. How his abstract pieces depict the warmth and energy of emotions. The paint flowed off his brushes as images danced on his fingertips. Hearing Ian blatantly lie talking about his inventive style fried her patience.

Ian's success would fade. It had to because it didn't calculate. To keep herself calm, she focused on her happy place; her computer filled with hundreds of digital masterpieces. The endless hours spent behind her screen devising intricate, thought-provoking, one-of-a-kind immersive and interactive images. Colors, dimensions, projections, overlays, and dilemmas.

Over the last year, her art had been inspired by the complexity of her crazy, dysfunctional relationship. She had developed her own unique specialty—blending contrasting images to make a statement. Her recent favorite included a complex piece with sound and movement illustrating a library filled with hundreds of books and wild and exotic musicians playing loud music within the confines of the perfectly manicured typically quiet library. A drummer drumming on an open book. A guitarist strumming chords on sentences instead of guitar strings. A singer getting lost in a tunnel of poems.

She also was putting the finishing touches on two additional pieces; a trashy hospital operating room, and a tree growing up through frozen water with fish swimming in cotton candy. The opposition of the images was striking and conversational. She kept her eyes closed and blew out a slow breath, trying to block out the activity in the next room.

"Rach, come see what I drew," Rodney said from the dining room table.

Rachel turned and looked at her quiet and unassuming brother. His jet-black hair was textured cut, managing the natural waves on the sides of his head. His beaming smile melted Rachel's irritation. She walked over to the side of him and peered over his shoulder at a 10x10 piece of paper with an accurate depiction of a black camera spread across it. Through the five-inch wide drawn camera lens was the silhouette of a woman with a magic wand in her hand sprinkling magical dust all over a computer screen. The picture drawn on the computer screen was a stunning display of bright hues of pink, yellow and orange popping in 3D into what looked like a digital masterpiece. Rachel picked it up in awe. Her brother should be getting his picture taken, not Ian.

"Is this supposed to be me making my own special magic? I love it! You need to sign this one, Rodney. This one is going to be my personal inspirational piece. You are amazing." She bent down and kissed the top of his head.

"No, Rach. You tha mazing one."

Rachel cleaned up the items in the sink and then went out to the now empty garage. Ian had moved into their house last week and was converting the garage into his makeshift studio until the lease began on the public studio he was opening at the Artist Warehouses. She still couldn't believe she'd convinced her mother to let Ian move in after his father cut him off financially.

The empty space was a huge reminder of the enormity of the recent household transformation. Rodney had been very agitated when he heard the news. He kept shaking his head and saying, "Our hows, our hows." Rachel had to convince him it was only temporary until Ian could put enough money away to find a place of his own. Even as the words came out of her mouth, she felt like she was telling a fairytale. And just like most fairytales, there was danger hidden in the details.

Ian could barely afford to pay the rent for the leased studio space on his part-time wages as a bartender. Rachel warned him that having a couple of commissioned art pieces under his belt didn't guarantee business would continue, especially after the TikTok died down. But after he was asked to do this interview, he went ahead and signed the lease and showed up on their doorstep with all his luggage.

Rachel stared at the empty garage, remembering the disturbing conversation from the fateful night that changed the course of their relationship into her unforgettable reoccurring nightmare.

"Babe, you're going to love waking up next to me in the morning. You can make breakfast for me before I go to the studio, and we can come up with inspirational ideas together in the garage. I'll even put a desk in there so you can work on your silly computer hobby. Since we'll be living together, we won't have to go out on dates anymore, and Lily will appreciate having you around more to help with Rodney. It will be great. I only need a couple of months under my belt before I'm sure my dad with crack open the vault again. He never goes dry for too long. The more famous I get, the more he'll want to help me. The most successful builder in Walton County and his famous contemporary artist son. I can see dollar bills rolling my way."

Ian entered their house as if he already lived there. He walked into the living room, purposefully placing his luggage by the treadmill Rodney performed his daily physical therapy on.

"I don't think this is a good idea, Ian. We've only been dating on and off for four years." Rachel winced in her head as she thought about the loss of four years of her life. "Moving in together seems like rushing it. My mother's got enough on her plate. Besides, Rodney is a full-time job. You know how much time my mother and I spend going back and forth to therapists. Even if you're here, I don't think I'll have any more time to spend with you than I have now between work and his doctor appointments."

"Babe, if people are stupid enough to pay me to slap some paint on a canvas, then I need to take advantage of this situation. Hell, I could let Rodney paint my commissioned pieces and no one would be the wiser." He picked up the basket full of Rodney's pain and inflammation medications and therapy lotions and examined them as if he playing the bad cop in an interrogation. A subtle reminder that her decision was the reason the basket was full.

Rachel could feel the anger boiling in her gut. Rodney was ten times the artist Ian was. People would pay thousands of dollars for Rodney's life-reflecting imagery. If her mother would let her, she would fill every inch of the walls with his artwork. How dare Ian criticize Rodney. Ian shouldn't even be in the same sentence with Rodney, never mind the same house.

"Besides, Rachel, if you don't let me move in, then I might have a lapse in memory and share with the world how you abandoned your twelve-year-old brother, leaving him all alone on a dark night at the beach. He texted you and you promised to pick him up. Promises were made to your mom. She wouldn't have gone out if she knew her daughter would recklessly abdicate her sisterly duties. Your selfish decision changed your brother's life. It's a shame to think how bad decisions run in your family history. Do you really want me to expose family secrets?" Ian picked up the last surfing championship award Rodney had won before his accident and spun it around carelessly in his hands. Another non-verbal stab in the gut.

He knew how to get under her skin. Why didn't she have the balls to stand up to him?

Rodney limped into the room. Immediately his demeanor changed when he saw Ian. "It late. Why you here?" Rodney asked.

"Hey, little man. I'm going to be moving in. Rachel and I are going to be roommates. Guess you're not going to be the only man getting waited on hand and foot anymore." Ian smiled at Rachel as he threw the surfing award into her hands and walked out of the room.

"Rach. Not true?"

"I don't know Rodney. I hope it will be a temporary thing."

"Not good."

"It's temporary. I promise. He's not worthy of being on our family Christmas card. I'll fix this, Rodney. Be patient."

"No Idea, Rach. No idea."

Rachel wrapped her arm around him as they stood in front of the hall mirror. "You and me, Rodney. I've got your back. I promise."

She remembered calling Tony after Ian went to sleep for the first time in her bedroom. They talked for hours, helping her manage her frustrations. She vented about the household financial burdens, the difficulty of juggling her career, supporting her mother and being a sister and a friend to Rodney. She explained how the stress of medical bills, automobile insurance and student loans was crippling her self-esteem and desire to pursue an alternative career.

When she got to the part about Ian moving in, she self-consciously cringed, knowing it would break Tony's heart, but she needed to share her irritation with someone. She had lasted four years with Ian because they had their separate spaces. Now the place she escaped to feel whole, to feel accepted and loved, was going to be defaced by Ian's ego and lack of respect. Plus, eating his way through the pantry, Ian would add to her financial burden, not alleviate it.

Tony listened, never judged. He didn't guilt her or question her life choices but rather attempted to paint a bright future, telling her today's decision are only today's, not tomorrow's. He reminded Rachel of her mom's words of wisdom: commandeering life's challenges was like watching acrylic dry; each layer added strength, character, and beauty.

Rachel shook her head, back in the real world, listening to the camera shutter over and over again. She could feel the stress creeping into her shoulder muscles, and the beginning of a headache. She wished Tony was here to help her get through this afternoon. Rodney was trying to help, but she needed Tony's strength of character and calm energy to make her feel less like a worm caught on a fishing pole—hooked, hanging in midair and analyzing her daunting inability to escape.

A few minutes later, the photographer asked to see some of Ian's work. Ian excused himself, saying he had a portfolio in his car. While he stepped out, Miss Rich walked around the dining room table, which was covered in partially used paints, a paint-splashed palette, and a slotted container filled with Faber-Castell graphite pencils of varying hardness. Eraser shavings and small wads of used kneaded Blick eraser blobs were sprinkled all over the table next to several different sized pencil sharpeners.

She picked up several pieces of art, and Rachel could hear mutters of appreciation under her breath. The photographer began taking photos of Rodney's work, moving the images around as she clicked.

"These are magazine worthy. Does Ian sell these? I would love to show these in the article."

Rachel was about to answer when she heard Ian drop his attaché case and stomp over to the table.

"These are silly scribbles and practice. You don't need to look at those. Come over here and let me show you some high-quality pieces of art." He pushed all of Rodney's work onto the floor. The flutter of pages and the crash landing of Rodney's creativity felt like knives raking over Rachel's skin. She was about to say something when she felt Rodney grab her wrist.

"Be bet than. Strngrrr."

Rachel looked at her younger brother. Really looked at him. He understood. All her anxiety, all of Ian's negativity, the repeated demoralizing comments Rachel put up with. Rodney seemed to understand she was doing this for him. Rodney took her hand, slowly moved it to his heart, and pressed it there. He took his other hand and raised it to her eyes, protecting them from the scene in front of her. She could feel the slight tremble as he held it blocking her vision.

"Feel."

She let herself feel the pulse of his heart beat against her palm. One thump. Another. She let the darkness seep into her soul. *This is temporary. You are going to figure out a way out of this, this thing, whatever it is. Take this anger. Use this emotional energy. Let your disappointment, your desperation fuel you. Breathe.*

She gently took his hand and removed it from her eyes and placed all four of their hands together on his heart.

"Go." Rodney pointed to her computer on the desk.

She smiled and released her hands. For the next four hours, Rachel sat at her computer and created the most powerful soul searching digital masterpieces of her life.

Flock To Florida

Chapter Ten

Present Day

S etting her sights on the horizon, Trina held the boat railing tightly, as if she were securing a toddler's hand in an amusement park. She was excited about the experience awaiting her, but the rocking of the boat was making her stomach queasy. A very limited number of people were invited to witness first-hand the annual Underwater Museum of Art deployment. Trina felt privileged to be sitting on one of five small, covered pontoon boats transporting eight passengers within viewing distance of the deployment vessel. Rachel had been provided two passes as an honorary guest, and Lily asked Trina to fill in for her since today was a huge supply delivery day at the café.

As the boat rocked, Trina's mind transported back in time. A foggy memory from her youth when she felt as if she had been riding in a horse and buggy. Startled by the negative flashback, Trina squeezed the railing a little tighter and took a deep breath of Gulf air. *You can't erase the past. Lily needs you to be in the now. You turned your past into a better future, so now do the same for Rachel. Focus.*

She let the breeze awaken her senses and re-centered herself. She casually wiped the railing down with her T-shirt, the memories having agitated her nervous habit of leaving no trace behind. She turned and found a seat between two ladies she didn't know, as Rachel was riding in another boat with the four artists being recognized today.

"Hi, nice to meet you. My name is Trina. Is this your first time watching the deployment?"

"Hi, Trina. Nice to meet you. I'm Roberta. Roberta James. This is not my first experience, but each annual installation feels like I'm seeing snow for the first time; it's pretty incredible. I'm a reporter with the PCB News Herald. How are you connected to the program?"

"I'm filling in for someone who couldn't make it today, so I'm not sure what to expect as this is my first rodeo. I'm excited to see all the sculptures, but to be honest, I'm morbidly curious to see Mr. Scott's sculpture."

"Good or bad, his death has definitely brought another layer of publicity to this year's event. I'm glad his apprentice, Victor Nevad, was able to complete the *Unflappable* sculpture. They finished evaluating the structural integrity last week," Roberta said as she flipped through her small notepad.

"Such a sad ending for a young man, and a very unusual set of circumstances for the art community," Trina said. "On the bright side, I bet the Cultural Arts Alliance has been googled more times over the last three weeks than the last Elon Musk tweet. Though, it is unpleasant to think the loss of someone's life has brought the gift of more admirers and more livestream deployment viewership. But I've learned so much about this project over the last couple of weeks. What an incredible collaboration of art, diving enthusiasts, marine life, and environmental benefits. I bet new artists will be clamoring for their chance to be on next year's elite list of honored artists."

"My understanding is one of those spots is already taken. The artist who lost her spot this year was given a guaranteed spot for the coming year's installations. Let me see. I have her name someone here," she said as she flipped through the pages. "Samantha Grey. I've heard she is extremely talented and deserved to have her spot reclaimed."

"How did she lose her spot?"

"Her design proposal had received national recognition because the governor referred to it during a news conference, but she had a bad skiing accident soon after being selected. The artists only have five months to complete their designs before the final work is brought to Orange Beach, Alabama, where the sculptures are attached to their concrete pedestals. After her injury, she voluntarily backed out as she knew she wouldn't have physically recovered enough to finish her piece in time. Ian Scott was selected as her replacement. However, since she missed her original opportunity due to a medical situation, the committee guaranteed her a spot for next year."

"Really? That's interesting. How did the governor get involved?"

"He was meeting with members of the South Walton Artificial Reef Association (SWARA) in regard to potential state funding of another project. During their discussions, the governor was shown several of the top UMA proposals submitted by various artists. Samantha's grabbed his attention. Let me see, I have some information. Ah, yes, here it is. Her piece was called *Flock to Florida*. Embracing the tropical and cultural diversity of the state and highlighting the freedom of expression embedded in the Florida way of life. The design was a concrete spiral symbolizing the constant churning of new ideas supported by Florida's "Open for Business" philosophy. The spiral was to be accentuated by hand-etched images of ten of the most successful entrepreneurs in the state's history. Anyway, she will be one of next year's artists." Roberta waved her hand apologetically as her cell phone rang. "I'm glad we are close enough to shore that we still have reception." She stood up and walked toward to edge of boat to accept the call.

Trina remembered meeting an artist at the crime scene whose name was Samantha. She hadn't said the most pleasant things about Ian. But then, nobody had. Still, Samantha's angst was more meaningful now. Trina wondered what process had led to Ian being selected as the replacement.

Trina turned to her other side and introduced herself to the woman sitting nearby, who it turned out was a local artist who had previously submitted a proposal to the UMA.

"I heard you talking to the reporter. Samantha *was* injured in a skiing accident, but the real story is in who she was traveling with on that ski trip."

"Okay, you have my curiosity stirring. Who?"

"Ian Scott. How ironic is that? Samantha told me Ian invited her and two of his friends on a trip soon after the committee selected her. All weekend he complained his proposal should have been one of the finalists. On the last day of their trip, he asked her to go up with him for one final run. Looking back, she said wished she'd declined because he was already showing signs of having had too much to drink. But she said he laid on the guilt, telling her she owed him since he'd invited her on the trip. Details are a little murky because she doesn't really remember the accident, but somehow Ian plowed into her on the slopes, causing her to fall and break her arm and sprain her ankle. He walked away scratch free and was picked as her replacement by the end of the week.

"She said she understands that her injuries prevented her from being able to fulfill her duties, but she did think it was odd how fast Ian was selected as a replacement. She turned over the full $7,500 design stipend to Ian, and rumor has it, he also borrowed money from his father to finish the project because he was paying other artists to help him finish it by the deadline."

"Does Samantha think Ian ran into her on purpose?"

"I've never heard her claim he did, but the timing of events was a little suspicious to me."

"I assume Samantha recovered from her injuries over the last five months. Why didn't she get picked to finish Ian's artwork after he died?" Trina said, contemplating the intensity of anger and disappointment Samantha must have garnered after not only losing her spot but forfeiting it to the person that caused her injuries.

"She had no desire to finish what he started, and she knew she was allotted a spot for next year. The only reason Victor agreed to finish it was because they agreed to give him full recognition as the artist. Supposedly, after Ian died, Ian's father tried to use his influence to stop the deployment of Ian's design. He wasn't powerful enough to defeat the combination of excessive publicity and community pressure to honor a dead artist's contribution, but a compromise was negotiated to ensure the Scott family name would only show up as a supporting contributor on Victor's final piece. Strangely enough, Ian's original proposal was subpar in comparison to other artists. He submitted an impeccable sketch, but he had no clear messaging to associate with it. Plus, his 3D renderings were not very detailed. It was like he scanned the sketch and tried to rework it using old software. The fact he was picked as the replacement to begin with still rubs people the wrong way.

"This is only my opinion, but once Victor had full control over the process, he completely transformed the piece in a very short window of time, taking the original premise and designing a sculpture worthy to sit alongside so many other creative and ingenious sculptures that give back to marine life while infusing symbolism and artistic flare to the world beneath the surface."

"You've piqued my curiosity. Now I wish I had seen the before so I can appreciate the after. Were there any rumblings of concern regarding the transfer to Victor since he didn't go through the typical application process?"

"There's always someone willing to throw a punch, but most of us within the community already knew Victor and Ian's girlfriend had performed the majority of the manual labor. From what I heard, she had no desire to finish it, and Victor was willing."

"Interesting, but it makes sense."

"Ian was, how do you say it? He was like a known author who secretly had ghostwriters doing all the work, if you know what I mean. I talked to Victor several times over the last couple of months. Although he was a little green in terms of knowledge as a new artist, he easily recognized failures in Ian's original methods. He said he had to fix structural deficiencies throughout the process and teach Ian processes he should have known all along. I think most of us would agree Victor deserves the full recognition, and I'm glad they let him rename it to *Ray of Hope*. It gives the rest of us artists hope that someday we'll get our shot."

"Thank you so much for sharing an enlightening perspective. Don't give up. Someday you'll get your chance to display your own creation in the Underwater Museum."

Just then, the skipper made an announcement as the boat approached the deployment barge. In order to secure the best viewing positions, the boat was going to drift in the waters near Grayton Beach in a synchronized ballet with four other observation boats, each filled with a select group of spectators, reporters, and artists. About two hundred feet away, resting in the middle of the Gulf, was a large blue vessel with an Empire State Building-sized crane positioned to the side. The crew onboard were carefully preparing the first piece of sculpted beauty for liftoff. Each piece of art was affixed to a six-inch thick, rectangular concrete base that had U-shaped metal loops affixed to each corner. From the peak of the crane, thick rope hung down from a huge stainless-steel carabiner and looped through each of the corner hooks, securing the first piece of cemented beauty.

The crane raised one of the 3,500 pound sculptures into the air.

Witnessing the extraction of a delicate piece of art that represented over 150 days of one artist's commitment, love and creativity was electrifying. The massive structure was slowly lowered, and the piece hovered over the crystal-blue waters of the Gulf of Mexico like a diamond dropping into a treasure chest. Each piece would rest on the ocean's floor and be integrated into the natural habitat of marine life, promoting biodiversity. The large platform splashed as the weight and magnitude of its entrance into its new neighborhood sent ripples cascading throughout. As celebratory air horns blasted from each watercraft, history was unfolding like a slow-motion movie as a unique piece of art was submerged sixty feet below the water. Cheers from all five boats erupted as the boat crew high-fived each other in recognition of success.

The process of moving all the sculptures into the water transpired over a two hour period, but it only felt like minutes to Trina. Victor's piece was the last to take the plunge. Even from a distance, his refined metal work glistened off the original sun concrete base. It was spellbinding. Kudos to him for pulling off an amazing creation under pressure.

The ride back to port was filled with prideful conversations about the deployment's triumphant success. Visualizing all of the fifty plus sculptures placed in the Gulf of Mexico over the years energized Trina to sign up for a private diving experience with Dive 30A. Each piece, covered in natural algae and home to thousands of breeds of fish, created an amazing artificial reef, which the local professional dive team expertly navigated, promoting exploration and discovery.

Trina exited the boat and met up with Rachel in the parking lot for the drive home.

"What an awe-inspiring experience," Rachel said as she twirled a piece of black hair in her fingers, her other hand rested on her growing belly. "I watched the prior year video online, but to see it live was so incredible. My mind is spinning with new artistic inspirations. I can't wait to get home and start sketching out the designs flashing through my mind."

"I wish everyone could see it up close and live. Thank you so much for letting me join you today," Trina said. "Lily really wanted to be here, but I feel honored I could sit in her place."

"Rodney and I are used to it. My mother's café schedule keeps her from 90% of our life's events. She does her very best to make up for it by grilling us when we come home and then sharing the event with her customers like she was there to witness the accomplishment. I appreciate everything you've done to help. My mother really appreciates our community, which has been her core support system since the accident. We really couldn't have managed without our friends and neighbors."

"I've forgotten what normalcy feels like. I've had a difficult time over the years juggling a full-time job, Rodney's appointments, and my own personal life, so I greatly respect her for building a business from scratch. Especially a restaurant. It's a twenty-four-hour, non-stop demand. If it's not inventory or staffing issues, it's an unexpected equipment repair or a disastrous plumbing failure. I know she wanted to be here. I'm sure I'll be watching the entire deployment all over again on YouTube with her and Rodney before the weekend is over."

"Did you know the artist who took over Ian's project?"

"Yes. Victor worked under Ian. Well, honestly, it was the other way around. Ian worked under Victor. He hired Victor right out of college as an apprentice, but Victor had more knowledge and artistic talent than Ian. Victor and I tag-teamed and completed most of the work. Anything Ian touched needed repair and eventually he stopped trying and let us manage the bulk of the process. The only time Ian produced a piece worthy of appreciation was when he was completely inebriated. Which the latter, lately, seemed like a daily occurrence."

"You've mentioned that before. Did he ever seek counseling?"

"Several times. But he checked himself out too quickly and changed sponsors more times than I can count. Most of the time, he would hide under sunglasses and his arrogance. Sometimes it was hard to distinguish between drunk Ian and normal Ian. The only big difference was he forgot everything he said and did when he was under the influence, but he acted pretty much the same sober."

"Was Ian a skilled artist in your opinion? And you don't have to answer if you don't want to. I know he is the father of your baby, and I don't mean to put you in an uncomfortable position."

"It's fine. Anyone who hangs out with Ian gets used to being uncomfortable. Let's say my boyfriend didn't know how to cultivate his inner creative juices. I witnessed his talent once or twice over the years, but his limited skills only flowed through a paint brush not building a 3D fixture. He was lucky to have Victor supporting him."

Rachel was wringing her wrist as she spoke. Trina felt bad for dampening Rachels' excitement by talking about Ian, but she wanted to find out more about Victor. Detective Trent would appreciate any insight into who could have had a motive. She hoped she wasn't putting undue stress on her and the baby, but Rachel seemed contemplative, not stressed.

"Do you think Victor held any grudges against Ian?" Trina continued as she drove down Route 98 toward the 30A turnoff.

"Most definitely. Everyone who came into contact with Ian walked out of his studio with a grudge. Ian was not above begging, bartering, manipulating, and forcing other artists to help him. I swear he spent more time finding dirt on people so he could hold it against them when he needed to finish a piece than he did actually creating art." Rachel clasped her hands together over her stomach and repositioned herself in the passenger seat. "To be totally honest, the list of people who would have had a reason to dislike Ian was longer than the line at Grand Boulevard during the 30A Songwriters Festival."

Trina smiled at the reference. "I'm so sorry to hear that, Rachel. It sounds like you've had more than financial and medical hardships to manage throughout your life."

"Just a few," she said softly and slowly, as if she was carefully pronouncing each letter.

"Please stop me if I'm crossing the line with my questions." Trina paused, waiting for a sign to not proceed further. "Has it ever crossed your mind that Ian might not have died accidently?"

The gravity of the question seemed to resonate with Rachel. She remained silent for several seconds longer than normal before responding. "When I first arrived at the scene, they told me it looked like an unfortunate accident, but my gut told me otherwise. I don't know how the investigators will uncover the entire list of potential suspects, because Ian crossed so many people in his lifetime."

"Have the police sat down with you yet? I bet you could provide them with a list of names that would be good place to start."

"Yes. I met with two different detectives several times. I've provided them with as many names as I could. Unfortunately, though most of the names are people Ian pissed off, that doesn't mean they're crazy enough to commit a crime. But it felt really good to tell someone and get it off my chest."

"It sounds like Ian left quite an impression on people. As you eventually adapt to his passing, I do hope you find strength and happiness. Having a little one will bring you so much joy."

Rachel nodded in silence.

"I haven't personally seen your digital creativity but based on the glimpses of your tattoos and Lily's motherly stories of pride, I can see you are extremely talented. I'm curious, did Ian respect you as an artist?"

Rachel began to twist her wrist again. Her skin was red from the repeated skin to skin contact. "No. Ian wouldn't waste an ounce of energy on anyone but himself. Sadly, the only thing he respected was liquor store hours. He treated AA meetings like a networking event instead of a therapy session. Gosh, you must think I am a horrible girlfriend, but we were not in a typical girlfriend boyfriend relationship. And what we did share was not the most positive thing in my life. It's hard to explain. It was sort of like a small snowball that kept rolling down a hill getting bigger and bigger. The longer it rolled, the harder it was for me to pick up and smash, so I let it keep rolling."

"I am not in a position to judge, Rachel. Everyone has their reasons to live life the way they choose or the way they need. I'm not making any assumptions about you, or him. Watching the events today had me wondering about the circumstances of his death. I'm sure you're curious too."

"I'm curious, but I don't want Ian absorbing any more of my energy. Our relationship had its purpose, and now that purpose has ended, I'm eager to move forward."

"How often did you work with Ian on his painting commissions? Maybe you could take over and build a new revenue stream."

"Unfortunately, once he moved in with us, he saw our mounting pile of medical, cafe and household bills. He then manipulated me into helping him. I ended up assisting him on a regular basis, but he would only share 30% of the proceeds. I really should have earned 75% since I did most of the work, but I didn't mind getting lost in the painting process. Especially knowing I was helping my mother pay bills. But painting is not really my genre. There are an endless supply of local artists who can satisfy Ian's client list."

"Have you had any free time to start exploring your own work since things have calmed down?"

"My mom surprised me with a brand-new Inkjet printer with all the bells and whistles. I know she can't afford it, but she's been extremely supportive of this new phase of my life by pushing me to explore and create. She started sending me links for art grants, art industry award applications and digital art exhibitions. I promised her I would pay her back once I sell Ian's work, but she blatantly refused to accept. So, I promised I'd give 100% to this new phase of my life."

"It's exciting to hear you are diving back in and rediscovering your talent. Lily told me your new business is going to be called DreamInk. I love the name."

"Thank you, Mrs. Scotsdale. The process of renovating the garage into my own tattoo parlor and diving into digital art full-time has been invigorating. I haven't felt this free in years."

Trina pulled into Rachel's driveway and recognized Lily's car. They both got out and walked up the path to the house. Rodney opened the door, letting Charlie out. Rachel reached out to give the poodle a cuddle. As she fawned over the dog, Trina caught a glimpse of her forget-me-not tattoos, which previously had looked like a pair of handcuffs. Trina had researched the flower and discovered it was associated with various symbolic meanings, including broken promises and regret. Trina assumed the flower chains that adorned her wrists represented Rachel's sisterly promise to protect Rodney post-accident.

But to Trina's surprise, her wrists were now free of the symbolic chains. No longer were the flowers tattooed in a vise grip around her wrists, but rather they had been reworked into beautifully crafted bouquets. Trina didn't know how difficult the process of redesigning a permanent tattoo into an altered image would be, but the simple fact Rachel made the change to her body art reflected the impact Ian's death and departure from her life must have had.

It was impossible to stand on the outside looking in and expect to grasp the motivation and illogical complexity of remaining in an unhappy relationship, but the unspoken message of the reworked tattoo said more than any verbal one. The redesign screamed freedom, contentment, and appreciation for the beauty of her new life as a soon to be mother and as a woman unbound by the tethers that previously restrained her.

Trina hated to admit it, but when it came to Ian's death, Rachel had the greatest motive of all. Trina didn't expect to understand it, but she'd gathered enough intel to recognize a possible red herring. Rachel had been released and was happy to be free from the negative influence of Ian's life and companionship, and she would gain financial freedom with the pending sale of Ian's now-coveted artwork.

Vincent was not too far behind in the motive department. Samantha too.

Trina stood inside the doorway looking at a happy family photo of Lily, Rodney, and Rachel from several years earlier. Even with all her previous interactions with the Fairfield family, she had not realized how badly their level of happiness had been drained by an unwelcome guest constricting the household.

As the three of them now stood in the foyer in a warm and genuine family embrace, Trina saw that joy had returned to this special family. Lily was eagerly interrogating Rachel to hear all the details of today's adventure. Rodney was holding Rachel's hand, resting his head on her shoulder, and staring at her like she was Cinderella. Rachel stood in the center, bursting with energy, detailing every tiny aspect of the boat ride, crane extraction and the waves that rebounded off the sculptures causing nearby boats to sway as each massive concrete design was given a new home for all the enjoy. Rodney threw out several technical deployment questions, and Lily asked to see pictures. They were lost in a once-in-a-lifetime recreation of watching history unfold under the blue crystal waters of the Gulf.

Feeling like an intruder watching the symbiotic family dynamics, Trina nodded at Lily and slowly retracted from the house. As she walked back to her car, she wondered what drove Rachel to stay in an unhealthy personal relationship, while also being constrained by the irrational demand to perform as a painter with what appeared to be an unjust financial split of proceeds. She didn't have the right to know, although her desire to understand was growing.

While Trina teeter-tottered between feeling sorry for Rachel and feeling unnerved by her animosity toward her deceased boyfriend, she desperately wanted to ask her if she knew the singer Jax. But she felt like she had pushed the boundaries enough in one day.

Promises Promises

Chapter Eleven

2022

"I'll pay you back. I swear, Dad. I won't disappoint you." Rachel hit the end call button on her cell phone. "Damn it!"

She grabbed her laptop and checkbook and headed out the back door. She laid her computer on the patio table and walked to the edge of the property overlooking the beach. Several blue chairs and umbrellas lined the water's edge. Small children were digging holes in the sand, while others took naps in the midday sun. Groups of people mingled in waist-deep water wearing hats and sunglasses to block the glaring rays of the sun. Couples holding hands walked slowly down the beach, bending over periodically to pick up a seashell. Rachel caught sight of a pod of dolphins swimming behind a group of kids throwing a football back in forth in the water, oblivious to the natural beauty of the marine life dipping and diving through the waves.

She was so frustrated. Angry even. Why did she trust him? What made her think he would follow through? Stand behind his word? Stop drinking? He'd manipulated her into a relationship. Squeezed himself into their household. Stolen her dream of becoming a recognized artist. Treated her mother like an employee. Overexaggerated Rodney's limitations, treating him like a toddler instead of a grown adult. Checked on her whereabouts like she was untrustworthy. No wonder his family abandoned him.

Rachel started pacing back and forth in the yard, waving her hands around like she was practicing for a part in a play. Berating herself for becoming that girl everyone felt bad for. The one who people said had so much to offer the world; what happened? What began as a silent conversation slowly became a verbal one.

"He is the most illogical, disrespectful, lazy, frustrating, mean, drunk of a boyfriend."

An arm gently touched the back of Rachel's waist.

Rachel winced. She hadn't realized she was speaking—or for that matter, yelling—out loud. She looked up and tried to put on a smile for her brother. Although almost a decade younger than Rachel, as an adult now, Rodney surpassed her in height. He frequently teased her that he should be the older sibling since he could reach the tallest cabinets in the kitchen. She reminded him that Lily only spoiled the youngest child, so if he still liked eating the 5-Cheese Bomb grilled cheese sandwich at the Meltdown food truck in Seaside every Friday night, he better own his rightful place as the younger sibling.

She sighed as she responded to Rodney's touch with a sisterly embrace, remembering why she was putting up with Ian in her life. She was the reason Rodney had to spend an hour a day pulling on an elastic stretch band, practicing on a balance board, and completing leg raises and knee extensions over and over again. If her brother could work with a speech therapist three times a week and spend the rest of his life with physical and mental disabilities, she could deal with Ian.

"Remember when we would sneak out of the house after dinner and chase crabs back into their holes up and down the beach? And you used to sit in the brackish water in Allen Lake for hours with your snorkeling mask trying to find the mullet. I'll always remember when you turned ten and caught your first redfish after a trip to Stinky's Bait Shack. You were so proud holding that fish and then it slipped right out of your hands before we could take a picture. Do you remember that?"

"Slipree sucr," Rodney said with a silly grin, and Rachel laughed. "I miss fishg," Rodney said pragmatically.

"We need to get you back out there. If you can carry trays full of food, I bet you can hold a fishing pole."

"Can't bait line. Hand shake too much."

"I'll help you. Let's do it this weekend, okay? You can teach me what bait to buy, and I'm sure we can find your old fishing pole in the garage."

"Not Ian," Rodney said, shaking his head emphatically.

"Okay, Rodney. I won't tell Ian."

"Wut Dad say make you anggee?"

"You heard that too, huh?"

Rachel squeezed both her hands into tight fists. She took in a slow, deep breath of fresh air and forced a controlled breath out, then grabbed his hand and led him back to the patio table.

"Remember when Ian moved in and we helped him open up his art studio? He'd been adamant he needed to lease studio space if he was going to invite clientele to examine his art. He needed first and last month rent to secure the lease, and five thousand to buy art supplies. Well, I convinced Dad to loan Ian the money since his parents refused. Ian begged me to ask and promised to pay Dad back by the end of last year. Ian had six substantial commissioned projects to work on before he signed the lease, so I felt pretty confident that once he was up and running he would be able to pay Dad back. Well, you know how stingy Dad is with money even though he has plenty of it. He refused to lend a penny until I put together a whole business plan with a twelve-month forecast to support his investment. I also had to sign the loan agreement as Ian's guarantor, which basically meant if Ian didn't pay it back, I'd have to.

"Last week, Ian finished two of his most expensive commissioned pieces and was finally going to have enough money to pay it back in full. Instead of coming home Friday after work and wiring the money, he called me from Las Vegas. He decided to celebrate with his friends for the weekend. This morning, I found out he lost it all. Every penny of it. He's not only broke but now owes the casino money. It's going to take him months to recoup what he lost and still pay his studio expenses. He's borrowing money from friends and other artists to help pay next month's rent, but the original debt to Dad still has to be paid."

"Ian's mistake. Not Rach."

Rachel flipped her laptop open. "I agree, Rodney. But I made a promise, and I have to stand behind it. I need to pay Ian's debt by the end of the month. Between my wages at the tattoo parlor and the couple shifts at the café, even after helping pay household bills, I've saved a pretty decent amount." Rachel showed Ian her screen, which displayed her bank balance.

"Your money. You keep."

"I made a promise. Just like I promised you that I'm going to protect you forever." Rachel held her wrists out with her palms touching, her forget-me-not chain tattoo clearly visible.

"I am never going to break a promise again. I saved this much money once; I can do it again. And when I do, you're going to help me open the coolest tattoo studio on 30A. Will you promise me?" Rachel held out her pinky finger, and Rodney reached out and twisted his with hers.

"Still not right. No idea, Rach. No idea. Crummey."

Rachel nodded, still curious why he always repeated that phrase. "It's okay if you don't understand, Rodney. Financial transactions are hard for most people to grasp. This is my mistake, not yours, and I'm going to make it right."

Rodney went back inside and sat at the dining room table to let his frustrations out on pieces of paper. Rachel sat at her computer for the next two hours number crunching her way through her monthly expenses. She signed up for a couple of extra shifts at work and figured out how she could reduce costs. She'd been taking an online digital arts class to keep herself current with the latest technology, but she was going to cancel the remaining sessions and ask for a refund. She could also skip her daily Beach Cowboy Latte from Hotz Coffee and end her yoga membership at Studio Thirty A.

After devising a financial plan, she switched over to the Affinity Designer software to disappear into the design world and forget her troubles. She played with brush width and opacity variances, fine tuning her pen strokes and manipulating the vector scales while transforming her images with the vector warp tool. She lost herself in developing a dramatic new design and almost missed dinner even after her mother gave her a fifteen minute warning. She examined the Pantone color library and ensured she had selected the most visually appealing complex combination of colors and hit save.

Rachel pulled herself away from her computer and rubbed her neck, feeling the tightness slowly release. She went downstairs into the kitchen and gave Lily a hello hug. Lily placed a large casserole dish on the dining room table next to a feta, cranberry, and arugula salad.

"Dinner smells amazing. What is this?" Rachel asked as she scooped out a serving for Rodney.

"It's a new recipe from Half Baked Harvest. It's called the Creamy Caprese Quinoa Bake. I used Rao's tomato sauce, quinoa, fresh mozzarella, and basil from the garden."

"Thank you so much for cooking. I'm sorry you had to prepare dinner after working all day. I sort of got lost in a train of thought upstairs."

Ian walked in the front door, dropping his golf bag at the entrance. Obviously under the influence, he barely walked a straight line through the foyer into the kitchen, bumping into furniture along the way.

"Didn't even have enough class to wait for me? Since when do we eat before seven?" He grabbed a beer out of the refrigerator and plopped down next to Rodney, sliding Lily's plated dish away from her spot to his.

"You're welcome for this home-cooked meal, Ian," Lily said with complete disgust and frustration.

"Well, that's your job right? You are a cook. I would hope you can provide dinner for your family every night. Don't think you deserve accolades for cooking tomato sauce and cheese. Doesn't take a genius," he said as he stuffed a mouthful before Lily even filled a plate to replace the one he took.

"How can you afford to go golfing? Rents due in five days," Rachel said with a clenched jaw.

"Eh, we hopped on the course in the middle of hole four. Nobody noticed Mike and me. We played four through sixteen. The old folks behind us couldn't even catch up. They had no idea we even jumped on the course."

"Doesn't your father have a membership at the Vue? If you get caught, he's going to—"

"Going to do what? There's nothing my father can do to me that he hasn't already done. You need to learn to live life, Rachel. Let go of all those rules you live by. That's why you'll never be an artist like me. You need to release the chains that bind you. Take your laughter, your love and your anger and let it pulse through your fingertips. Let your mind relax and the art will flow."

Ian banged his hand on the table and started laughing; really laughing. He was almost choking. He wiped tears off his cheeks from the exertion and stood up. "I'm good. I'm so good. I even fooled myself. Do you believe any of that shit? I had you all going there for a second." Ian walked to the kitchen with his empty plate, dropped it on the counter, and grabbed another beer. "Relax your mind and art will flow. What a crock of shit," Ian said to himself as he plopped down in front of the TV while Rachel, Rodney and Lily sat there staring at him from the table.

Rachel wanted to tell him he was a real piece of shit but instead shoved a forkful of quinoa into her mouth. Her relationship with Ian was impossible to understand and frustrating for her family to interpret.

She would never tell them the real reason she was torturing herself was pure, selfish guilt. She had broken the family promise years ago by not putting family first. She'd put her own desire above that of her brother's safety, and she was paying the price. Although lately, it felt like her whole family was paying the price.

After eating, she cleaned up the kitchen and took the dog for a walk. By the time she got back, Ian had passed out on the couch, and Rodney and Lily had retreated to their rooms. Rachel grabbed her laptop, sat on the porch, and called Tony. He could tell she was frustrated, and he let her spill all of the details of Ian's most recent fuck-up. Tony offered to help her pay Ian's debt, but Rachel refused. He eventually changed the subject in hopes of bringing her some positive energy.

"How are you coming on your design for next year's Underwater Museum of Art application? Are you almost finished?"

"Initially, I was designing a piece called *Choices*. It was going to symbolize how life delivers a Monopoly board of challenges depending upon the cards you draw. I had designed a corner of a Monopoly board with two human-sized sculptures of the race car and thimble. Each sculpture would have been built to allow easy access for fish and an abundance of surface area for algae to grow. I was really proud of the design, and the message behind it. But life isn't really about choices. It's about decisions. I've made my fair share of bad ones—like not picking you."

"I would agree. Who wouldn't want a scruffy, sentimental, laid-back southern boy with a guitar and a business degree? And don't forget my tight ass."

"Oh, I can't forget that ass, but I could do without the wimpy sentiments. I need hard core. No empathy. No feelings. Otherwise, I'm going to regret the decision to leave you for the rest of my life."

"Remember, Rachel, no regrets. I have a tattoo to remind me of that."

"Unfortunately, I have to live with my regrets every single day. That's why I scrapped the previous design and created a new one called *Decisions, Dreams and Death*. A person lying in bed with a dream bubble. The bubble would have the jaws of a shark clamping down ready to pounce."

"Rachel, babe, I don't mean to burst your bubble, literally or figuratively, but that sounds so morbid. I don't think that's quite the vibe the Cultural Arts Alliance is going for."

"I'm only kidding. That's how I feel at the moment. I did rework something tonight, but it wasn't for the Underwater Museum. I'm going to ditch the museum application. I have another dream I'm chasing. And this time, I'm not going to let anything stand in my way."

What You See is Not What You Hear

Chapter Twelve

Present Day

S itting on her porch watching the dogs play, Trina ended her call with Detective Trent feeling inept and worthless. He called to inquire if she had uncovered any details that would lead him in a new direction. She was apprehensive to point fingers since she had nothing concrete. Her gut was leaning toward Rachel, but her heart was aiming toward Samantha or Victor. The singer Jax had also stirred her curiosity. Unfortunately, she had no proof. Gossip, inuendo and little moments of butterflies dancing in her mind were not enough to send Trent on a wild-goose chase. She needed to find something, but she didn't know what she was looking for.

Wouldn't it have been nice if the killer left a note saying, "My motive for killing Ian is blah, blah blah, blah." Finding a clear motive was like finding a misplaced cell phone; way too many places she could look. Ian's track record for treating people like Michael Scott from *The Office* left a list of suspects as long as the line at the DMV. The value of his art rising post death provided a great motive, but the overall perception of the quality and desirability of his art toggled between absolute contempt to modern phenomena. Did someone orchestrate the spike in value, or was Rachel the only one who would benefit from the sudden increase? Did Rachel's pregnancy have anything to do with his murder? Would Ian's father kill his son in order to protect his reputation? Did someone dose him with a tranquilizer?

What about those flowers at the funeral? When she researched the note on the condolence card, she discovered it was associated with Lacey Sturm, formerly of Flyleaf, who sang "Let Me Love You" on the *Perfectly Preserved* album. Her own personal struggles with the blows of life gave her reflection into the ripple effect that death causes. Trina wasn't quite sure what the message on the note was implying, but she was motivated to find out who the sender, EDAD, was. She also admonished herself for not paying more attention to who had come to the funeral services.

She had too many suspects and not enough factual evidence.

Trent mentioned they found over ten unique fingerprints on the metal sun rays found in Ian's studio, but the sheriff's office didn't have enough evidence to require the long list of artists to submit their fingerprints for comparison. The fingerprints alone were not proof of anything since Ian had leaned on so many people to help him throughout the building process. She knew as well as the detective that helping did not necessarily translate to hurting. She wished she could find the one thing that moved the investigation in the right direction.

Today, David and Trina were headed to Trina's favorite annual event, the ArtsQuest Fine Arts Festival. She called the dogs back to the house and went inside to get ready. Over one hundred artists from all over the country were brought together to share their creativity with the Emerald Coast community. All the artists were eager to share their stories to help customers gain an understanding of their medium, whether it was clothing, furniture, jewelry, art, photography, pottery, or metalwork.

She loved to stroll through the white tents sprawled on the Grand Boulevard Town Center examining the hundreds of mixed media and authentic handmade pieces. The quality of the various pieces shined a light on the incredible talent that exists in today's art world.

She was also on a mission. Her boss at Grayton Loft & Gifts wanted her to identify five new potential artists she could partner with to help support the local art community in her retail shop. Trina had her favorites, including handcrafted jewelry by Beth Christina and Mary Dilley, quilted clothing by Mary Ellen DiMauro, and contemporary art by Bradley Eiland, Lindsay Tobias, and Ginger Leigh. But she enjoyed discovering artists she was not familiar with just as much. She was enthusiastic about the hunt, though she knew David was going to lose his patience, as she liked to take her time appreciating the event; it was like getting a free pass to a VIP museum. Before they left the parking lot, she gave him the "Get out of Jail Free Card" and told him after an hour he could head over to Vin'tij Food & Wine and wait for her at the bar.

The festival was busy; each tent crowded with ten to twenty patrons browsing or whipping out their credit cards. The first couple of booths displayed customizable hats, oyster shell artwork, garden sculptures and freshwater pearl jewelry. Trina was fascinated by the mixed media designs by Bobby Lowe, which created a sense of movement, life and color that made you want to reach out and touch it. Trina also discovered three mediums she thought would sell well in the store, so she grabbed a couple of business cards and snapped photos of their products. She continued to stroll, looking at a tent filled with handsewn bohemian pants and tank tops as David was immersed in a conversation with a wood carver who made custom tables and benches out of cherry wood.

After checking out a glass fusion artist and a customized dog collar tent, Trina became transfixed in a photography booth called *Today's Specials*. All the photographs were black and white images of restaurants across the country. Close-up, zoomed-in images of swivel bar seats, customer engravings on old wooden bars, torn leather booths, broken napkin holders, greasy grime on grill pans, crates filled with aging produce, ingredient-splashed chef aprons, and the crud hidden in a kitchen mat. Although the images were shockingly realistic, they also invoked the comfortability and familiarity so many could associate with.

The lack of color accentuated the raw intensity of the restaurant world. The pressurized hourglass a kitchen staff operates within. The warm, tender memories of old-town diners. The physical remnants of an endless rotation of food orders. The insanity of maintaining the image of cleanliness under the hidden truth of perpetual kitchen sludge. The camaraderie of staff. The joy of regulars.

So many perfectly imbalanced and unrelenting trigger memories conjured in her mind. Working at a beach bar for several summers herself during her teens, the images conjured raw, powerful emotions in Trina. She never thought much about the Salty Bar, even though she had spent hundreds of hours, took thousands of steps, and engaged in endless conversations there. The one image that struck a chord within her was the close-up of a restaurant dumpster. The open metal door on the side of the decrepit container spilled out empty liquor boxes and bags and bags of trash. It sent shivers down her spine and made her want to backtrack her steps and erase her history. She felt a squeeze on her arm and broke out of her reminiscent trance.

"Hey, I've had my fill. I'm heading over for a beer. How much longer do you think you'll be?" David asked.

"I haven't made it down the last aisle. You know what I like to eat for lunch so text me in an hour and I'll walk over."

David took her two shopping bags filled with unique gifts she had found along the way and left her standing at the edge of the photography booth. Trina took in her current surroundings. The laughter coming from two couples as they drank spicy margaritas in plastic cups. The concentration on a graceful lady's face as her long, slender fingers measured a custom-built coffee table. The pride exuding from a jeweler as a customer tried on a pearl beaded necklace in a mirror. A young mom with her hip extended supporting a toddler as she attempted to use her free hand to examine a bottle of organic face cream.

As an older man with a pink collared golf polo walked by with a steaming lobster roll from Cousins Maine Lobster food truck, she breathed in deeply to accept a tiny bit of pleasure from the smell. She listened to a yorkie barking protectively at a greyhound as their leashes intertwined, causing a grin to overtake her frown. She pushed thoughts of her past out of her mind. She was living a full, active, and pleasant life and was determined to focus on the present and not get distracted by distant memories.

She migrated away from the photography booth and turned the corner to begin her trip down the last aisle. Another photography booth called *Art in Art* by Phillip Jenson grabbed her attention. The pictures hanging on the inside of the tent's wall were of the inner workings of so many other unique art studios. He had captured moments of pure intensity as artists created their own inspirations. His pictures were carefully cropped so that only a glimpse of the subjects' own art was visible, focusing on their paintbrushes, camera, saws, or beads. Although she recognized several of the faces, studios, and styles of local artists, there were hundreds of photos of people and places she did not know. Trina read the photographer's biography, which simply stated: *Capturing the essence of art in process.*

Trina flipped through the stack of framed images, finding herself admiring the effort that must have gone into developing trust with fellow artists allowing him access to their sacred workspaces. She examined each image in the three bins on the display table and noticed a small box under the checkout table. The box was labeled *Unedited.* She bent down and slowly flipped through 5x7 images of scrap pieces of quilts near a sewing machine, remnants of wood shavings carved off a handmade end table, and a zoomed-in image of a jeweler wearing a pair of magnifying loupes glasses.

She continued flipping through the photos but stopped suddenly when something triggered her mind. Not sure what it was, she went back six or seven images and looked at the pictures again. The picture that had pinged her was of a painted canvas with a hand-drawn sketch clipped to the corner of the canvas's frame. The sketch matched the painted canvas and was signed "Crummey."

Trina pulled the picture out of the box and waited for Mr. Jenson to finish checking out a patron who had purchased a 10x12 image of a photographer setting up his tripod on the beach at sunset.

"Excuse me, Mr. Jenson. First, I'd like to say I greatly appreciate your attention to detail in capturing other artists at work. The angles and lighting are captivating. Such an interesting take on creating your own artistic style."

"Thank you. I have loved photography my entire life and found that discovering art through the eyes of other artists adds not only perspective but appreciation and value. I hope you find something that speaks to you," he said as he turned around to replace the blank space on the wall with one from his inventory after the last customer walked out with their prized possession.

"I did find one particular piece of interest. Do you remember where you took this photograph?" Trina handed the photo to him, desperately trying not to sound to enthusiastic. She felt the vibration in her skirt as her cell phone signaled the arrival of a text most likely from David.

"In the plastic sleeve should be a brief description." He pulled out a small piece of paper and read it out to her. "Artist Warehouses – Route 393 – Ian Scott. I remember taking this. I'd spent an entire week at the Warehouses gathering an understanding of how and why each artist chose their line of work. I remember taking a couple shots of Ian's idea station. He had several hand-drawn images splayed out on a table in the back of his studio. I didn't like the final image enough to edit and refine it for one of my framed pieces, but if you admire it, I could always work on it a little more and generate a larger framed image for you," he said, handing her back the photo.

"Oh, no I like it the way it is. Do you happen to date your photos?"

"Yes, the date is printed on the back. If you remove it from its protected sleeve, you can see the date. Why?"

"I'm not sure if you know but, Ian passed away recently. I'm friends with his girlfriend's mother. I thought she might like this photograph. Do you have any other unedited photos from his studio?"

"Oh man, so sorry. Let me look. Hold on." He opened another plastic tub and flipped through. After a couple of minutes, he pulled a tan envelope labeled Scott on the outside. "Here, you can give these to Rachel. I don't know why I didn't think of that myself."

"Oh, I would be happy to pay you for them. This is your time and skill and—"

"No, really. Take them. I have hundreds of photos. I can always reprint them. Take them. Tell Rachel that we miss seeing her around the art community." He smiled and handed Trina the envelope as another potential customer walked up and began asking questions.

As Trina walked out of the booth, she received another text from David that her lunch was ready, so she headed over to the restaurant. She sat down at the bar next to David and ordered herself a glass of white wine. She barely ate her Cuban sandwich because she couldn't stop thinking about the envelope. David entertained himself talking to a man sitting to his right who was from Texas and was here visiting his niece. Trina feigned interest but was mentally thinking about Rodney's signature on the sketch in the photograph.

As she fiddled with her food, Trina received a text from their eldest son, Trevor, who had grabbed an Uber at Northwest Florida Beaches International Airport after spending two weeks in London on a business trip. He was going to spend a couple days visiting, mostly playing golf, before heading back home to Austin. She showed David the text and then asked for the check so they could get home about the same time

Trevor would. On the drive home, she texted her boss and shared the artists' contact information and pictures of potential new inventory. She did her best to keep the envelope sealed until she could examine the images in private, knowing David would admonish her for sticking her nose in where it didn't belong.

They arrived home and were met with tail wags and excited dog spins. Trina grabbed the clean sheets out of the dryer and remade the bed in the guest bedroom, then pulled out the container of homemade cookies she had cooked the previous night and took out a cold bottle of Carlsberg beer to welcome Trevor back home. The moment her son opened the door; she forgot the envelope and overindulged in travel stories and updates on her son's career and relationships. It was almost nine thirty when she retired to the bedroom, while David continued watching an episode of *Breaking Bad* with Trevor.

Trina sat on the side of her bed and pulled out the stack of images in the envelope. She scanned through various images of Ian's studio. Two images focused on the stacks of canvases, which looked like abandoned ideas, and one solo image of Ian staring out a window. Two of the remaining pictures sent fireworks through Trina's brain. The first was an overhead view of Ian's desk at the art studio that was covered in pencil drawn sketches.

The second photograph was of a hand-drawn sun with a cylinder cone extending off the back. It was a detailed, perfectly drawn image of Ian Scott's *Unflappable* sculpture. But what had triggered her attention was the fact each graphite, fine-lined drawing was signed "Crummey" with a hand over a heart.

Ian's big Underwater Museum sculpture wasn't even his idea. This photograph is proof that Ian stole Rodney's creation. It was one thing to beg and borrow for helping hands when building the sculpture but submitting Rodney's idea as the basis for a sculpture and never giving Rodney any recognition was immoral, disrespectful, and blatantly evil. She wondered if Lily and Rachel knew where the idea came from. Or maybe the crucial question was when did they find out?

How many times had Ian stolen ideas from Rodney?

What if it was Rodney who recently discovered it?

Could Rodney be complicit in his death?

At the End of the Rainbow

Chapter Thirteen

2023

"What's the big deal? It's a harmless lie. The people who sit on these advisory boards could care less if I have a college degree or if I studied art," Ian said as he sipped his third glass of straight bourbon. "These nonprofit organizations have to ask those questions on the grant application, so they cover their asses. All they care about is picking people who have clout or people who will get them clout. I was rewarded the $5,000 artist of the year grant because I still have a huge TikTok following. The organization will benefit from free publicity by giving me the money. It's a win-win."

"Ian, thousands of artists clamor for access to grant funds. They work for years to compile their portfolio in hopes of receiving a grant. I wouldn't have helped you with your application if I knew you were going to go back and change your answers. Plus, the funds are to be specifically spent to provide an artist training or research associated with the specific artwork submitted. You can't take the money and pay your rent. They will be following your progress and expect to see the design come to life."

"I'll sign up for some cheap art classes, and the rest I'll say I spent on supplies. You can help me create a mural that mimics what I submitted.

If the end product isn't as good as you described on the application, they can blame it on bad training. They won't ask for the money back. I'll pay a couple of Influencers to take some videos promoting the mural and the nonprofit organization. I'm sure you can paint a decent picture, right? It will get thousands of views, and the organization will get more publicity than they could ever dream of. No one needs to know I didn't work on it. That's between you and me."

"Ian, the grant was for a mural on the side of the Draper J office building in Blue Mountain Beach. I can't paint it. People drive by there every day. You have to be the one to complete it."

"Good point. You and I can work side by side. No one will be the wiser that you're doing the bulk of the work. I can do touch-ups and paint the generic sections, but I need you to complete the details. I mean look at this concept photo you submitted," he said, showing her his online application. The mural depicted a realistic image of two legs resting on the beach from the perspective of the sun worshipper, with a detailed, distinguished heron standing in the water during a sunset that was vibrantly brought to life with over a dozen hues of perfectly blended color.

"There is no way I can paint that. You had to know that when you submitted it. Did you think I was going to magically learn how to paint? Either you have to help me, or I have to pay Samantha, Zee, or some other artist to help me. And you know how pissed they are at me already. Especially after last week."

Rachel cringed. "Why, what did you do last week, Ian?"

"I'm surprised you haven't heard about it yet. During the Open Studio night last Thursday, I got a little tipsy. I knocked over several pieces of pottery, spilled a case of jewelry beads, stepped right through a sold canvas, and tripped over a couple buckets of paint which leaked all over Zee's inventory. It was rather comical if I do say so myself. They're all a bunch of babies. Seriously overreacting. It was near the end of the event anyway; the customers still milling about were there to drink the free champagne and eat the hors d'oeuvres, not buy art."

"Zee must have lost it. This is the third time you've damaged her property. I thought you were banned from her studio. Did you help them clean up? Did you pay them for the lost inventory and necessary repairs?"

"Stop being such a worrywart. They aren't going to do anything. I know all their little secrets. Zee abandoned her last studio and owes her ex-studio partner back rent. Felicia's having an affair with her studio partner's husband. Johnni's living in the studio right now because he's in the middle of renovating his house. Jennifer is—"

"Stop. I don't want to know their secrets. Everybody makes mistakes, Ian. You, of all people, should know that. How can you hold their mistakes over their heads? Would you want them to do that to you?"

Ian shook his head, shut his computer down and walked to the liquor cabinet to pull out a bottle. "Rachel, when will you learn? People can't hold anything over my head. They can scream from the top of their lungs. It doesn't matter. My screw-ups are already public knowledge. I don't hide from my mistakes. It's a great strategy, actually. If you don't care what people think, you can do anything you want. You should try it sometime," he said as he guzzled straight from a whiskey bottle.

"Hey, speaking of my screw-ups, I need you to paint a commission tonight. I told the guys I would meet them at Beach Camp Brewing

Company to watch the game. I'm supposed to meet the customer tomorrow. Here's the description of what she wanted. She's going to pay me $2,000 so don't screw it up. The money can help pay back a big chunk of your balance with your father."

Ian grabbed his cell phone and walked out the door as she heard his friend Mike honk his horn. His lifelong friend always seemed to be ready and waiting to be at Ian's beck and call. Ian relied on their friendship, as Mike was a willing punching bag—big enough to take the hits but not coordinated enough to hit back. Rachel never quite understood why Mike agreed to be Ian's rescue inhaler; always there for a quick escape and opening the way for future calamities. Although who was she to judge? She'd put up with Ian's erratic and self-absorbed behavior for years, so how could she criticize Mike?

She grabbed the piece of paper, slammed open the sliding glass door, and ran out to the yard. *My balance?! It's his damn debt not mine!* She stood by the edge of the dunes and screamed. Her neighbor's dog began barking, and Charlie, their doodle, came running out the door.

Ian was a master manipulator, waiting until the day before the commission was due and dangling a $2,000 carrot in front of her. He knew having $2,000 would cut four months off her efforts to pay her dad back. He knew she'd do it. He was such a weasel. A rat.

It was bad enough she had to constantly fix his art, but now he expected her to paint an entire painting on her one day off this week. Plus, he'd get all the damn credit. He'd been getting commissions left and right, but she did most of the work because his drinking had gotten so bad he couldn't even hold the paintbrush.

But $2,000 would bring the balance due down to $1,000. She could pay her dad back in two more months and start saving again.

"Fuck."

She went back in the house, grabbed her AirPods and an energy drink, and walked out to the garage, their makeshift studio. She sat down on the stool and read the client email. It had been sent two months ago, and the deadline was tomorrow. She noticed the client's name. *Oh my gosh.* This wasn't just any client, it was Lorna Soreto. She had been the top real estate agent from Coastal Blue Brokerage firm for the last ten years. Rachel remembered reading about her in a magazine; she had surpassed other agents' annual sales figures by more than ten million dollars. She was not someone you wanted to establish a bad reputation with in this town.

She was paying Ian to paint a picture for the foyer of a recently sold property, and the new owner was moving in this weekend. The email, which appeared to be written by Lorna's assistant, stated how important this piece was to the new owners. Although it was not a large painting, it was a sentimental picture of a paddleboarder on the well-known Western Lake. The image was taken by the owner of his daughter, who passed away last year. The email said if her client was pleased with the result, she would guarantee Ian a steady reoccurring income. This could be massive for Ian.

Then the realization hit her; if she knocked this out of the park for Ian, she would be responsible for fulfilling all of Lorna's future orders because she would expect the same level of talent in the commissioned pieces for her listings. *Should I put forth the effort to ensure Ian earns the $2,000, or do a half-assed job and let Ian's reputation take the hit?*

She needed advice and texted Tony. He responded quickly, telling her he was at a gig and couldn't chat, but he'd check in with her later tonight or tomorrow. Feeling like she needed a moral compass, she texted her mom. The response surprised her, but she liked the recommendation. She sat pondering the idea for a while. After fifteen minutes of self-reflection, she guzzled her Red Bull and got to work.

She began sketching the outline on the canvas and naturally became mesmerized by the process of painting. Layering the base of the light-blue sky followed by a gray and translucent green hue of the water, then the light-tan base for the sand. Before changing colors, Rachel read the labels on each acrylic paint to ensure she was using the correct tones and color combinations she had mastered through years of studying how colors are made. She made several test batches of the intended shades on a palette and compared them to a cheat sheet chart Rodney had helped her create to ensure she correctly identified all the red and yellow hues since she was unable to identify them herself.

Around midnight, she laid her brushes down and examined her work. She rubbed her shoulders and back and twisted her wrists in a circular motion to relieve the strain. She was satisfied with the result and was mentally counting the dollars as she crawled into bed.

The next morning as she sat on the bench swing sipping a cup of coffee on the patio, she could hear Ian grumbling through the open kitchen window. Lily had left for the day and Rachel was going to drop Rodney off at the café before heading into work.

"Rachel, where's the canvas? I need to take it with me so I can meet the client this afternoon. She's coming to the studio around four to pick it up." Ian stepped one foot out the sliding glass door holding his flask in his hand.

"I left it right by the front door. I wrapped it in bubble wrap and some paper to protect it," Rachel said as she pushed herself into a gentle motion, keeping her eyes focused on the beach.

"Where's my lunch? Did you pack it?"

"There's a container on the second shelf with leftover chicken piccata."

"Again? Is this yours? You know I don't like your mother's."

"Yes. I made it. Hey, I told my dad we should be able to send him $2,000 this week."

"Really, Rachel? I haven't even gotten paid yet. And I didn't say you could have all of it."

"Ian, It would really take a huge chunk out of the amount left. Remember, if you nail this one, she's going to send you lots more, so you'll be making more money in no time." Rachel stood up and walked back into the kitchen with her empty coffee cup. "Remember to call Mike or an Uber if you need to," she said, looking out the window at the beach, reminding him he shouldn't be drinking and driving.

"Fine. I'll see you later." Ian grabbed his lunch and picked up the canvas on the way out the door with not a word of appreciation for either.

Rachel went upstairs and took a quick shower. When she returned to the kitchen, Rodney was at the table drawing. After making sure he had eaten breakfast, she walked over to see his new creations.

A graphite drawing of a sailboat with a striking side view of a fisherman reeling in a big catch, truly capturing the triumph in the man's face. He had labeled the drawing *Death and Joy*. Another, labeled *Peace,* reflected a dolphin as it breached the surface of the water, causing ripples of water cascading out in a beautiful halo. A third image was a giant sun with delicate, translucent, yet tangible rays bursting out from its circumference, with one particular ray focused like a tunnel out toward an image of the earth. It was a complex drawing, despite the enormity of the sun, the focus of the ray on the earth was directly on Florida. Rodney had labeled it *Florida Foreva.*

"Rodney you must have eaten a hearty breakfast this morning. These are incredible drawings. How would you feel if we hung some of your art on the wall? Maybe we can make a collage in the garage since it's become an art studio of sorts. Would you like that?"

"Hang some yours too?"

"Sure, I can print some of my digital designs and grab some of my paintings. How does that sound?"

"Like it. Let me pick some," Rodney said as he walked over to the boxes in the corner filled with his artwork.

While he was picking his pieces, Rachel cleared a space in the garage by moving some shelves around. Thirty minutes later, they had covered one wall with twenty pictures Rodney had drawn and about ten Rachel created. The wall looked like a graphite mural with random pops of color from the digital art prints mixed in. They stood back and stared at their accomplishment.

"I feel like we are looking at a museum exhibition. Your work is truly magnificent, Rodney."

"Thanks. Good together," he said as he grabbed her hand and held it up to his heart.

"We are, Rodney. We are very good together. Okay, I hate to burst the bubble, but I've got to run an errand before work. Are you ready to go to the café?"

"Yes, let me grab bag."

Rachel walked up close to the collage and ran her hand gently over the images. Her brother was extremely talented. His work was as accurate as the real thing, while being emotionally thought-provoking. She stared at the contrast of her colorful images with his black and white graphite images. She wondered if her art was better than what she saw since she relied on Rodney's color charts to create them. Her mother always told her the colors were perfectly curated, and Rodney was constantly gushing compliments, but it was difficult to distinguish between the truth and family appreciation. She was glad Rodney was her rainbow expert. After finishing any digital piece, she would ask him to examine it for color deficiencies. Thankfully, he was not bashful at pointing out her flaws, and they worked well together to make small tweaks in the color palettes.

She smiled and took her hand off the wall and held it up to her heart. *I've got your back, little brother.* She went back into the house and grabbed her purse and keys. She told Rodney to get in the car and ran back to the garage to grab a canvas wrapped in protective paper. She dropped Rodney off at the cafe, ran in to say hi to Lily, and grabbed a to-go sandwich from the refrigerator. She was back in her car and on the way to her errand in less than five minutes.

She pulled into a real estate office and walked up to the receptionist to introduce herself as a local artist who was providing samples of her work to brokers in the area to see if they might be interested in partnering with her to redecorate homes before they go on the market. The receptionist accepted the gift and told Rachel she would pass along the information.

Rachel drove to the tattoo parlor with a little spark of joy in her heart. She worked a full day and left the parlor a little after six. When she got in the car, she looked at her cell phone, which had been blowing up with texts from Ian. Rachel grimaced. Tonight was not going to be a fun, but she was mentally prepared. She didn't bother reading the texts, just drove home with a steady heart and firm head in anticipation of the arguments forthcoming. As she pulled into the driveway, she noticed she had also received a voicemail earlier that afternoon. She clicked on the message.

"Hello, Rachel, this is Mrs. Soreto's assistant. You and I spoke earlier today when you dropped off your painting. Mrs. Soreto was very pleased with the quality and depth of the work you presented, and she would be interested in meeting with you to discuss a potential partnership. If you can call me back, I can help arrange a meeting. I sent you an email with potential times and my phone number. Thank you."

Rachel sat in the car smiling ear to ear. She raised her right hand and rested it on her heart. *I've got you, Rodney. We are going to change our world. You and me.*

Before she even opened the front door, she could hear the muffled sounds of Ian scolding someone. She had texted her brother and her mother earlier in the day to give them advance warnings that Ian was most likely going to come home with his feathers flustered. She told them she would be home as soon as she could to deal with him and apologized in advance for whatever horrible things he said. Rachel pushed the front door open and calmly walked into the kitchen.

Rodney and her mom were at the table eating dinner. Her mother had a large glass of wine at the ready, which was atypical. Rodney had his AirPods on, but he looked up and smiled at Rachel as he raised his hand to his heart. Ian was not in the house, but she could hear him ranting through the open garage door. Rachel took a quick bite of the Philly cheesesteak her mom had plated for her and snagged a huge gulp of her mother's wine. Lily reached up and rested her hand on Rachel's arm. She squeezed it gently and said, "You're not going to like what you find out there. Rodney's fine, and I know you are doing the right thing."

Rachel closed her eyes and breathed in a purposeful breath, holding it for a moment before releasing it slowly. She walked into the garage and was greeted with a floor covered in papers. Some were torn, some were stepped on and the rest were scattered.

"You! How dare you fuck up my commission? That was a total piece of shit. What were you thinking giving that to me? It looked absolutely nothing like the girl on the paddleboard. Do you know how angry that bitch of a lady was? She specifically wanted a realist recreation of her client's daughter. What you painted was an abstract blob of colors slightly mimicking a person on a paddleboard. She is going to destroy my reputation in this town. You royally screwed me over. The damn lady took the canvas too. Said she deserved to take something after waiting for two months! Then I come home to find your brother's crappy art and your silly digital crap all over my wall. How dare you hang his art in my garage studio? What sort of crazy pill did you take?"

"I'm confused. I swear her email said she wanted an abstract painting. I don't know how I messed that up. I'm so sorry, Ian. I spent hours on it too. I really thought she would love it. Did she tell you what she was going to do for her client?"

"She was blabbing about some other artist she was going to set up a meeting with. I stopped listening to her after she refused to pay. I'm going to go have a drink at the bar with Mike. Clean up this mess and don't hang crap on the walls again." Ian stormed out the garage, leaving Rachel to her own thoughts.

She carefully knelt on the hard concrete floor and began gathering up Rodney's and her images. Most of the pictures were intact, with only a fraction having a small tear. She made a pile of the dismantled pieces and laid them on a table by the art supplies. She sat down on the garage step and typed out a reply to the real estate office setting up a meeting early in the morning. She had completed two additional pieces of art the previous night in anticipation of her inquiry. One of the canvases she planned to bring to the meeting was almost an exact replica of what Mrs. Soreto had originally hired Ian to complete. Rachel also printed and framed five of her digitally created art pieces to bring to the meeting. She hoped if Mrs. Soreto saw the potential in her graphic designs, she would commission her to create contemporary, colorful, and exploratory images for her clients' homes.

This was the first time she had stood up to Ian's demands, even though he didn't really know the extent to which she had screwed him. He would never come in contact with the lady again, though, and most likely never find out.

Rachel felt good. She felt like she'd discovered the pot at the end of a big, beautiful rainbow.

Ladder of Secrets

Chapter Fourteen

Present Day

"**D**o you want to go for a ride?" Trina said with an elevated baby voice as she clipped the leash onto their older dog, Phoenix. She patted their other dog, Freckles, on the head and promised she would be back soon. Today, her schedule was tight. She had an 8:30 a.m. vet appointment, followed by an 11:30 a.m. dental cleaning, then she was heading to the Digital Graffiti Festival in Alys Beach with girlfriends.

She held the small dachshund on her lap with the window down. Clutching her pup's leash with one hand to ensure the dog's safety, she soaked in Phoenix's joy like a sponge—breathing in the fresh Gulf air, enchanted with the wispy waves of the palm leaves, and curious about the various people they rolled past. The seven-mile stretch of 30A between her house and the vet was populated with bungalows on stilts, expansive beachside condos, burger huts, souvenir shops, a golf course, a couple of dune lakes, and an endless loop of walkers, bikers, and runners. Small drips of saliva dripped on the car door as the tiny dog panted in anticipation of the unknown destination and exuberance over the overabundance of sights and sounds.

The drive put Trina in a good mood by the time she reached Kindness Pet Hospital, which was in complete opposition to her pet, who knew this place meant prodding and exploration. Turning right into the dirt driveway, she parked in front of an adorable blue and white beach house with a small front porch. Trina said hello to the receptionist while holding the leash at a safe distance to prevent Phoenix from approaching a cage occupied with two hissing cats. Sitting on the wooden bench, she waited ten minutes before being called into one of the two small examination rooms. The vet assistant performed the annual weight exam and filled out preliminary questions and then Dr. Connor entered the room to complete Phoenix's full annual exam. Trina was only half listening to what the doctor said because she was mentally devising an appropriate way to ask about the tranquilizer.

"Dr. Connor, in addition to flea prevention, could you refill her allergy and anxiety pills?"

"Yes, we can give you two weeks supply, and then when we get her blood work back, we can provide you the complete prescription, or you can wait and pick up the full prescription by the end of the week." Her assistant was standing at the ready to write down the details based on Trina's response.

"I have enough to get me through, so I'll wait for the full dose. I do have another question for you. I'm curious why you prescribe Trazodone pills for Phoenix for her thunderstorm anxiety. I heard the receptionist suggest to a customer that they could give their dog Gabapentin." Trina internally blushed knowing she was fibbing in order to get more information. "Is one better than the other?"

"They were talking about pre-surgery. We administer Gabapentin before surgery as it can help relax the dog prior to a procedure. But we can prescribe either Trazodone or Gabapentin for a reoccurring treatment for anxiety. Is Phoenix experiencing side effects with Trazodone?"

"No. She's fine. I assume one would have to administer a lot of Gabapentin to have the same impact on a human?"

Dr. Connor and the assistant both stared at her.

"Trina are you needing anxiety medication?" the doctor asked incredulously.

"Oh no. Sorry for the confusion. Let me explain. When I take walks, I sometimes pick up litter on the side of the road. The other day, I found a bottle of 500 capsules of Gabapentin. It seemed really odd to find what appeared to be a full bottle just lying on the side of the road. I googled it when I got home and learned it could be used for human or animal consumption. When I heard one of your clients mention it, my curiosity got the better of me."

"Well, that makes me feel better. I was about to make you a personal therapy referral." The doctor laughed a little. "Both these medicines can be purchased online and are commonly administered. I would agree that it is odd that you found a full bottle on the side of the road but if Phoenix is handling the medicine well and it calms her down during thunderstorms, there's no reason to switch her medications. Everything today looks good, but if you have any additional concerns, please let us know. We'll see you next year." Dr. Connor shook Trina's hand and left the completion of the paperwork for her assistant.

The assistant reviewed the renewals of the prescriptions and then asked, "Mrs. Scotsdale, I'm curious. When did you find the bottle of Gabapentin?"

"It was about a month ago. Such a strange thing to find on the side of the road."

"That's so weird. About a month ago when we received our monthly inventory, the delivery driver told us several boxes were damaged in transport. When we compared the delivery to the invoice, we discovered one bottle of Gabapentin was missing. Any time medications are unaccounted for, we're required to file a claim with the vendor to properly report the discrepancy, as well as file a special claim with the delivery company. I've been working here for ten years, and that was the first time that had ever happened."

What are the chances? Believing this was not a coincidence, Trina asked, "Did the delivery driver tell you how the box was damaged?"

"The truck was rear-ended that morning while the vehicle was stopped making a delivery. Several customers' boxes fell out of the back of the open truck. We accepted the delivery as is because we were low on inventory. We ended up filing a missing property claim, though. It's possible that bottle fell out during the accident and rolled to the side of the road, and that's where you found it."

It was possible a random passerby could have found the bottle at the accident site and pitched it in the trash can at the cemetery, but why not take the contents if they opened the seal? The red splotch of blood on the bottle, however, made her think it was not random. Trina asked a couple more questions and took some notes before checking out and heading back home.

Finally, she had discovered a detail worthy of sharing. It was odd someone would go through the effort of stealing it, though, especially since Trina's research had proven ordering Gabapentin over the counter was a possibility. Of course, purchasing it would leave a paper trail. Maybe Detective Trent could investigate the vehicle that caused the accident. It was a possible lead worth following.

Trina dropped Phoenix at home and jumped back into her car to head over to the dentist. She arrived at Dr. Cook's office minutes before her designated appointment, said hello through the open window and sat down in the waiting room. She was flipping through a magazine when she heard the receptionist talking to the previous patient behind the closed glass door.

"Feeling better? Did Dr. Cook relieve your pain?"

"Yes. Thank goodness. I didn't think I could go through another day. I've been so stressed out. I haven't been sleeping much at all."

"So sorry to hear that. I don't mean to pry, but are you stressed out at work or is it personal?"

"Personal. I keep obsessing over decisions I've made and actions I've taken. Sometimes actions I didn't take. As a mom, I would do absolutely anything to protect my kids. Even though they are now grown-ups, they'll always be my kids."

"Ah, kid stress. A lifelong challenge," the receptionist said with empathy.

"My nightly grinding had gotten so bad, I'm embarrassed to say I needed two crowns."

"Hopefully, you can find a way to separate yourself from the family stress, but I'm sure it's easier said than done."

"Well, thank you again for squeezing me in today. I better get back to work before the place falls apart." The customer thanked the front desk staff and pushed open the door to the waiting room.

Trina looked toward the door with curiosity, as the voice sounded familiar. "Oh, Lily, what a surprise to see you here. How strange we both had our cleanings on the same day," Trina said, covering the fact she had overheard the conversation.

"Trina. Oh, my goodness. I wasn't expecting to see anyone out here," Lily said, slightly flustered. "I'm glad you're here only for a cleaning. Unfortunately for me, I required more extensive repairs. But luckily Dr. Cook fixed me up. Nerve pain is the worst."

Trina stood up and gave Lily a hug. "Oh, I feel for you. I've been in a similar situation before. Dental repairs are never fun, but living with the discomfort is not fun either. I hope you feel better now. Let's try to schedule a night out. It's been a while since we sat and chatted with a glass of wine. Send me a couple dates and we'll get it on the calendar."

"Sounds good. I've got to run. When they called to tell me they could fit me in, I left the café in a rush. Hopefully, it's still standing when I get back. Good to see you."

Trina mentally replayed what she had overheard. No, no, no. She couldn't let herself think Lily had anything to do with... Lily was a dedicated, loving, hardworking, selfless, protective mother. There was no way she— Trina couldn't even let her thoughts finish. But the reality was, Lily had been talking about protective actions and by the sounds of it, actions that had caused quite some stress.

"Mrs. Scotsdale, we are ready to see you now."

Trina blinked and gave her a head a slight shake to physically remove the negative thoughts. While in the dentist's chair, Trina replayed all her conversations with Lily, trying to discern if she'd had blinders on and missed a clue. The only positive affect of having these thoughts was she completely zoned out her dental cleaning and was back in her car in less than an hour and a half.

Driving home, she ran through potential ways in which Lily could have played a part in Ian's demise. Lily prepared Ian's food, had access to his alcohol, most likely visited the studio during off hours, knew Ian's schedule, and regrettably had a motive. She had relented and allowed Ian to move into her safe haven, subsequently witnessing her daughter's mistreatment and Ian's lack of couth. It could have been enough. Rachel was expecting Ian's baby. Maybe Lily didn't want to risk having the child exposed to Ian. But Trina had to trust her gut. She had spent hours with Lily over the years. Lily would never cross that line.

When she arrived home, she pulled out the bottle of Gabapentin she had tucked away in a plastic bag. Admittedly nervous to call Detective Trent, she swallowed her pride and placed the call. She explained where and when she had found the blood-spotted container, how she had stored it and relayed the story provided by the vet's assistant. He was curious since the autopsy drug test revealed similar drugs in Ian's system, but he remained doubtful the container was related to the case. If Trina hadn't been previously helpful, she got the impression he probably would have politely dismissed her tip. But he listened with intention, clarified the necessary details, and validated her gut instinct by acknowledging the possibility it could be related. He arranged for an officer to pick up the medical container and agreed to dig into any recent accidents relating to delivery vehicles.

Feeling satisfied she finally had added some value; she spent some time googling the effects of the drug in humans. The side effects included feeling tired, dizziness, coordination problems and double vision. If someone wanted Ian to be less likely to fight back, a dose of Gabapentin would do the trick. And if he had been consuming liquor, the combination could have been deadly.

After getting sucked into various internet searches over the course of two hours, Trina's phone beeped, and her friends said they were on their way to pick her up for the Digital Graffiti event. She cussed to herself for being so distracted she hadn't got ready. A quick dash into her closet, a brush of the teeth and a glance in the mirror, and she was slipping on her walking shoes as she heard the horn beep in the driveway. She stopped in the garage to tell David there were leftovers in the refrigerator and the dogs had been fed, then grabbed her purse and was out the door.

The bubbly chatter and relaxing ride down 30A toward Alys Beach cleansed her mind of the ugly Lily accusations and drug overdosing theories. Laughing with her girlfriends and sharing in the excitement for this year's event quickly transformed her mindset. The ladies arrived an hour before the event to enjoy a cocktail at the classy coastal seaside tavern The Citizen.

They left the elegance of the white, navy-blue, and gold restaurant and walked toward the entrance into the Alys Beach community, which had been cordoned off for the night's event. The crowd of spectators patiently stood in line to have their QR codes scanned, and wristbands - affixed to readily accept an empty plastic goblet to enjoy the many locally crafted cocktails made by distilleries and breweries spread throughout the event. The cobblestone, winding paved streets lined with meticulous gardens and Greek inspired architectural stucco homes transformed into a live-action, stunning display of art, color, inspiration, creativity, emotion, and complex movement.

Attendees were dressed in coastal clothing, as if they were attending an elite charitable fundraiser not an outdoor art show. Some of the most highly regarded, influential and financially successful people attended the annual event to witness the digital illustrations and graphics projected on the exterior of countless homes. Annually, over 300 artists from around the world competed for under forty spots, from which, Best in Show, Curator, and Special Recognition awards would be given.

As her group completed check-in, they were immediately transfixed within steps of walking down the path by the stunning display of colors and images displayed on the walls of the first several homes. Strolling casually through the neighborhood, Trina was impressed by the mini movies, interactive art and unexpected use of architectural lines and contours to enhance the artists' visions.

In addition to the displays occupying her eyes and ears, her stomach was spoiled by tent after tent of premier Emerald Coast chef delights specifically crafted to entice her tastebuds. The streets were bustling with admirers, judges, curators, entertainers, and artists from various genres. Witnessing the wall of a home—previously a blank slate of windows, doors, shutters, and gutters—transform into a kaleidoscope of light, geometric shapes and complex yet subtle and harsh messages was a mind-expanding phenomenon.

The ladies initially stayed together but eventually got separated in the ever-flowing body of arms and legs moving throughout the outdoor museum. After two hours of exploring, Trina found herself at the end of a cul-de-sac as it was nearing ten p.m. She texted the group and agreed to meet at the entrance at ten-thirty. As she approached a large, two-story building with several dozen admirers standing starstruck at its perimeter, Trina read the artist's summary in front of the display.

The artist dubbed themself "The Protector," and the digital design was called *Octopus*.

> *The Octopus represents the everchanging*
> *shape one must contort to appease*
> *predators and hide from critics.*
> *The interactive scene reflects the endless*
> *steps one must climb to protect oneself.*

Projected horizontally across a 350-foot, multiple home complex was a digital picture of a massive ladder with steps constructed of wet, dripping paint brushes. A woman wearing a black and white striped prison jumpsuit was attempting to run up the ladder. The interactive digital reel reflected her struggle to climb the mysterious ladder constructed of rungs randomly vanishing and reappearing, causing her to falter and desperately grasp for a higher rung. Periodically, she would be within reaching distance of the top, but a man standing on the desired landing stood looming over the precarious ladder pouring black paint on the woman's hands and down the ladder rungs. As she slipped further and further down, he nonchalantly refilled his paint can and then turned and meticulously fixed and polished awards affixed to a floating shelf behind him.

As he remained preoccupied with his personal accomplishments, the woman relentlessly climbed the ladder, donning a different outfit every ten seconds, camouflaging with the images displayed behind the ladder like an octopus. Sometimes she was a waitress, a mother, a student, a banker, and a sister, but she was always climbing. Never giving up. No matter how wet and sticky and slimy her hands were, no matter how often she slipped, no matter what environment she was in, she continued to set her eyes on the goal.

Trina was fascinated by the imagery; the sadness and perpetual fight reflected on the side on the building. She studied the fine detail hidden within the larger design and noticed the sides of the ladder were wrapped in forget-me-not flowers and every outfit the woman wore had an image of a hand over a heart hidden on one of the pockets. At the very bottom, a stream of words were displayed, almost indecipherable. Trina put on her glasses and walked up as close as the temporary border allowed. She read the words: *Once a regret, twice a lifetime promise; becoming whomever you need.*

This is Rachel, Trina thought. To be selected as one of these artists from around the world was a massive accomplishment. The clues were boldly staring at her, emitting secrets, though the general crowd would have no personal connection to the scene unfolding before their eyes. Feeling as proud as a mother and as curious as an investigator, Trina could not turn away.

The crowd also seemed completely transfixed by the display. The clarity, the motion, the desperation, and determination emanating from the images forced spectators to become mentally intertwined with the woman. It was impossible not to empathize. It was like trying not to smell freshly baked bread or not to desire a bite of ribs roasting on a smoky barbeque pit. The human natural connection with the scene portrayed was inescapable.

Trina heard murmurs that this could be an award-winning selection. Reporters were clamoring to shoot a clip and record a sound bite.

Professionals were congregating together discussing the intricacies and visionary complexity of the piece. It truly was a stunning digital display combining emotions and common struggles so many people could relate to.

Trina stood watching the short video play over and over again for several minutes, fascinated by the images floating on the wall, popping over the house windows and bouncing off the patio decks. Each time she watched it, she identified a small detail she missed the previous time—like watching a TV series twice and being amazed at the tiny tidbits of information you overlooked the first time.

Then, unexpectedly, the image changed. The man on the landing dropped the paint can and fell in a black hole that burst into orange flames, followed by the triumphant success of the woman reaching the pinnacle and smashing his awards on the floor. Trina was confused, because she had been watching the same scene over and over again and the woman had never made it to the top. Trina scanned the area in front of the building and realized there was board propped in front of the display that had been blocked by the crowds of people. Trina walked over and saw an interactive button for viewers to select between two choices to manipulate the images on the screen.

One button was labeled Ladder of Success, the other, Ladder of Secrets.

She hit the success button and watched the woman continue her hopeless climb. Then she hit the secrets button, and the man plunged into the fiery pit of flames.

Trina's stomach churned.

Oh, Rachel, what have you done?

Who's Going to Know

Chapter Fifteen

2023

S he walked the beach after dark to escape the crowds, escape her stress, and escape her past. As Rachel sat on the sand, the dampness seeped into her shorts, but she was too tired to move. The last seven days had depleted her youthful energy. She had worked every day at the tattoo parlor, hosting two bachelorette parties and completing over thirty individual elaborate designs. Ignoring her exhaustion, she had woken up four days in a row to help the breakfast staff bake croissants, bagels, and muffins.

She had been working fifty to sixty hours a week for almost two years straight and was feeling the physical and mental strain. Although weary and exhausted, today she felt invigorated because she was finally debt free. She had paid Ian's debt back in full using her earnings from Mrs. Soreto's painting commissions. However, her bad luck charm continued to lavish her with love because within a week of making her final payment, her car broke down and Rodney's annual brain scan set her back financially. Lily scraped every spare penny she could, but the overall financial strain had put an unexpected crick in Rachel's neck, literally.

Trying to think positively, she was looking forward to having her first paycheck that would not belong to someone else.

Adding heat to an already bubbling pot of life's challenges, she was turning twenty-seven soon and was feeling sorry for herself. She had been living her life through the lens of other people's life events: birthdays, weddings, promotions, and child births. Remembering the details and the emotional connections of the last decade of her lackluster life was like trying to examine the wings of a hummingbird; furiously blurry but incredibly beautiful.

So many of her high school friends had married, had children, and moved up the corporate ladder. Some had divorced and already remarried, while she was stuck in an ugly standstill relationship. Ian and Rachel spent as much time together as the pest control person spent tapping poison into the corners of her home—brief conversations, random dead topics, and a smell only those close to it can tolerate. Her evenings were filled with lonely nights reading books, swallowing her pride, and testing her patience.

Rodney was old enough now to be generally self-sufficient. Although he could handle an e-bike, he didn't have his driver's license, but he was living a full life. He had an intimate group of friends, a passion for customer service, and had started paddleboarding in the calm lakes to get back into the water. He was happy, and she wanted that too. She wasn't getting any younger, and she needed a way out. She desperately needed to make changes in her life.

She could deal with her dysfunctional relationship if she spent her day doing something she loved. Although she had hundreds of happy clients, she still had an internal itch to explore other means of cultivating her art.

She was earning additional income from the real estate broker's periodic painting requests, but she fulfilled those orders with as much lackluster energy as she did opening her monthly bank statement. She knew she had to do it, but she would rather be engaging her soul by mastering her digital craft.

Sitting on the beach was calming her flip-flopping emotions. She had so much to be thankful for, so much to be proud of. But there was a big hole, a chunk missing. She needed a personal connection; a physical one too. So many years dancing with no music and eating with no tastebuds felt like she was petting a soft puppy with thick leather gloves on. Something was missing, and she was not only craving a change, she ached for it.

Feeling reckless, she swiped up on her cell phone adding a bright glow in the charcoal-black night. She texted a message to Tony. *Ian's gone for the weekend skiing. Let's meet at our old hangout. I get off at 3.* She stared at the screen waiting to see three dots, but she assumed he was probably asleep as it was almost midnight. He could be with another woman. He should be cuddled up in bed next to a loving and dedicated girlfriend... but she hoped he wasn't.

After two minutes with no response, she stuck her phone in her pocket and turned toward the dunes. She stopped when she heard repetitive splashing in the silence of the night. Returning to the damp sand, the moon shined like a director's light on three dolphins jumping out of the water. They were leaping so high, it looked like they were playing on a trampoline. Trina was jealous of their freedom, playfulness, and obvious contentment and freely accepted the natural transfer of joy. She watched them for several minutes, then finally turned to head home as she had an early start tomorrow.

A symphony of high-pitched whistles and clicks stopped her in her tracks. She turned back to see all three dolphins resting in the water with their heads above the surface. It was like they were cheering her on. Like they were saying, "It's your life, Rachel, don't let it go to waste."

I hear you. Today, I promise. I'm going to listen.

She heard the beep of a text alert. She glanced at the phone and smiled, then said out loud to the dolphins, "I think Tony heard you too. It's about time I take my life back." Rachel walked home, climbed into bed, and let her exhaustion take over.

After helping her mom at the café for several hours in the early morning, she spent the next six hours at Mercy Tattoo Parlor and then headed straight home. She took a shower, changed into a blue mini skirt and a black crop top with a blue pocket. She brushed her hair and braided it into one long braid, the blue streak popping out from the dark black. She adorned her fingers with several rings and hung silver peace earrings in her ears. Applying a light shade of pink lipstick, and black eyeliner, she gave herself a once-over. She may be almost thirty, but she still had sex appeal. She felt confident. Pretty. At peace.

She walked downstairs in her platform boots and found her mother and brother in the kitchen discussing their dinner plans.

"Are you joining us for dinner tonight? I'm making your favorite, shrimp and grits," Lily said as she stood peeling shrimp over the sink.

"Save me some leftovers. I'm going to meet a friend for dinner. I've got the day off tomorrow, so I may be home late tonight. Love you." She kissed them both on the cheek on her way out.

She drove to McTighes and sat in her car staring at the previous night's text from Tony. He had told her he had a surprise for her. Tony was the one thing she relied on for her sanity, so she was hoping he hadn't got engaged or, even worse, had plans to move out of state. She didn't know what it could be, but she was looking forward to seeing him. They hadn't spent quality time together in several months. His business travel and music career had kept him busy.

A soft knock on her window startled her. She looked up. Damn, he looked divine, like the fictitious character on the cover of a romance novel. *Gosh, how did I screw up so many years ago? This man is a dream. Those eyes, that smile. Good god, those muscles.* She turned her cell phone off, peeked in the rearview mirror, grabbed her purse, and pushed her door open.

"Tony. Hi." Her eyes diverted as she felt like a high school wallflower talking to the quarterback.

"Rach," Tony said as he bent in and kissed her cheek, resting his warm hand on her naked waist. She could feel the rough texture of his fingertips and the strength in his grip. She felt like a marshmallow in a s'more—melting and gooey.

"Thanks for meeting me. You look, umm, good," she said, blushing with internal appreciation for the hotness standing in front of her.

"Well, thank you, kind lady. Blue and black are definitely your colors. You're becoming more beautiful with age."

Rachel blushed in the darkness.

"Your eyesight must be getting worse with age. I'm on a date with an old geezer who can't see clearly," Rachel said as they walked toward the front door.

"Oh, is this a date? I thought this was a high school reunion," he said, opening the door for her.

They grabbed a corner booth and ordered drinks. Catching up on the generalities of day-to-day life, they split a pizza and some wings. Laughing at several memories from their teenage years, they were relaxed and comfortable with one another. They finished their last round, paid the bill, and left. He directed her across the street where his truck was parked in front of the closed bakery.

He pulled down the tailgate and pulled out a blanket for them sit on. The dim glow from the celestial bodies in the sky provided the only light in the perfectly clear night. Their conversation continued to flow seamlessly. They discussed the old days and how much the town had changed. Rachel gave him updates on Rodney's progress and Lily's booming business. After covering every topic that was not focused on her, he gently coaxed her into talking about herself. Not wanting him to feel bad for her, she described a bustling career and a growing painting business. She told him she was finally debt free and feeling weightless. She inquired about his recent success, as his song had hit number one and he was ready to switch to music as a full-time career.

"I'm so proud of you, Tony. Or would you prefer I call you, Jax, mister famous musician," she said with a little friendly teasing. "Seriously, though, you deserve it. You deserve all of it. With your voice, musical talent, and good looks, you're going to be a superstar. Are you going to handle your own production and marketing?"

"Thank you, Rachel. Making you proud is my biggest motivator. I'm hoping to manage my career by myself. I'm nervous but I'm ready."

"Does this mean you're moving? Is that the big secret? Are you moving to a big city? New York? No, that doesn't fit. I bet you found a record producer in Austin and your packing up and moving west? I'm happy for you if you are. I'm jealous too."

"Would you come with me if I was? You're not married. It's still an option."

"Don't tempt me, Tony. You know my life is here. It will always be here."

"Thought I would test the waters. I still have big news, but I'm not headed to the Big Apple or Austin." He snuggled up close to her, thigh to thigh. With her mini skirt on, she could feel the heat from his legs. She could also smell his earthy cologne with a hint of patchouli; it was organically doing things to her body she had no control over.

"Okay, let me guess. You're moving to Nashville. Have you hooked up with Taylor-Rae, bought a house on a hill, and plan on writing music in the back of a pickup truck with your ten children? Wait, don't tell me the answer. I really don't want to know."

"Damn, am I that easy to read? Yup, you guessed it. I'm packing my guitar and cowboy boots and headed to the land of honky-tonks and fried chicken."

She stared at him, mouth agape as her hand reached out and squeezed his thigh in horror of hearing her worst fear. "No! You're lying."

"Gotcha. No, I may have a little Nashville running through my veins, but my cowboy boots have found their forever home in the sand. But I'll keep telling you fibs if it makes you touch me that way."

She quickly retracted her hand.

"I know you don't believe me, but I will wait for you, Rach. What-ever lock restrains you, I'm still holding the key. Simply ask for it. Hell, I'll tattoo the combination across my chest." He reached out and took her hand, holding it to his chest. He locked eyes with her, then raised their hands in unison to his lips and gently kissed her hand.

"Rachel, I'm serious. You're the woman I dream about, the one who cradles my emotions and drives me to succeed. I am so proud of you for doing what you believe to be the right thing. Not putting yourself first." He slowly separated. "I will always respect your deci-sions even though they're difficult for me to comprehend. But I'm mentally making a list of the ways I can show you I'm the right decision. I may receive applause and hit the top of the music charts, but you're the one who deserves all the recognition."

He unlocked their hands and kissed her tattooed wrist. "You are the most selfless..." Kissed her upper arm. "Thoughtful..." Kissed the crook of her neck. "Caring..." Her earlobe. "Sensitive, amazing woman," he whispered in her ear. "You are more than beautiful; you are as mystical as the northern lights and as mesmerizing as the embers of a fire. It's you who deserves to be on the top of the life charts."

Rachel gulped. Her crop top felt like it was bouncing off her chest as her heart was racing. She held the edge of the truck bed for dear life.

"I mean it. Every word. I will wait for you."

"Tony," she said in a desperate attempt to separate herself from him. "You are the person, the man... the one." She closed her eyes and held her breath. "Can we go for a walk on the beach?" she said as she let go of his hand.

"Yeah. Sure. Let me grab something real quick from my truck." He hopped off the back, helped her down and grabbed an envelope out of the truck. He took her hand in a comfortable embrace, and they walked down the dark street toward the public entrance to Blue Mountain Beach. A little past nine thirty at night, the beach was deserted. They took their shoes off, held hands again, and silently strolled through the silky soft sand listening to the waves crest the edge of the beach.

After several minutes of silence, Rachel stopped and asked, "I have to ask you again. Are you moving? Is that what you were going to tell me? Are you leaving me?"

"No, Rachel." He squeezed her hand. "I'm focusing on my singing career, but there is plenty of opportunity for me right here in Santa Rosa Beach."

"Okay, selfishly, I feel a whole lot better. What was it then? What was your big news? Did a record company sign you? Are you touring with someone famous?"

"No. Tonight is not about me. Tonight is about you."

"What do you mean?"

"Don't be mad. I did this because I believe in you."

"Now I'm nervous. What did you do, Tony Jackson Miller?"

"Rachel Evergreen Fairfield, you are officially the winner of this year's worldwide A' Digital Art Award." He handed her the envelope he had folded into his back pocket. Rachel stood there with her mouth open and eyes wide. The international A' Digital Art Award was one of the highest honors an artist could strive for, providing them with global recognition and exposure.

"I knew you would never submit an application, so I contacted your mother, and with a little help from Rodney, we downloaded the project you've been diligently working on. You won, Rachel. Your life is going to change. Even though you don't believe in you, the world believes in y ou!"

He did what? When?

She won?

They picked me?

Impossible! All those hours hidden in her bedroom clicking away at her keyboard, envisioning, crafting, eliciting emotions, dappling with motion, experimenting with color, pinpointing a message, all of it.

They picked me!

Rachel's grip on the paper was so tight it was ripping from the strain. She threw the paper in the air and jumped, hugging Tony with her legs and arms. Laughter exuded from her. He spun her around, saying, "You did it. You really did it."

"Tony, I cannot believe it. You're crazy. I must be crazy. Is this for real?"

He stood ankle deep in the water and held her tight. "Yes, Rachel, it's real. I am so proud of you. I love you." His muscular arms wrapped around her back and her waist as he stood still, smiling proudly. The moon was shining, and the silence of the night air brought the reality of what he said to a crescendo.

"I love you, Tony Jackson Miller. I always have and I always will." Rachel, still clamped around his waist, bent her head toward him. "I don't deserve you, but I want you. I need you. I don't want to lose you." She let her lips touch his. He was reluctant, knowing she was in a relationship, but her presence and proximity were too much to bear. The gentle acceptance was refreshing.

She let her arms slide down his muscular forearms. Arms she had not had the pleasure of exploring but had witnessed their transformation. She ran her fingers through his curly locks and let herself experience his gentle kiss. The tenderness of their touch was electric. Ten years of waiting, wanting, needing, and dreaming.

He gracefully walked out of the water and carried her up the beach to a flat area. Lying her down, he caressed face. "I didn't do this to manipulate you. I did it because I love you. I believe in you."

"I don't deserve your attention. Your kindness and support. You have truly always been there for me. From the days of teaching Rodney to surf, through my freshman year at SCAD, through years of family chaos and financial burdens. And worst of all, you've stayed with me emotionally even when I abandoned our relationship for so many unexplainable reasons. You have always been there for me. You are my backbone when I can't get up, my heart when I can't love. You are my words when I can't speak, my color when I can't see," she said with tears in her eyes.

"Be with me tonight. Can you please.... be... with me," Rachel whispered, pulling him toward her.

He let his eyes rest on hers, gently caressing her with his concentration. "I will be with you if you will be with me. Just me."

"Just you, Tony."

Never once rushing, their evening on the beach was more than they could have dreamed. A decade of love, tenderness, desire, and passion materialized on the sand under the darkness of night.

As Rachel lay next to Tony, he whispered, "If you will be mine, I will do whatever you want. Whenever you need it."

Tony followed her home sometime after three in the morning. He parked and met her at her car door. Their fingers locked as he walked her to the house. "You have me forever, Rachel."

She held his hand to her mouth and kissed it gently, breathing in his essence. "Thank you for tonight. It was the perfect end to a perfect date."

Holding the crumbled, damp, sandy paper in her hands, she unlocked the door and quietly turned the door handle. Slipping off her platforms, she tiptoed upstairs barefoot and went into the hall bathroom. She stood in front of the mirror. Her hair, braid released earlier in the night, was tousled, sandy, and wet. Her lips slightly plump and red. She ran a fingertip over her lips, remembering. Seeing the reflection of the forget-me-not flowers enclosed around her wrists, she twisted her arm, staring at the vines in the mirror. A reminder of her chains.

She had never known what it felt like to feel so wanted. So needed. She felt like her body had been in a medically induced coma for a decade, and Tony was a specially concocted injection that jolted her awake. He was her fairy dust, pink clouds at sunset. The special sand dollar on a beach stroll, the smell of freshly baked, warm bread. He was her Valentine's bouquet, her diamond ring, her first sprout from a spring garden.

But she still had a boyfriend. At least everyone thought she did.

Morally, it was the worst thing she had ever done. Well, not the worst. Abandoning Rodney was the worst. She'd had a couple of one-night stands over the years, but sleeping with Tony felt different. Meaningful, purposeful, and emotionally connected.

Yes, tonight, might have been wrong morally, but it was right in every other way.

She didn't want to shower afraid to lose his scent. She smiled to herself thinking about her incredible award. Reminiscing about Tony's electric touch, she knew exactly what tattoo she was permanently affixing to her skin—her back and her chest. Dolphins; magical, mystical, and romantic.

She climbed into bed and fell soundly asleep.

Saturday morning, she woke up and texted Tony. *Thank you. I'm whole again. Let's keep making dolphin magic.* They made plans to see each other on Monday night. She was inspired to create, to break up with Ian and start a new life. She spent the day cleaning her room and organizing the garage. When Lily brought Rodney home from work, Rachel convinced them they needed an afternoon of family time. They bought some bait and sat at the lake fishing for several hours through sunset.

To celebrate Rachel's award, they texted the owner of Crust Artisan Bakery for a reservation, took the bottle of 2019 Cimarossa Cabernet Sauvignon that had been gifted to Lily by a patron, and headed out to feast on lump crab salad, stuffed rice balls, a large bowl of steaming Seafood Cioppino, handmade gnocchi Bolognese, and perfectly grilled grouper with spinach.

The night was a rare moment in time. The three of them lavished themselves in culinary delights, sipped expensive wine and immersed themselves in each other's company. It was like they had been pieces of broken Play-Doh, and someone had scooped them up and remolded them back together, making them as strong, creative, and as promising as they originally were. The three of them went home with smiles on their faces, bellies bloated with goodness, and thoughts of a positive future.

Enjoying another day without Ian's presence, Sunday morning she focused on submitting an application for the upcoming Digital Graffiti event. Feeling empowered by her award, she confidently submitted the concept she had previously worked on. She tweaked it here and there, and by noon, she hit the submit button. The light and heat from the sun had been reflecting on her computer screen for the last several hours and finally seduced her into the backyard. She put on a bikini, poured a tall glass of ice-cold lemonade, and grabbed a magazine before heading down to the beach.

Eventually, Rachel fell asleep soaking in the beach heat, naturally exhausted from a long, enjoyable, self-aware weekend. Her dreams took her on fairy-tale strolls in the forest with butterflies dancing amongst the branches and ladybugs parading in lullaby marches. She felt weightless, spirited, and carefree, letting her fingers touch the light-blue delphiniums growing tall and proud. Her hand eventually met with the contrasting color of vibrant blossoms. She stopped when she saw a unique, stunning, arched flower blooming in stark contrast to the emerald-green stem that supported it like a chandelier in a ballroom. The bleeding heart flowers hung in a crescendo of light-pink, heart-shaped bulbs. She held them in her hand as gently as she would a newborn baby. Lovely, graceful, and free.

"Hey, Rachel. Wake up! You're as red as a lobster. Did you spend your entire day at the beach? Seriously, don't you have more important things to do? I need your help. Get up." Ian shoved her arm, almost pushing her out of her beach chair. He turned sharply to walk away, sending an explosion of sand into her face.

She wiped her eyes and saw the sun was dipping slowly below the horizon. She must have been asleep for hours. She pressed a finger on her arm and then released it, leaving a bright-white fingerprint quickly fading on her sunburnt skin. *Ouch, that's going to hurt.*

The realization hit her then—Ian. He was back.

She hadn't thought how or when she was going to break up with him. She had only been brave enough to tell herself she was ready to do it. The reality was suddenly staring at her like tsunami wave.

She grabbed her belongings and begrudgingly walked back to the house. She reached out and touched the blades of beach grass in an attempt to calm and center her soul. Reaching her backyard, she turned to stare at the waves. *You can do this. You deserve a life.*

Ian stuck his head out the back door. "Are you coming? I have something to show you."

She reluctantly walked into the house, dropping her belongings on the bench. Her mother and brother were sitting at the kitchen table. In the center of the table was a big bottle of wine, a dozen red roses, a box of chocolates, a brand-new box of elite graphite pencils, a stack of high-quality paper, a new BEST MOTHER AND COOK apron, an unopened box of brand-new pots and pans, and a table set and served with what appeared to be dinner from 3Sons Bar-B-Q.

Rodney was looking at her anxiously, eager to dive into his plate. Lily was sitting still with a vacant expression on her face, as she was holding a check for one thousand dollars.

"What's going on?" Rachel asked incredulously.

"I know I told you I was going skiing this weekend, which I did. But the whole time I was gone, I couldn't help but think how lucky I am to have such a spectacular girlfriend, a funny and creative future brother-in-law, and a warm, giving, and talented cook of a future mother-in-law. I couldn't wait to rush back home and treat you all to your favorites. Rodney has new art supplies and the best brisket in town. In addition to some new kitchen supplies, I paid Lily back for feeding and housing me.

"And for my special girlfriend..." He pulled a box with a brand new computer out from under the table, picking it up and displaying it. "I know how hard you work and how much you want to follow your dreams. I decided you deserve only the best. It's a top-notch, Apple MacBook Pro 16-inch with M3 Pro/M3 Max chip. Seriously the best laptop you can buy."

What the bloody hell?

She felt like she had stepped into a *Game of Thrones* scene where mutiny was about to explode before her eyes. Why was he showering them with gifts? Gifts that actually made sense. Gifts that reflected someone who observed, listened, and paid attention to their loved ones. And where did he get the money?

What happened this weekend while he was skiing? Did he rob a bank? Smoke too much weed? Get hypnotized by a gypsy? Did he bump his head on a ski jump? Did he stop in Las Vegas and win at roulette? Her brain couldn't synthesize what she was seeing and hearing. This could not be happening.

Why now?

Did he have someone following her? Did he know what she'd done? Was this his cruel way of punishing her? Was this an act? Was he going to start laughing his annoying creepy laugh and take the gifts away? Rip the thousand-dollar check into a million pieces? She stood absolutely still, feeling her jaw hang like a swing left alone on a tree branch. She blinked, blinked again. She looked at Rodney, his hand hovering over the plate with a fork. She looked at her mom, tears dripping down her cheeks. She squinted at Ian and then looked away at the pile of snow gear, a winter jacket, and snow boots leaving a puddle of dirty wetness on the doormat. She searched the room for a clue. Any clue.

What the hell did he need her to do? There had to be an ulterior motive behind this show of affection. She looked at the laptop and dreamed of all the incredible things she could create. Her mother could really use a thousand dollars. Rodney would appreciate a new set of pencils, and gosh, he looked like he is going to snort barbecue if she didn't say something.

Her eyes locked with Ian's. His smile was as devious as Jack Nicholson in *The Shining*.

She breathed, closed her eyes, and held on to the back of a dining room chair. She remembered last night, Tony's hands, his gentle loving touch, his admiration, his award-winning giving performance. His heart. His soul. His smile.

She opened her eyes. Rodney said, "Can I eat now?"

Lily held the check up to her chest but was shaking her head, wanting Rachel to stand firm.

Could she deal with Ian for one more week? One more month?

Fuck!

You Can't Pick Your Parents

Chapter Sixteen

Present Day

"Where did you put it?" David asked from the open porch door.

Sitting on the couch swing in her backyard sipping a cappuccino with both dogs cuddled beside her, Trina was relaxed and content. She had woken up early and watched the welcoming rise of the sun filtered through the pink, puffy clouds making them look like cotton candy-stuffed animals. The heat slowly rose as the sun gradually and gracefully moved up into the sky, reminding her she was living the life so many people dream about.

She took another sip of her coffee and tilted her head as the dogs jumped down to greet David. "Trina, where are my readers? I put them on the counter, and I can't find them anywhere. I need to sign this contract and scan it back to the office before I leave for my eight o'clock hair appointment. Also, what happened to my wallet?" He stood at the door expecting a confession.

"Weren't you reading a car magazine last night while we were eating dinner? I bet you left them on the dining room table, and your wallet is probably in your truck's cupholder. You said you would grab it after we unloaded groceries," she said as calmly as a school teacher.

"Are you sure? I swear I left them both on the counter," he said as he went into the house, leaving the door ajar. She could hear him say, "Ah, there they are." Five minutes later, she heard him holler goodbye on his way out the door.

She found it amusing she was involuntarily designated as the gate-keeper for all physical possessions in the house. She admittedly kept an orderly household. She was slightly obsessive about keeping the jars in the refrigerator organized by category, and the labels in the pantry all facing in the same direction. It bugged her when things were left on the counter for more than ten minutes, and she was a drill sergeant about keeping the kitchen sink empty. She had always been a little OCD. Even as a teenager, she was the only one in her family of six who could find anything and was always tasked with putting laundry and groceries away. As she grew older, her teachers admired how she organized the classroom supplies, and her bosses appreciated her detailed email responses and meticulous presentations.

Sometimes her OCD went a little overboard. She worried about hair left in her brushes, the invisible DNA remnants in a bathroom sink, and she always brought her own utensils to restaurants, claim-ing she had teeth sensitivities. After retiring and moving back to her parents' bungalow in Florida, however, she felt like she had chilled out a bit. She no longer wore gloves to the grocery store, and she'd stopped bringing a handheld vacuum to the hairdresser. Previously she used to have dozens of weird over-compulsive cleaning habits; now, she only had a few.

In reality, she also knew it wasn't only cleanliness she worried about; it was her constant concern that someone could track her down. Find her if she didn't want to be found. It all started after one of her childhood friends went missing from the beach. The pit in the stomach, the fear in the adults' eyes. The sad, dark tone of the sheriff's voice addressing the crowd after hours and hours of searching. She never wanted to be the girl everyone searched for. The girl they wished they had kept an eye on. The girl they wished they had said those special things to. She never wanted to be taken. Therefore, she made sure couldn't be found. At least in her mind, erasing her past would make it harder to find her in the present.

She finished her last sip of coffee and went back into the house. Remembering she needed to find some plastic tubs to bring to Lily's so she could pack up art supply donations from Rachel, Trina grabbed the key to the shed and went back outside. Allowing the dogs entrance first, she pulled the light and peered around the shed. Several months ago, she had spent some time opening her mother's old storage bins in an effort to organize the chaotic mess left behind. She scanned the shed, looking for plastic bins. Seeing an opportunity to consolidate, Trina walked to the corner and reorganized beach things into one large container, freeing up two she could take to Rachel's.

As she walked by a wall of shelves, she stopped and turned to look at eight boxes stacked in the corner. Boxes David had unloaded from their attic back in Georgia. She had packed the kitchen and the closets, but David had taken care of the attic. There had been so many belongings in the U-Haul, she had never taken the time to examine the contents of the attic boxes after moving. Still thinking about the irony of how she was the keeper, storer and organizer of all things, it made her reminisce about her past. She rarely thought of her youth. She'd had a full life and a successful career, but the journey she recently experienced in helping Detective Trent with the unsolved case had popped the bubbles of her past, spilling details she had forgotten about.

She put the two empty plastic bins down and read the labels on the stack of boxes. The kids' athletic trophies, middle school awards, science projects, and her daughter's prom dresses. She moved boxes off the stack until she got to the second to the bottom; a box labeled *Trina's college memories*. An instinctual nagging rose from the pit of her stomach. A box filled with decades old junk was not important and definitely not worth her time, but her inner self was peer pressuring her to peek inside.

She broke the tape and popped the top. The box was extremely organized, with yearbooks aligned to one side, college magazines in which she had published articles stacked in a pile, sorority swag, and other paraphernalia stored in Ziplock bags. The items elicited strong memories of growing into an adult and breaking free of her youth.

As she removed each item, she stacked them gently on a nearby shelf. There were a couple mementos she had forgotten about, and she smiled at the memories jostling in her mind. She continued to pull miscellaneous items out until her eyes lasered in on a small black box at the bottom that was hiding under a journal. She cautiously picked up the securely taped box and spun it around. There was a small handwritten note tucked under the corner of the lid. She removed the paper and unfolded it.

Find Jasmine

Seeing Jasmine's name was more lethal to her gut than a surgical knife cutting without anesthesia. A jolt of pain coursed through her entire body. It felt like a message from the grave. It was her youthful handwriting, but she had no recollection of writing it. A young, innocent teenager struggling with the mystery of a missing friend. A Trina she had tried so hard to forget about.

Find Jasmine, she read again.

I tried to find Jasmine. No one could find her. Why would I have written this note?

Five minutes later, Trina was still sitting in the shed. She wasn't really looking at the box. Nor was she reading the note. She was a fifteen-year-old girl again. Looking in sand dunes, searching sheds in Grayton Beach, examining any item which seemed out of place searching for a clue for beautiful, sweet Jasmine who was never seen again.

What's in this box, and how come I never opened it before?

A text suddenly came through from Lily. *Rachel's headed to Ian's art studio to pack up more supplies. Police finally released access. Can you pick up donations later this week?*

Trina responded yes and told her she would coordinate directly with Rachel. The interruption had broken the spell. She stared at the black box while repacking her college belongings. Closing the lid, she straightened the remaining boxes accordingly and carried the two empty bins and the small, secretive container to the house.

With the name Jasmine repeating in her mind like the chorus of a pop song, she hid the box in the rear of her dresser drawer and jumped in the shower. *Find Jasmine. How am I supposed to find her?* As desperate as she was to open the box, she was twice as fearful. What could she possible have in the box that would help her find Jasmine? Maybe the box didn't have a clue. Maybe she wrote herself a note to make sure she never forgot about Jasmine. Either way, the shock of finding the box, a box she subconsciously knew was tucked away, was giving her bad vibes. Trina needed a diversion.

Trying to be logical about her discovery, she redirected her focus. It was unrealistic to think she could solve a thirty-year-old missing persons case, but she could help Lily and Rachel put Ian's death behind them. Although she was worried her friendship with both of them was clouding her vision, Lily and Rachel were looking guiltier than Trina was comfortable accepting. For her own peace of mind, she wanted to assume they had nothing to do with his death. Detective Trent must have checked their alibis and run their fingerprints to cross them off the list.

Who would still be at the top of the possible suspect list? Ian's path of destruction and lack of respect for the art community would have generated motive for numerous people. The motive puzzle piece fit a fellow artist, but her gut told her the theory might be the correct color but not the right shape. How could Trina generate casual conversations within the art community to continue investigating without appearing abnormally inquisitive? She had an idea. She texted a couple of her friends a suggestion. Within minutes, they had agreed to participate in a hands-on art experience and picked a time and date. Forcibly trying not to think about Jasmine, she sent another text to arrange an artistic collaboration that might provide her with an excellent investigative opportunity.

With an unexpected free morning since her donation errand was delayed, Trina sat at her computer catching up on emails and bills. David had returned from his hair appointment and was in his office working. She perused garden websites and then found herself adding unnecessary things to her Amazon cart. Her thoughts periodically slipped back to the black box, but she forced herself to find activities to focus on. She made lunch for the both of them and told David she was taking Freckles for her daily walk.

Feeling stuck in a mental gridlock, she needed something to dismantle her mood. She tugged on the leash and decided to explore a different neighborhood about two miles from home. She picked up litter, stopped and chatted with two frequent customers she knew from her part-time job, and let Freckles lead the way. Wanting to be free of outside intrusions, she listened to country music instead of her current mystery novel, *Ask for Andrea*.

On her return home, she stopped to grab a smoothie and was standing behind a tall, lean woman with wild auburn hair—wavy and straight all at the same time. She was wearing athletic shorts and a runner's top, with sleek sneakers. Trina guessed her age to be late twenties, as the woman was enthusiastically explaining to the cashier she was recovering from an all-nighter at AJ's and needed some healthy greens to replenish her dehydrated body. Trina pined for youthful exuberance and stamina but was personally satisfied she had completed a three-mile walk and only had one more mile to go before returning home. As the woman accepted her green smoothie, she turned and smiled at Trina, looking at her as if she were caught by her own mother. Admiring her freckles and delicate complexion, Trina joked she should be able to go all night again tonight because a For the Health of It smoothie worked magic. The woman smiled, feeling less ashamed of her public oversharing.

As Trina placed her order, her phone vibrated in her pocket. She finished the order and stepped aside for the next customer and examined her phone. She had a long text from her son Trevor.

Forewarning. Some guy headed to house. Took his golf bag in error. Same color. Same brand. He was heading to course. Realized not his bag. He sounds like an ass. Tracked me down by raising hell at clubhouse. I left mine in garage.

Trevor had visited them recently and spent several days at the local course. Not sure how he could have mixed up bags, Trina called David to warn him, but he wasn't answering. She texted him the facts and told him she would be home shortly. She grabbed her smoothie and navigated Freckles toward the door, pulling her away from additional friendly customer pats. With her curiosity stirring at the potential of a disgruntled member of the community headed to their house and a mysterious bag swap, she increased her pace.

As she neared the house, she saw a fancy high-end car in the driveway. She subconsciously adjusted her hair and rubbed her tongue over her teeth. Their garage door was open, and David and a well-dressed man were standing at the edge admiring David's dark-green 1968 Triumph TR250 he'd been restoring for the last six years. There were two black identical golf bags propped up against the side of the house, and she could hear an air of pompousness as the man spoke.

"I'm not a big fan of low-end British convertibles. I prefer German engineering. I own a '69 Mercedes 280 SE 3.5 convertible, a 280 SL, and my wife's favorite is my Mercedes 300SL Gullwing. It's all about the precision construction and the world-class performance. I only invest in timeless classics exuding power in their design."

"Can't argue with you there," David said. "I can hear the rumble of the high-caliber engines just thinking about them. I would love to see your car collection. By the sound of it, you must have quite the museum of classics. Do you restore them yourself?"

"I used to when I was younger. I'm too busy now. I am a self-made millionaire. Been building homes up and down Walton County for years. I started the best architectural firm in Destin and then began my own construction company over twenty-five years ago. I've built over sixty homes in Santa Rosa Beach, Panama City, Destin, Freeport, and DeFuniak. When you're as successful as me, you pay people to do manual labor. I haven't picked up a wrench or a dirty oil rag in years."

"Kudos to you. Especially if you've been lucky enough to find people you can trust. I enjoy tinkering. Some people play golf or pickleball, I hide in my garage."

Trina stood behind them, quiet as a mouse. She admired David's ability to converse with a man who obviously thought he was better than they were. As she stared at the man's profile, Trina realized she recognized the man's face and was trying to place it in her memory.

"I take it you don't own your own company. If you had the same level of responsibilities on your shoulders, you would understand. I don't really have free time. I may spend half my day on the back nine making eagles, but what I'm really doing is building my forecasted revenue. Fifty percent of my deals are struck on the fairway. If you have time to tinker in the garage, you must be working for someone else."

"You got me there. I work on someone's else's dime. I can't imagine the stress of not only running a business but starting one from scratch. Do you have any kids? I bet they've been watching your every move so they can take over one day. Maybe then you can sit back and relax," David said nonjudgmentally.

The man grunted. "My son didn't have the same blood running through his veins. I groomed him to be a successful businessman. Dragged him to client meetings, forced him to read contracts and work alongside my construction crews, but he was a complete failure. No ambition. No drive. He had no desire to succeed. I think he dedicated his life to embarrassing me. I leaned on every relationship I had to get my son a job, but he was useless in the corporate world. I figured that out real quick. Couldn't even graduate college with an associate's degree never mind a bachelor's. He was fired from so many jobs, the kid received dozens of W-2s at the end of every year."

The man started pacing back and forth. He saw Trina but gave her zero acknowledgement. Trina put two and two together. This man was Ian's father who had been so detached at his own son's funeral.

"He didn't understand respect comes with responsibility. Building trust and fostering relationships. Giving a little to get back. He could have been the next big developer in Walton County. I would have set him up with his own independent business. We could have competed against one another as he learned the ropes, but no, not my son. Do you know what my son decided to become? A damn artist. Can you believe that? He lathered paint on a piece of paper for a living like a kindergartner. I'm attending prestigious city council planning meetings, voting on infrastructure and beach access and he's fingerpainting." Mr. Scott's voice had elevated to a level slightly below yelling.

David picked up a car part and began polishing it. "Artists possess an entirely different talent. I can barely draw a stick figure. It takes a steady hand, vision, and meticulous attention to detail. You know the saying: you get what you pay for. There are artists out there making five times what I earn in a year. They must be delivering a perceived value. I would rather spend my money on a new car part, but that doesn't mean I don't recognize their efforts and talents," David said, attempting to politely disagree.

"It's a bunch of bull if you ask me. I'd rather spend a hundred dollars on a painting at HomeGoods than spend a couple thousand on one because the artist is well recognized. Working with your hands is not as respectable as working with your mind. He was always a disappointment. It was an embarrassing career choice. He wasn't even good at being an artist. He had to hire other people to help him finish paintings, and he had an army of advisors helping him build a sculpture for the stupid underwater thing. Damn kid had more people touch his work than he did. I saw him the night before he died. He was desperately slathering solder on metal like a carpenter using duct tape to build a house. The kid couldn't swing a golf club, couldn't finish a piece of art even if it was paint by numbers, and definitely knew absolutely nothing about structural integrity. His stupidity ruined our family legacy."

"Sorry to hear about your son. I heard about his unexpected death. I hope you and your family are adjusting. Do you have a daughter who can take over the business and maybe inherit your car collection? We have two sons and one daughter. All three of them are sharp as tacks. Our oldest son conducts business with an international firm, our daughter is a manager in a marketing firm, and our youngest is pursuing his law degree. But honestly, I would be proud of them even if they were working at the local car wash. As long as they are self-sufficient and happy, I have no issues," David said with honest pride.

"You don't have to put on a show for me. I don't believe that for a second. I'm sure your pride comes from their accomplishments. It sounds like you raised them right. I don't have a daughter, but I bet if I did, she would have been a better businessman than my son. I guess my grandchild will inherit my wealth. He'll be born soon, and I'm hoping my brains skipped a generation. Guess I'll be enjoying my cars all by myself for the next twenty years. Hey, I've got to run. I've got to meet a partner for tee time. Next time, tell your son to pay more attention before grabbing someone else's golf bag. Our bags look similar, but my Americana Edition leather headcovers should have been an obvious clue. Here's my business card. Let me know when you want to knock down this old bungalow and build a 21st century home."

He grabbed the golf bag, nodded to Trina, stowed his belongings away, then revved his engine before peeling out of the driveway.

"Let me guess. Mr. Pierce Scott," Trina said.

"Bingo," David said, handing her the card.

"Quite the proud papa. Sounds like Ian would never be successful in the eyes of his father unless he followed Mr. Scott's footsteps."

"I found it a little ironical that the guy only see faults in others but not himself. Trevor might have grabbed his golf bag first, but he took home Trevor's and didn't realize his own mistake until today. He might need to take a good look in the mirror," David said as he leaned in and began examining his engine again.

"Agree, I can see how Ian might have inherited some arrogance from his dad. Although, what I'm more curious about is what he was doing visiting Ian the night before he died."

It was No Accident

Chapter Seventeen

Present Day

"**N**o. No. No." Rachel sat down and tore open another package. She finished, rested it on the counter, and paced back and forth. She tore a piece of toilet paper off the roll and began rolling it in the palms of her hand.

"This has to be a mistake." She braided her hair, then unbraided it. Twisting her hands around her wrist, she stared out the small second-story window into the backyard. Rodney was sitting on the picnic table with two friends after playing a game of cornhole. Lily was swinging on the porch swing, relaxing on her day off.

"Five minutes. It's all going to be fine in five more minutes." Rachel laid her cell phone on the counter and typed the phrase 'false positive' in the internet search box. A stream of information populated her screen. She scanned it, seeking refuge in the words.

She pulled the toilet seat lid down and sat, holding the upside-down pregnancy stick in her hand. She closed one eye and peeked through the other. She turned the stick over.

Two dark-pink lines stared back at her. She dropped the stick and grabbed the pamphlet from the box. *Was one of the lines supposed to be a plus sign symbolizing positive, or did two lines mean yes?* She read and re-read the instructions.

She was pregnant. She was going to have a baby before she turned thirty. She had never felt so exuberant and completely devasted at the same time. She felt like she was riding a roller coaster with multiple, shortly spaced crests. As quickly as she made it over one hill, she was climbing up another one. She pulled up her top and felt her skin, resting her hands on her belly. She was going to be a mother. A beautiful, precious, fragile life was growing inside of her. She had dealt with a lot of unexpected challenges in her lifetime, but this one was a doozy.

As much as she was in shock, in the pit of her stomach, she subconsciously had known all along. She had been so focused on trying to grasp the changes in Ian, she hadn't paid attention to the changes in her body. The 180-degree turn in his behavior was confusing and irritating and had been completely distracting. She'd placated herself, convinced her recent stomach sickness was related to the Ian dilemma.

Why now? Why was he being a good boyfriend now? Not only had she not kicked Ian out of her life, she had mysteriously fallen under his spell. He had been kind, engaging, interested and supportive—taking Rodney to his doctor appointments, helping Lily count inventory and cooking dinner. He had taken her on a romantic date and lathered her with compliments. With shame, she had let herself be coaxed by the splendor of a brand-new laptop, the relief on her mom's face when she used the money to pay off medical bills, and the eagerness with which Rodney used his new art supplies.

She let herself be lulled into false hope, but it wasn't long before glimpses of the old Ian seeped out. Berating her for not responding to his texts or demanding a hot meal even though she was the one that had a long day at work. Rachel observed his efforts to hide his bad habits, but instinctually, she knew he was putting on a show for one reason only: Ian needed her for something.

Then he had dropped the bombshell. By some insane miracle, Ian had been awarded a spot with the Cultural Arts Alliance annual Underwater Museum of Art installation, and he had no earthly idea how to design or build such a monumental structure. He begged, pleaded, even cried his way into her generous heart. He said this was the biggest opportunity he'd ever had, and he would stop asking for her artistic services as soon as his *Unflappable* sculpture was completed.

She blatantly refused at first, raging inside at herself for falling for his tricks and schemes. He had played her like a fiddle. Giving her brother gifts, relieving her mother of financial stress, and filling a hole in their relationship with desperately needed acknowledgements and compliments.

Her dolphin tattoos danced in the steam of a hot shower while her skin turned rage red as she repeatedly admitted to herself that she had been used for too long. She was determined to stand her ground. She craved sympathy, empathy, forgiveness. Why did her life spiral in reoccurring circles? The never-ending cycle of giving and forgiving, helping, and hurting. Fighting her rising blood pressure and berating herself for her stupidity, she immediately told Ian to leave and never come back. She told him she would not help him anymore. She was tired of being used, emotionally abandoned, and stripped of her self-esteem.

However, after days and nights of Ian's pleading, blunt reminders of his recent generous gifts, and his promise to never ask again, she broke down and agreed to help. This would be the very last time. Never again, she promised herself. She promised Rodney and her mother she was going to leave Ian after this.

She had no experience building sculptures, and this was a massive undertaking. The design was complex, the materials required numerous, and the structural engineering would be challenging. She began working with Ian every night after her shift at the tattoo parlor. As the days progressed into weeks, she noticed Ian's rapid decline. With each advancement in his career, he fell farther off the wagon. He was drinking 24-7. She would find him passed out on the studio floor, empty bourbon bottles all over the studio. Rachel forced him to hire an assistant to work with him during the day because Ian was never going to make the deadline based on his lack of progress during the daylight hours.

When Rachel showed up at the studio, she would be bombarded with stories from the various artists who assisted or provided guidance to Ian during the day. Ian's daily alcoholic escapades were becoming its own form of a soap opera, about which everyone had an opinion. He was burning bridges where bridges didn't even exist. People were angry he had been given this rare and sought after opportunity as unqualified as he was.

Ian called on every favor he could think of, threatened to expose personal confidences, and threw money at roadblocks. After a couple nights of witnessing his lack of vision, engineering knowledge and physical stamina, she sent Ian home in an Uber and told him she would complete the tasks necessary to keep the project moving along.

On the positive side, she was developing relationships within the art community. She was garnering the respect and admiration of her peers, and their deepest sympathy. Many of them tried to convince her to stop working on Ian's sculpture; let him fail and fall on his own sword. But the artist in her could not walk away. She started it, and she needed to finish it.

Secretly, she was enjoying the nightly escape. The studio was quiet, big, and completely separated from her normal life obligations. She felt relaxed and comfortable there. She wasn't guarded and was feeling her inner artist thrive. After the third night of working on Ian's sculpture by herself, she extended an invitation to Tony. Ian's temporary personality change could not dampen the internal flame that had ignited between them that memorable night on the beach.

She asked him to keep her company, so she wasn't in the studio late at night by herself. If he wasn't performing a gig, he would bring her dinner and play his guitar while she worked. He enjoyed watching her work and would test out lyrics and practice new melodies. She was living on a teeter-totter, feeling elated whenever Tony showed up but disappointed in herself for not breaking it off with Ian. Ian was like an invisible noose around her neck. She couldn't latch on to it to break it, but she could feel the constraint.

At the same time, she felt like she was floating on a cloud when she was with Tony. She loved Tony and didn't want to lose him. Initially, she had promised she would break up with Ian in a week. Then once she started working on the project, she begged Tony to give her a little more time. One more day, one more night, one more weekend.

Some nights when Tony showed up, she was so deeply imbedded in the sculpting process, she barely realized he was observing her. Then there were those random romantic moments they found themselves alone in the studio. Tony lathering his hands with sculpting sludge, attempting to mimic what she was doing. He would try, repeat instructions, and fail miserably. Wearing more cement sludge than the sculpture itself, they would end up laughing themselves into hysterics, only to find themselves romantically entwined on the small studio couch in the back ro om.

When he sat with one boot on a rung, whispering his soothing, soulful songs, chills spread across her skin. His poetic love language melted her tough exterior, making tears stream down her cheeks as she worked. Tony would lay down his guitar, gently humming the beat, and wrap his hands around her exhausted, fragile frame. She craved his comfort, and his presence fueled her artistic energy.

As time progressed, she went to the studio even though there was no work to be performed. They spent the evening talking and sharing their fears, obsessions, self-doubts, and pet peeves. Tony's messy hair, sheepish smile and tight jeans were as irresistible as Edward Cullen in *Twilight*, and as endearing as *It's a Wonderful Life's* James Stewart. On those nights when he melted her on sight, she had his shirt off before he even crossed the threshold. Tony knew exactly where to touch her, how to elicit her inner desires and coax her into submission. His heart expressed itself through his hands, as his love for her showed in so many ways.

The yin and yang of her situation was like riding an elevator—speeding to the penthouse, where she explored luxurious love, kindness, and emotional connection, then plunging to the basement, where guilt, chains, and a life full of bad decisions greeted her as the doors opened to an escape room with no discernable clues in sight.

Her breasts started to become sore, and she was hugging a toilet more times than she could count. Initially, she had dismissed it. Blamed her insane work schedule and the late hours at the studio, eating in a rush, not getting enough sleep, and drinking too many energy drinks.

She didn't know how to react now that the truth was staring at her in the form of two pink, parallel lines — a road with no clear beginning and no end. She was expecting a baby.

But somewhere deep in the recesses of her mind, she had wondered. Had she remembered to take her pill? Did Tony put one on? As the days past her expected cycle slipped by, her mind had been in a defensive fight with itself. She was going to have Tony's baby, so why did her heart feel shriveled up like the petals on Ian's cheap grocery store flowers?

As she sat slouched on the toilet seat holding a stick that represented a magic wand instantly changing her life forever, she didn't know if she should run jumping up and down to her mother or run screaming in frustration down the beach.

Months later, when she was holding a thin piece of paper with the black and white image of her unborn child, it felt like she was holding a lottery ticket with the winning number. It looked real, but was it fake? Did it represent a future full of promise, or had she heard the numbers incorrectly?

The frequent trips to the restroom made it impossible to hide the news forever. She eventually told her family and reluctantly told Ian. She was due soon and had no real parenting plan, but she only had to last until deployment day. She was going to be free from an unhappy, horribly matched relationship.

Even though it was not Ian's baby, Ian had been yapping around town about becoming a father and how he was planning to attend AA meetings regularly to get clean. Ironically, he did the most blabbing while sitting at local bars as he rang up nightly tabs higher than most people accumulate in a month. Rachel decided to let people believe it was Ian's since she was his girlfriend, and after the deployment was over, she could break up with him and let the truth be known.

Once word had spread about Rachel's pregnancy, Ian's father had reached out to Rachel and requested a one-on-one meeting. Although she had interacted with Mr. Scott a couple of times over the years, the interactions had always been brief and lacked any semblance of true family bonding. She left the Scott holiday gatherings feeling like she had sat through a county board meeting. Rachel granted his request, regardless, knowing there was no way to escape him forever. He was extremely well connected and could pull, or cut, strings where and whenever he wished.

The meeting had been brief, a total of ten minutes. They met at a sandwich shop in Panama City, a good forty-five minutes away from home. She assumed he did not want to be seen or recognized. His message was not only clear and concise; it was cold and emotionless. He would only assist Rachel financially in raising the child if Ian completed a paternity test and if Ian agreed to not be a part of the child's life. It was neither a request nor a demand, simply a statement of fact. He didn't promise any specific amount of money, didn't promise to buy her a house or pay for his grandchild's college education. He simply said if his two demands were met, he would be there for Rachel and the child.

She was flabbergasted. How cruel and selfish was this man? Who did he think he was dangling a financial carrot over an unwed mother?

She knew the truth; Rachel had never slept with Ian. They slept side by side but had never been physically intimate. She didn't bother correcting Mr. Scott. Let him boast around town that he would soon be a grandfather. For once, she had the power, and she was thankful her child would not have the Scott family genetics.

It had been difficult letting people believe Ian was truly her boyfriend. She should win a Tony for the Best Actress of the "Decade;" a convincing performance in a play that lasted way past its prime. Ian had been holding a flamethrower pointed directly at her for years. Any wrong move and he would hit the button. She was protecting herself, her family, and her past. The thoughts and assumptions other people made could not change the predicament she was in, so public misconceptions had free range to grow unabatedly.

Walking to her car after meeting with Mr. Scott, she decided right then and there she wasn't going to prove anything to anyone. She had lived her life thus far fighting and kicking her way to the top.

She was not going to finally cut ties with Ian to finally be free of his irrational hold over her life only to join forces with another man, especially another Scott, and live the next phase of her life under his thumb. She was done living someone else's life. She had a baby to protect. She was no longer going to let any man, even a powerful well-known man, manipulate her actions. She had no plans to contact Mr. Scott in the future.

There was one man, however, she was willing to let influence her future as a mother. Tony and Rachel had been plotting and planning their next phase of life. Tony was ecstatic about the arrival of the baby and thrilled that the approaching birth had been the eye-opening moment for Rachel to act selfishly for the first time.

The Three Dots

Chapter Eighteen

Present Day

I'm desperate. The text came through to Trina's phone, piquing her curiosity.

I need to send my tax accountant my annual financial data for the café. I'm at work with Rodney and Rachel's at work. Could you run over to my house and grab a password? I wrote it somewhere on my desk calendar. Look for a seven-digit phrase under the words Square Retail System.

Trina replied, *Can do. Key in same spot? I'll text it as soon as I find it.*

Trina turned her left blinker on and maneuvered to the left lane. She was on her way home from a short shift at work and rerouted herself to head over to Lily's. Glad she could be helpful, she stopped at Bastide Home and Garden and picked up a beautiful potted plant to bring some joy to Lily's stressful life.

She pulled into the driveway, walked up to the front door, and grabbed the key from under the garden mushroom. Letting herself in, she could smell the remnants of freshly baked bread mixed with sea air from the breeze coming through an open window. Leaving the plant on the center of the kitchen table amongst several of Rodney's sketches, she walked by the kitchen toward Lily's office. The desk was covered in café receipts, open pads with lists of ingredients, menu changes and recipes. Trina saw several colored folders labeled insurance claims, medical records and doctor bills stacked in the corner of the desk. Trying not to rearrange too much, she scooted papers aside and saw a large desk calendar. She perused phrases and words which might indicate the password.

Finding nothing, she flipped months on the paper calendar looking for the words *square retail system*. After flipping through a couple of months, the weight of the papers landed on the mouse, causing the computer screen to come to life. Lily's eyesight must be as bad as hers, because on the screen was a magnified email. She knew it was inappropriate to read a personal email, but Trina noticed the sender of the email was EDAD@gotitmail.com. The condolence flowers at the funeral with the unique note had been signed by EDAD. Trina hesitated briefly, then read the email with as much shame as interest.

Lily,

I'm so happy Rachel is rebuilding her life. Her new computer equipment, personalized studio and infusion of start-up cash will provide her with the infrastructure she needs. While her current tattoo clients will provide a steady stream of reoccurring revenue, she can build her digital art reputation on the wings of winning the prestigious Digital Award. She'll be at the top before the baby turns one!

As we discussed, I met with my lawyer last week and the trust for the baby is in the works. I'll send both of you a copy as soon as it is all finalized. Call me if you need anything – ever!

Always here to help.

Trina sat down in the office chair. A trust for the baby? Trina didn't know why, but something about the email was sending her Spidey senses on high alert. Was this a family member of Ian's? EDAD had sent flowers to his funeral. After meeting Mr. Scott, it would be a shocking turn of events if the Scott family stepped up to support the baby. Maybe Lily had a significant other in her life? Maybe it's Lily's ex? Either way, Lily must be thrilled to know her grandchild would have a financially secure future.

The amount of allotted time must have slipped by, as the computer screen went black. Trina's hand rested midair over the mouse in consideration of digging further. Talking herself out of her disrespectful behavior, Trina continued flipping through the calendar until she found a code written in the top corner of the month of January. She texted Lily the information and straightened the papers as best she could.

You've already seen more than you should. Walk out the door and don't stop. What's the right thing to do? No more prying.

She casually walked to the kitchen, grabbed the plant, and gave it a little water from the kitchen sink. She found a dog bone and gave Charlie a dog treat.

You're stalling, Trina. You have snooped enough. Leave. They trust you. Lily trusts you.

Trina walked to the front door and grabbed the door handle. She stood there and thought about Ian. He was a young man whose life had been taken. Based on what she had heard, he was not well-liked, but did he deserve to die? *What harm would it do to take a quick stroll through the house?*

She spun around and took her first steps to the second floor. She had never been upstairs and found the second floor to be as warm and welcoming as the first. Adorable pictures of Rachel and Rodney when they were much younger hung on the wall. A bookshelf in the hallway was filled with coffee table quality art books and surfing magazines.

Trina walked into Rodney's minimalistic room, which had physical therapy equipment organized on hooks on the wall, a small table with pencils, paints and paper, and an old computer. He had two large windows overlooking the beach. There were two blown-up photographs of Rodney surfing when he looked to be about nine or ten years old. His genuine joy exuded from his smile as he was riding waves.

Not seeing anything of interest, she left his room and went into the next room. Various graphic design images hung on the wall of what she assumed was Rachel's room. Color, movement, and curiosity burst from each one. Her wall was layered in imagery. Bright, emerald-green landscapes with stunning varieties of flowers, colorful birds, butterflies, and insects mixed with gleaming coast lines, majestic waves, and land masses out of reach. The complexity of the wall was mesmerizing, because as breathtaking as the images of earth's bounty were, they were in stark contrast with the abstract images of haunted souls. Anger, fear, stress and anxiety permeated from the silhouettes, profiles and portraits of the various women captured on the wall. Goosebumps and a deep pang of empathy stirred within Trina. There was so much emotion and beauty in Rachel's work. It was the same feeling Trina had when she watched the Protector's film at the Digital Graffiti event; the uncontrollable urge to be sucked into the soul hidden within the art.

Trina took a couple steps back and tried to take it all in. As a mother, she couldn't help but be proud of Rachel's talent. To possess the naturally born skill to create pictures that elicited immediate and strong emotions was a powerful and commendable skill. This was why the art world exists. Value, essence, stability, and instability exuding from the canvases.

Mystified by the wall, she assessed Rachel's life, which had generated so much negativity but was seemingly counterbalanced by a love for all things real and natural. Her relationship with Ian caused the majority of the strain, but the stress of managing Rodney's medical issues while helping her mother maintain a financially secure household must also be very demanding.

Like the email had insinuated, Trina hoped Rachel's life would take a turn for the better. She was still young enough to have a bright future. Plus, the birth of a child would bring joy and a fresh perspective, which could help offset life's stresses.

Taking a moment to process the thoughts blending in her mind, Trina walked around the room, scanning an open closet filled with black and blue clothes and a basket full of silver rings and chunky earrings. In the corner of the room, a closed laptop rested on a small table. A couple yellow sticky notes were stuck randomly on the adjacent wall—doctor appointments reminders, lists of supplies, people's names, and phone numbers. Each note was dated in the corner MM-DD-YY. Trina was surprised by Rachel's penmanship of big, bold, block print letters written with precision. The writing was simplistically perfect, reminiscent of Learn to Write kindergarten activity workbooks. Being so artistic and creative, it was surprising to see her rudimentary writing style.

A bulletin board hung above the table with several pictures: Rachel and Rodney fishing at the lake; all three of them sitting at a picnic table in front of Pickle's restaurant in Seaside enjoying hand-spun milkshakes, burgers, and fried pickles; a classroom picture of Rodney prior to his accident. Wrinkled concert tickets, flyers for upcoming tattoo exhibitions, a car mechanic's business card, and a menu from a local pizza place were peppered around the photos.

Trina scanned the items, looking for anything indicating Rachel's guilt or innocence. Disappointed, nothing stood out and feeling ashamed she had broken trust by stepping into their private world, Trina left the bedroom and stopped at the bathroom.

While she was washing her hands, a text came through from Lily. *When I talked to Rachel about finding a pediatrician, she said it was on her list of things to do. Maybe you can text her. I think she is tired of me nagging. She would listen to you.*

Trina was confused. Why would Lily want her to talk to Rachel about a finding a doctor? She had gotten closer to the family over the last month, but it seemed a little odd to ask her to meddle in such a personal decision. She wasn't sure how to respond.

Three dots appeared on her cell phone.

Oops. Sorry. Replied to wrong text chat. Please ignore.

Trina typed a reply with a laughing emoji. *I hope you had success getting data to your CPA. About to leave your house. I got sidetracked staring at your beautiful views of the beach. Let me know if you need anything else.*

The response came immediately. *Those views have gotten me through a lot of rough days. Data downloaded and sent. Thanks so much for helping me!*

Trina assumed Lily must have been texting her ex, although she doubted Rachel would listen to her estranged father over her mother. Could it be this mysterious EDAD person who set up a trust for the baby? About to take her first step down the stairs, she pivoted and returned to Rachel's room. *One more look.*

Returning to the small table, Trina scanned the sticky notes looking for a clue. Seeing nothing, she picked up a pencil and gently moved papers around on the bulletin board. Each concert ticket was marked with whom she presumably attended the show: Pink - Jennie & Cameron. Bruno Mars –Ian and Mike. Dua Lipa – Tony. Lacey Sturm – EDAD.

Against her better judgement, she unpinned the Lacey Sturm concert ticket. EDAD. Who was EDAD? Trina took a picture of the ticket with her phone and pinned it back up. Her excitement for seeing EDAD had her forgetting she was leaving a fingerprint trail on potential evidence.

She sat down in the small chair and opened up the only desk drawer. There were a couple of notepads, some bills, a few pieces of jewelry and hair ties, and at the very bottom was a stack of clipped handwritten letters. They were all signed EDAD.

Guilt was weighing on Trina, but she put on her investigative cap and kept going. She scanned the pile, making sure not to read the contents, and eventually she found one signed, *Love you, Every Day All Day.*

That's it. EDAD – Every Day All Day.

But who was it?

Trina's phone beeped. She took a picture of the signature and closed the drawer. Glancing at her screen, she left the room and descended the stairs.

One more favor if you're still close to the house. Rodney's riding his bike home to meet friends at the beach, and I have another hour to go. Could you help him get down the paddleboard from the side of the house and carry it down the boardwalk? Would be a huge help. Why don't you and David come join me for dinner? I've got some freshly made chicken piccata from the cafe I can bring home, and we can enjoy the bottle of wine we keep talking about.

Trina paused at the bottom of the stairs to respond. *Was walking out the door but happy to stay put and wait for R. Tonight sounds blissful. I'll bring a salad and a bottle of wine. See you tonight.*

Trina pocketed her phone and walked out the back door. She went around the side of the house and saw a paddleboard hanging on hooks. With a little maneuvering, she dismounted the board and dragged it closer to the boardwalk. She returned to the house and sat in the kitchen to wait for Rodney.

Suddenly, Charlie began barking and running in circles. The doorbell rang. Trina went to the door as the dog jumped up and down. As she reached for the door handle, Charlie bumped into her, causing her to stagger sideways and knock a frame off the wall. Luckily, there was a small basket with beach towels underneath that softened the landing, preventing the glass from shattering. Trina calmed the dog down and opened the door. An Amazon package had been placed on the doorstep. Trina called out a thank you as the driver stepped back into his vehicle, then retrieved the box and laid it near the basket.

Apprehensive to discover damage, she picked the thin metal and glass frame out of the basket. Inside was a stunning hand-drawn graphite image of forget-me-not flowers. The dark-black color of the stems was offset brilliantly by water-colored lavender, eggshell, and peacock-blue flowers. The flowers were drawn on a surfboard headed toward a photographically accurate painted sunset. There had been an inch of empty space between the canvas and the exterior of the frame, giving it the semblance of matting, but the paper had shifted awkwardly from the impact.

Trina carried the delicate metal frame to the dining room table and unfastened the rear so she could recenter the artwork. Removing a piece of black matte paper from the back, Trina saw a small handwritten piece of paper stuck behind the drawing. Trina recognized the block-print writing as Rachel's.

The page was filled with random phrases scattered all over the page like a decoder's scratchpad.

RODNEY / CRUMMEY

Crew Me, Cronies, Crumb Me, Clue knee, Queue See, Clooney, Crude, Karate, Kind to me, Crime to me — CRIME TO ME!!!

NO IDEA

No fear, No Care, Novocain, No rare, Know idea, Know Ear, Nowhere, I know where, No dear — NO DEER!!!

There was another piece of folded paper underneath, a small 3x5 drawing signed Crummey with hand over heart. It was a picture of a golf cart leaving a bar parking lot with a trail of empty liquor bottles. The golf cart's front end was mangled by the impact with a tree, and a small-framed boy was lying on the side of the road.

Trina examined the picture with the intensity of an archaeologist examining a 10,000 year-old parchment. Was she seeing what she thought she was seeing? Everyone knew Rodney's injuries were the result of a golf cart accident. The picture of this young boy lying delicately near a damaged tree and mangled golf cart had to be Rodney's attempt at reenacting the night.

Holy moly! The horrific truth was staring at her in the face. Ian must have gotten drunk and caused Rodney's injuries, which forever changed his life and the life of his family. The date signed at the bottom of the sketch was two days before Ian's body was discovered. This revelation must have been earth-shattering for Lily and Rachel.

A loud sound came from the backyard. Trina rushed over to the window and saw Rodney trying to pull the paddleboard to the boardwalk. She quickly restacked the three papers and centered them in the frame, locked the frame, and hung it back on the wall. She ran out the back door, greeted Rodney, and helped him walk the board to the beach.

Walking back up to the house, Trina contemplated everything she had seen. Rachel must have been trying to get to the truth about Rodney's accident. Ian had not hit a deer but actually had been drunk and hit a tree. All these years, Rodney had been trying to tell them a crime had been committed and there was no deer involved. The enlightenment must have been a crushing blow.

Rodney had known all this time but had difficulty explaining it. Rachel must have sat down with him again and figured it out... forty-eight hours before Ian mysteriously died.

What if Lily still didn't know? Was Rachel working alone? Did she manipulate Ian's sculpture to cause the fatality? Was there collaboration? Planning? With whom? Was Rachel working in cahoots with EDAD?

Trina's heart sank. It was too much to come to terms with now. She needed to leave. She scanned the house to ensure everything was back to its original state, locked the front door and hid the key. Mentally acknowledging the Fairfields' house might become an official investigation area, she pondered all the areas her fingerprints would have been left behind as she snooped throughout the house. She scolded herself for wandering and touching.

She didn't think she was ready to be face-to-face with Lily. She had too many questions, and she was scared to ask. Scared to know.

She texted Lily and told her she was going to have to pass on getting together, that something had unexpectedly come up.

Three dots from Lily

I'll take a raincheck, but we need to get together soon. I need a girls night to release thoughts swirling in my brain as Rachel's due date approaches. Catch you next time.

Revealing Art Class

Chapter Nineteen

Present Day

"It was never reported," Detective Trent said to Trina while holding a half-empty latte on the porch of Coastal Coffee & Cafe. Trina had run into him and Detective Jennifer at the popular shop located at the entrance to Topsail Hill Preserve State Park.

"There must be an accident or at least an incident report," Trina insisted. "The delivery truck was rear-ended and packages spilled onto the street."

"We checked our records and called Freeport, DeFuniak, Destin and Panama City," Detective Jenifer stated as she flipped through her notepad. "There was no report of a delivery vehicle getting into an accident or being hit. We canvassed camera footage from various streets from the days before and after the vet reported the missing container. We also reached out to the delivery company, and they have no record of an accident happening."

"We asked if we could speak to the delivery driver," Trent continued, "but the company refused to divulge the employee's name. The vet said the driver was filling in for someone who was out sick. Without a warrant, we really can't dig further. If we could access the prescription company's order records and check serial numbers on the container you found against the lost prescription bottle, we would have enough factual evidence to support a request for a subpoena. But we need more than a missing prescription bottle. We need something else to tie the two situations together. We also had the lab run tests on the blood smear, but there was no DNA match in the system. We appreciate the find. It may not have led us to the right person yet, but time will tell."

"I knew it was a long shot, but I really hoped we had something," Trina said, disappointed. "I hope you don't feel like you wasted valuable time digging into it. You're teaching me that investigating and validating evidence is much harder in real life than in the movies. Thank you for giving me an update."

"We're accustomed to taking trips down the wrong roads on the journey to the right one. Have a good day, Trina. It was nice bumping into you." The detectives stepped off the porch of the small cottage that had been turned into a coffee shop near the 1,640 acre state park that offered dune lakes, wetlands, campsites, and RV campgrounds to thousands of visitors every year.

It was a couple minutes past eight in the morning, still early for most vacationers to be starting their day. As a family with three young children joyfully walked into the shop to grab breakfast, Trina sat on the porch steps thinking about what she had heard. How was it possible no report was filed? The vet's assistant had been very detailed in her account of what occurred.

She had to work at eleven at the gift shop, and she needed to drop off the art donations she'd picked up from the Fairfields, so taking an unexpected diversion was not in the plan. Still, Trina had an urge to follow a feeling in the pit of her stomach. She walked back into the store, bought two bottles of cold water, two croissants, a couple of muffins, and a few protein bars. She headed back outside, holding the door for an elderly couple on their way in, and walked to her car on a mission.

The temperature was already approaching seventy-five degrees, and the palm leaves remained silent as there was no movement of air. With no natural relief from the heat, she could already feel the moisture forming under her T-shirt. She checked the time. She had an hour to search for Jen, the homeless person who'd been there when Trina found the Gabapentin, and still have time to drop off the art supplies and get to work on time.

Trina had not seen Jen since the incident at the cemetery, so she wasn't sure where she was sheltering, but she had a couple of options in mind. She drove around Stallworth and Allen Lake, looking for Jen's large pink and white shopping bag she tucked away near public restrooms. Not seeing it, Trina continued driving and parked near the causeway, then walked across the pedestrian bridge over Oyster Lake. Still having no luck, Trina drove a little further. She had once seen Jen resting under several oak trees on the backside of the Santa Rosa Golf Course, so Trina parked and strolled through several shady areas on the north side of the greens. Although she saw many people out on the fairway, there was no sign of Jen.

With only thirty minutes left before she needed to head to the Bayou Arts Center, Trina parked at Ed Walline Regional Beach Access. Hopeful she would run into Jen, she put her purchases in two reusable grocery bags, took off her shoes and meandered down the boardwalk. Leaning over the side of the walk ramp, she rested her arms and peered out onto the beach. Ignoring the umbrellas and beach chairs situated along the beachfront, Trina looked for a fully clothed woman sitting with a towel over her head to hide from the sun. Almost ready to give up, Trina caught sight of a green shirt hanging around the waist of a woman who was walking toward the outdoor shower. Trina walked down the end of the boardwalk and cautiously approached the woman from behind.

"Jen is that you?"

The woman, who was holding a bag overstuffed with belongings, kept walking, oblivious to Trina's question. Trina walked up to the side of her.

"Hey, Jen. It's Miss Trina. It's so nice to see you. How are you doing today?"

The woman turned, not expecting to be recognized. Her hair was ruffled, and her clothes looked a little damp. A couple of apples, a hair brush, a sun visor and what appeared to be a pair of worn-out flip-flops were visible in her open bag. Jen was wearing a white tank top that had aged to an off-yellow, with a green button-down shirt tied around her waist. Her colorful full-length skirt provided UV coverage for her legs while being light and airy. She was holding a toothbrush and small hotel-sized toothpaste in her hands.

"Hello. Have I met you before? You look a little familiar. I'm sorry I don't remember your name."

"My name is Trina. Sometimes I see you on my walks along the beach, and I ran into you a month or so ago at the cemetery. It was the same day you found the green shirt you have wrapped around your waist. Do you remember me now?"

"Oh yeah. I remember. I love my green shirt. I wear it every day. You're not here to take it back are you?"

"No, I'm not here to take it. I would love to look at it closer, though. Would that be possible?"

"Sure. You might be able to find your own. I see other people wearing the same one when I walk through neighborhoods." Jen removed it from her waist and handed it to Trina. Holding the shirt with a napkin from her purse, Trina examined it. A Specialty Express logo was embossed on the front of the shirt above the pocket, with an image of a truck with several swirling lines extending off the back. The delivery driver who claimed to have been involved in the accident worked for Specialty Express.

"Jen, would you mind if I take a couple of pictures of your shirt so I can be on the lookout for one myself?"

"Sure. I think only people who deliver packages get to buy them. I've seen another person wearing one when they were pushing a dolly filled with boxes. Sort of like the box I keep some of my stuff in," Jen stated as she pointed to a box hidden behind a crate that secured beach chairs at night.

"You're probably right," Trina said and then held out the two bags she'd brought with her. "I happened to stop at a store on my way to the beach this morning, and I brought you some cold water and some food." Trina stepped back to give Jen space.

"Thank you. That's very kind of you." Jen peeked in the bag, visibly smelled the baked goods, and an appreciative grin gently arose on her face.

"Can I see your box? Maybe I could get the contact information of the delivery company to see if I could buy a shirt?" Trina asked as she snapped several photos of the outside and inside of the shirt, including several of dried paint and possible blood stains, which now appeared faded.

"Good idea."

As they walked toward the box, Trina asked, "Jen, have you washed this shirt in the shower since you found it?"

"Yes. I try to wash my clothes at least two times a week in the outside showers or public restrooms. They dry really fast in the sun, so I don't have to worry about wearing wet clothes, although sometimes the dampness feels refreshing."

Trina bent down and examined the box. It was showing severe signs of wear and tear from transporting belongings while being out in the elements.

"Jen, your box doesn't look like it's going to last much longer. Would you like to keep the two grocery bags? I bet the breathable canvas bags will be easier to carry than a box, and the bags won't fall apart when they get wet. Also, sand can seep right through the tiny holes."

"Are you sure you don't need them back?"

"Yes, positive. Would you like some help emptying the box?"

"No, give me a minute." Jen slowly went through each item and deposited her belongings into the two bags. Then she sat down on the sand and opened one of the bottles of water.

"I can take the box for you. Thank you so much for letting me look at your shirt. I have to run to work, but it was great to see you. Find some shade, it's going to be a hot one today." Trina grabbed the side of the box with another napkin, waved goodbye to Jen, and walked back to her car.

She sat in the driver's seat and gently examined the box. The label clearly showed the box was being shipped to the vet from a medical supply company. She took a couple of photos of the shipping label and sent both the shirt and shipping label photos to Detectives Trent and Jenifer with an explanation of the pictures. She added another text to describe what Jen was wearing and where Jen was so they could find her. They had mentioned they needed something more substantial to help them garner the subpoena. She was glad she would not have to be the person to take the green shirt from Jen. She would leave that to the professionals, but she was excited this could be the break they needed.

Since she was running tight on time, she had told the detectives she would drop the box off at the police station tomorrow.

She didn't want to jump to conclusions, but it was beginning to look like the delivery driver, Gabapentin prescription, and Ian's death were all related. Whoever was wearing the shirt wanted to discreetly dispose of it. She drove to Bayou Arts Center thinking about why it was disposed of in the cemetery. She hoped the opportunity to obtain DNA evidence had not been destroyed by Jen washing the shirt and carrying the box all over town

Assuming this was the box that was damaged in the accident, it explained the source of the Gabapentin, but the absence of a vehicle accident report remained suspicious. The delivery driver could have arranged a financial settlement directly with the driver who caused the damage. She knew people circumvent filing insurance reports by arranging a direct payment for repairs so the guilty driver's rates would not increase.

Searching for an innocent alternate solution, Trina kept trying to manipulate the data in her head. Maybe the delivery vehicle itself was not damaged by the impact, but the box simply fell out because the door was left ajar. It was possible the driver didn't realize one of the bottles of medicine had rolled away and a random person grabbed the bottle. The unknown details were enough to drive her crazy.

She parked in the gravel parking lot near the Cessna Landing boat launch, opened the trunk, and stacked two plastic bins together. With her arms full, she slowly navigated the path, passing a basketball court and playground on her way to the entrance to the arts center. The two front doors were open letting the breeze flow in from Hogtown Bayou. She set the bins down, waved at the arts director, who was on a phone call, and returned to her car to retrieve the remaining boxes.

When she returned, the director was standing over the bins, examining the contents. "Trina, this is great stuff. Some of these supplies are brand new. Why is Rachel donating so much? Isn't she an artist?"

The table was slowly filling up with watercolor sets, paint tubs, bundles of synthetic and natural brushes, tube wringers, drop clothes, painters tape and palette knives. Trina picked up several unopened tubes of acrylic paint and several pouches of unused paintbrushes; mentally agreeing the quality of the donations were top notch.

She also found a huge color wheel and notations made by Rachel to help her discern the color combinations. Trina remembered Lily mentioning how proud she was of Rachel's ability to overcome her color blindness by using tools and cheat sheets Rodney had created for her. Rachel must not need the paint color sheets anymore since she most likely relied on various software tools to clarify colors for her when she created digital designs.

"Rachel is very talented. She can paint, draw, sculpt and tattoo, but her passion is digital art. I think these donations were the result of a deliberate effort to cleanse her past and begin anew," Trina said as she sifted through partially used canvases, sketch pads and random papers.

"Please pass along a huge thank you. We'll be able to use all of these supplies in our Prison Art, Art for All and Art on Demand programs. We truly appreciate her donation."

"I definitely will. I agree some of this stuff looks brand new, like these paint rollers and paint resin torch. What is this tool? It doesn't look like you would use it for painting. Do you know what this one is used for?" Trina said, pointing to a tool which looked like a liquid injector.

"Let me see. Oh, I think it's a portable desoldering gun. It looks like a relatively high quality one. I've seen smaller, less robust ones used by jewelers. This one must have been used to break down some sort of metal substance. Maybe there was a metal fabricator artist in the same studio. I'm surprised she's donating that too. It's an expensive piece of equipment. You can take it back if you think she put it in there by mistake."

"Gosh, she might have made a mistake if she didn't realize what it was. You said it's used to break down metal?" She didn't know the full details of how Ian's sun sculpture fell apart, but she remembered David talking about how one of the rays of the sun had broken off the sculpture causing his final demise. If this was left in the art studio, the police would have confiscated it. So how did Rachel come to possess it? And why was she disposing of it, considering the value?

Careful not to destroy any potential fingerprint evidence, Trina dumped a plastic bag filled with paint brushes to use the empty bag to pick up the tool. "Let me take it back to her to be sure. I can always return it if she tells me she doesn't need for it." Not wanting the director to think about it further, she changed the subject. "Do you mind if I look through this bin for a couple more minutes? Some of these sketches were created by Rachel's brother, and I think her mother might want them back."

"Of course, take your time."

"Thank you for letting me go through the boxes. I picked them up, but I'm curious what Rachel is giving away."

"I better get back and see how my pottery class is doing. Thank you for dropping everything off, Trina."

Trina sat down and flipped through a stack of sketches that displayed various trains of thought and inspirations. She ended up pulling out eight sketches signed Crummey. As she worked her way through the stack, she stopped when she saw the same sketch she had seen in the photograph at the Art Market. The sketch was an exact rendering of what Ian Scott had intended to build for his *Unflappable* underwater sculpture.

She had already dropped the envelope of photographs from the Art Market off at Lily's house but hadn't found an appropriate time to ask her about the photograph of Ian's UnFlappable sculpture. She knew Lily had boxes of Rodney's sketches, so she most likely hadn't taken the time to go through the photographs because she was preoccupied with café responsibilities and managing her household.

After discovering that Ian caused Rodney's injuries, and now seeing more proof Ian stole art concepts from Rodney, the Fairfield family motives for murder were growing exponentially. Who knew the lengths a mother or sister would take to protect their own. Adrenaline, anger, ethical disgust, and years of pent up frustrations were a recipe for unbridled action.

Trina repacked all items except the desoldering gun and sketches and left the boxes on the table. Afraid to point fingers at the Fairfields, she would wait to communicate these recent discoveries to Detective Trent. She needed to give Rachel a chance to explain. The gun had been sitting in a box for over a month; an extra day wouldn't change anything.

She drove to work in a personal fog of gray theories and black and blue coincidences all shining underneath a bright, blinking sign of motives. She attempted to plaster on a friendly customer-service smile all day at work as she was mentally drawing a Venn diagram of information. Her subconscious was putting certain data in the left or right sphere, not wanting the Fairfields to fall in the guilty center.

While she had a lull in customers, she took out a piece of paper and began compiling a list. After listing nearly a dozen suspects — ranging from Ian's family and friends to rival artists and random delivery drivers — and almost as many motives, Trina felt like she was staring at a laundry list of coffee flavors with endless available combinations, unable to pinpoint the mixture that would hit the spot. Was the motive protection, financial or revenge? Was it motive or opportunity that drove the perpetrator to the final act? Who would have been willing to put their freedom in jeopardy in order to take Ian's life?

Could Ian have self-medicated with Gabapentin while drinking alcohol and knocked over the sculpture on himself, causing this whole investigation to eventually lead to a dead end? But how would the bottle have ended up at the cemetery? And why would someone have deliberately blocked the camera security system?

Trina wondered how things always came together so easily in crime books and TV shows. How come detectives always seem to find the right clue at the right time? It was all so overwhelming.

The feeling of helplessness catapulted Trina's thoughts back to the little black box hidden in her dresser drawer. Was there a clue in the box that would have helped the police find Jasmine years ago? Would it help them find Jasmine today? Maybe this weekend she should open the Pandora's box, but for now, she needed to concentrate on the task at hand. She really needed to sit down with the Fairfields and ask them point-blank questions, but she didn't feel comfortable digging into their personal lives. It was one thing for the detectives to do it, but she felt awkward stepping over the line as a friend and confidant.

She locked up the store at five o'clock and drove home. She heated left-overs for her and David and then they went for a walk on the beach. The water was glistening off the dipping sun as slow and comforting waves crashed onto the shore. Their two leashed dogs gave them a workout, as they both attempted to chase sandpipers and seagulls on the beach. They walked for an hour and exited the beach at a different public access so they could grab a cocktail on the patio at Shunk Gulley.

Trina put forth an exerted effort to concentrate on David's stories and enjoy his company to help her mind cleanse of the day's information overflow. They walked home along the path on 30A as dusk set, relying on their cell phones to light the path.

The next day, she woke up excited to meet a group of her friends at Allison Wickey Art Studio for a painting class. Allison, a well-known 30A artist who was on the Board of the Cultural Arts Alliance, was also one of the original Underwater Museum of Art sculptors. As a Venetian plaster, acrylic, and glaze landscape artist, she had generated a dedicated following that allowed her the freedom to offer group art classes to share her love and passion with others. Trina had organized the painting class in an attempt to dig a little more into the inner workings of the art studio and possibly identify a new suspect to lead her away from the Fairfields.

Trina wished Allison's studio walls could talk. As one of the longest standing studios at the Artist Warehouses, she was sure countless juicy conversations had occurred within these four walls, as most artists would have visited Allison to discuss Ian's unexpected death as the discovery unfolded.

At the onset of the class, Trina and her friends reconnected while Allison finished setting up the blank canvases and paint supplies. After donning aprons and finding their spots around two long rectangular tables, Allison began the class by showing a completed Western Lake landscape she had painted and provided an introductory explanation of the first two steps in the painting process. Falling under the relaxing trance of painting, Trina forgot her initial intent and let her mind get lost in the sensory experience.

The ladies laughed as stories were shared, and painting experimentation filled up canvases. Trina glanced at her friends' progress and couldn't control the innate desire to contrast and compare. Allison walked around the table, providing guidance and offering suggestions. As the class progressed, Trina noticed several artists walk in and out, chatting with Allison and two of the other artists who shared the same studio. Trina kept her ears fine-tuned in an effort to pick up on any conversations that might be of interest, but nothing materialized.

After class, the ladies congratulated each other on the variety of talent and interpretation of the colors and paint textures. Her art looked like a kindergartener's attempt, while some of her friends had more natural talent and successfully captured the essence and image of Western Lake. Allison posed for a group picture and recommended everyone walk around and examine the numerous pieces of art available for sale by all the artists who worked in the studio. Trina walked, appreciating the skill and expertise more now as she realized how difficult painting a landscape truly was.

As her friends wandered, Trina approached two artists who were chatting in the back. She recognized Zee but didn't know the man talking to her. She politely interrupted them and introduced herself. Zee remembered Trina from the deployment day and introduced the other artists as Victor, who Trina now knew was the person who took over Ian's sculpture. With gentle nurturing, she inquired about their background and history and eventually massaged the conversation back to Ian's studio.

"Victor, I was lucky enough to witness the deployment of your final sculpture. How rewarding to see your hard work find a permanent home in the underwater gallery. Generations of people will cherish it for years to come. Were you surprised to be tasked with the completion of Ian's work under such a tight deadline?"

"I don't know if I would say I was surprised. He had hired me pretty early on in the process. Initially I was working a couple hours a week on his sculpture, but eventually it became a full-time job. Luckily, his girlfriend, who is also an artist, and I worked on the project together. She and I have many complimentary skills. Honestly, Ian spent more time slowing down our progress than speeding it up. By the end of the five-month construction process, Ian only came to the studio to critique because it made him feel like he was participating. He spent most of his time drowning in alco— um, I mean he spent most of his time dealing with personal demons and not really working on the sculpture. So, to answer your question, no I wasn't surprised to be asked to finish the job. I was expecting it."

Trina, synthesizing what she heard, allowed a brief pause. "Expecting it? Do you mean you were expecting something to eventually happen to Ian?"

"No. No, of course not. He was not a reliable individual, and he spent a fair share of his focus battling personal hardships, but no, I didn't mean to insinuate I expected Ian to become a victim of faulty structural integrity."

"Were you struggling with the integrity of his original design? I mean, you mentioned you and his girlfriend were doing most of the work. So, what makes you think it was faulty?" Trina knew she sounded accusatory but couldn't help herself.

"If Ian had left us alone, the sculpture would never have broken. His unnecessary meddling caused more harm than good. Sometimes after making great progress, I would come to work and find Ian adding slurry to the sculpture where it didn't need it or mending a portion he accidently broke. Rachel and I wasted more time reversing his mistakes than making headway," Victor said defensively.

Zee chimed in. "Who knows what Ian did to the design in last twenty-four hours. He was never someone who generated an aura of positivity, but lately, he was a walking disaster. He had been pacing the studios all week. Every time I saw him, he was in a panic."

"Do you think he meddled one time too many?"

"Well, we wouldn't be surprised if he did. The final nail in his coffin, so to speak."

"Were you surprised the Cultural Arts Alliance announced they wanted his sculpture to be completed by someone else?" Trina asked, then added, "Officially completed, since it sounds like you and Rachel had invested a majority of the time already."

"Uh, yeah. Exactly. With all the publicity and PR before the event, I knew they would want the sculpture to be finished. Once they decided to move forward, I knew I would be the most obvious solution to their dilemma."

"Ever since Ian's death," Zee offered, "the art community has been under a lot of pressure. We've been dealing with prying eyes digging into to all our lives. We wanted this event behind us, and Victor was the most logical choice." Zee looked at Victor and darted her eyes to the door.

"It was a great honor to be chosen," Victor said, "and I'm glad Rachel and her family can move forward. It was very nice to meet you. I hope you enjoyed your class with Allison. We need to get back to work."

Victor and Zee shook Trina's hand and then quickly scooted out the door. Soon after, a person walked backward into the studio pulling a dolly with three boxes.

"Oh great, my new supplies," Allison said. "I've been waiting for these specialty paints. You can put the boxes over here. Thank you." She pointed to an empty spot on the floor.

Recognizing the color of the green delivery shirt, Trina walked closer.

"Can you sign right here, Miss Wickey?" the driver said.

Trina examined the front of the shirt and recognized the logo. She looked up as the driver turned around and had a flash of recognition. *Where have I seen that face before?*

"Sure. I see you finally received a new uniform shirt. The color green looks good on you," Allison stated as she handed back the digital signature machine.

"Thanks. I'll take your word for it. I have no idea what green looks like, on me or otherwise since I've been color blind since birth. But, yes, I found a new uniform shirt in my mailbox at the office this morning. Finally, back to looking like a professional. By the way, I'll be switching back to my normal route soon, so I won't see you much anymore. Have a good day." The driver left, slowly pulling the empty dolly.

A missing green shirt and color blindness. Trina's adrenaline spiked and she could feel her heart race. Trina was more than curious about the identity of the driver and followed outside.

The back of the truck was wide open, and the music playing on the truck's radio filled the air. Trina stopped and listened as the driver loaded the dolly into the back of the truck. She recognized the lyrics and walked to the back of the truck.

"I think I recognize the song," she said to the driver, "but I don't know the title."

"It's 'Let me Love You' by Lacey Sturm. It's my all-time favorite song," the driver said, walking back to the driver's seat. Trina took a picture of the van, including the license plate, and hoped she captured an image of the driver as the van pulled away.

Returning to the studio, Trina asked Allison, "Is that your normal delivery driver?"

"No. She started delivering a month or so ago. Our normal driver has been out on sick leave."

The song "Let Me Love You" was sung by the same musician who was quoted on the strange condolence card. Those lyrics were ringing in Trina's head—million miles ahead, something about all you need, a harsh reality check. Trina was scrambling to solve this crossword in her head.

A strange message left for the Fairfield family after Ian died.

An email to Lily about a trust.

Going to a concert with EDAD.

Every day, all day.

The person Lily might have asked to talk to Rachel about a pediatrician.

Missing green shirt.

"Let Me Love You" favorite song.

Color blindness.

It was all filling in, horizontally and vertically. The details were beginning to make sense. Trina had met the mysterious EDAD. Now the real mystery.

Who was she?

The Last Straw

Chapter Twenty

Before

"Rachel, I need you. I fucked up. I really fucked up." Ian was slurring his words and barely able to hold himself upright. It was the afternoon two days before the UMA deployment. Lily had come home but was tired of hearing Ian and Rachel squabble, so she retreated to her personal space. Rodney was up in his bedroom playing video games. Rachel was sitting with her hands resting on her belly and her legs stretched out on the swing.

"Ian, I can't anymore. I'm done. You have taken advantage of me for too long. I have fixed every mistake you've made. I've invested more hours in your career than I have in my own. I'm tired. This is your damn project."

"I know, Rachel. I know. One more day, then I swear I'll leave you alone. You know I don't deal with stress very well. I've got the casino jumping down my neck for payment, I owe over $3,000 to several artists for their time and efforts over the last five months, and my father is being a bastard and won't open his financial chest. What am I supposed to do? I broke the damn ray right off the side of the sculpture when I fell over. I can't let them take it. And you know deployment day is in two days. I'm desperate."

"It's going to be your name on the art installation. Your name permanently listed on the UMA website as one of the final exhibits. Victor and I have done 95% of the work, but because your stupid ass got drunk again and broke something, you expect me to go and work over the next twenty-four hours and magically fix it. Are you insane?" The level of her voice was migrating higher and higher. She stood up and grabbed the bourbon bottle out of his hand and dumped the contents on the ground.

"Don't act like such a sad puppy who didn't get her way. I've shared my proceeds with you for years. You would've never paid off your father's debt and most of Rodney's medical bills if it wasn't for me. You relied on me as much as I relied on you. You have to help me." Ian grabbed both her wrists and squeezed.

"Let go of me!" Rachel screamed, and Ian reluctantly let go. "How dare you insinuate I need you. Nobody needs you, Ian. You could disappear and the world wouldn't blink."

"You've always thought you were better than me. Always the sweet and innocent one in high school. The teacher's pet. The girl everyone wanted to be friends with. The girl too shy to stand up for herself, but for some reason, people gravitated to you like bees to honey. But I saw your eyes always judging. Judging my choices. Critiquing my livelihood. Always offering to help so you would look like the kind and generous one."

Ian grabbed the empty bottle and tried to drip out any leftover remnants into this mouth.

"You are a such a…" Her face was twisting in anguish. "Such a selfish prick! Have you ever looked at yourself in the mirror, Ian? *Really* looked? The person who keeps track of people's mistakes like a statistician. The asshole who would cause a car accident and then sue the innocent victim for damages. The person who orders appetizer, steak, desserts, and the best bottle of wine but forgets his credit card. You couldn't pass a single class over three years of college, you can't hold a job, your family has disowned you, and your inheritance will end up going to some construction worker who your father loves more."

Ian grabbed her wrists again and stood up so close to her face. She felt like she might pass out from the intensity of the bourbon smell. "At least I have a family. Real bloodlines. The Scott family built this town, Rachel. My father will give it all to me someday. He sure the hell isn't going to give it to any of his numerous illegitimate kids. He made sure every one of those hussies signed an agreement to ensure that never happens. You don't think I've forgotten?"

Rachel turned, feeling the flush in her cheeks rise.

"Oh, poor little Rachel. *Sitting in a tree. K I S S I N G.* I fooled you into thinking I liked you, and you fell for it hook, line and sinker. I manipulated you to come to my house in what was that, third grade? I knew what my dad would be doing after school. I had caught him enough times with enough local sluts. But Wednesday was Lily's day. Your mother was rolling in the hay with my dad for years. He baited her with career promises, teased her with fancy dinners she could never afford. Told her he would take care of her and her sweet angel of a daughter. I listened to all his false promises while my mother had to grin and bear it."

Teardrops slowly began dripping down Rachel's cheeks. Her fists were clenched, and the heat of anger was rising up her chest. She could feel the baby kick as her adrenaline spiked.

"I told you to hide in my dad's office behind his credenza to wait for me. I knew you would see them. Hear them. I wanted you to know your mother was not as innocent as you made her out to be. She wasn't the perfect PTA mom. She wasn't the loving and caring wife she pretended to be."

Ian pointed his index finger hard directly on the center of Rachel's chest. Rachel could feel the repulsion rising in her stomach.

"On the other hand, my mother was. My mother did everything for my father, and he stomped on her self-esteem every single day. Your mother's affair with my father crushed her. All the other floozies were one-time things. He cycled through more women than a criminal going through defense lawyers. But your damn mother… She wouldn't go away. Every damn Wednesday for years. I was tired of it. I needed to put a stop to it.

"I was watching you through the window. I could see the shock and the utter despair in your eyes. Your mother doing the dirty with another man. When you walked out from your hiding spot leaving a trail of paper balls behind, I almost fell out of my perch on the tree. Witnessing the cracking of your innocence was one of the most rewarding memories in my life. And then the icing on the cake was watching them scramble to cover themselves up and get dressed. Your mother almost had a heart attack. I think about the shock on her face every time I ask her for my dinner."

"You should be ashamed of your family. Your mother should be wearing a scarlet X on her apron. This community would never forgive her for her sins. At least my father will leave a lasting legacy. He built this town. He may be an asshole, but he at least he has prestige. And money. Lots of money. Money you will never get. Money your slutty mother will never see. Money my stupid, illegitimate brother, Rodney, will never enjoy."

"That's enough! Don't you dare speak about my family ever again!" Rachel's eyes were popping out of her head. "Ian, you promised me. If I did what you asked, you promised to never divulge what your father and my mother did. You said you would never tell Rodney. Tell anyone. I have done everything you have ever asked. Everything." Rachel's tears were flowing, but she was standing next to Ian with determination.

"Seriously, Rachel? Promises are so easily broken. The night after Rodney's accident, I made sure you understood it was your actions that led to his injuries. Guilty like your mother. You abandoned your brother because of your selfish needs like your mother abandoned her husband every time she stripped her clothes off for my dad."

"Shut up, Ian. Shut up! Rodney is upstairs. Stop it before he hears you!"

"Did you really think I wouldn't use this against you for the rest of your life? The first time I promised to keep this secret; you helped me pass high school. Then I let it go for years. But then you texted me and asked me to pick up Rodney. You must have been desperate to text me of all people. I've gotten into more car accidents than a race car driver. It was your stupidity that put you in this predicament, Rachel. Rodney's accident fell in my lap. When I saw how guilty you felt at the hospital, how desperate you were for me to not tell anyone you were too busy working on your stupid college thesis to pick up your brother, I knew I was going to lean hard into you. Threaten to expose your cheating mother. Watching you fall apart was the best entertainment I've ever had.

"Listening to you cry for hours and hours at your brother's bedside. Listening to your mother stress over the mounting medical bills. Your panic the night I told you I was going to call the local newspaper and let them know the sweet, innocent, likable café owner the community leaned on for guidance and therapy was really a life-long cheater.

"That's when I realized I'm like my dad. I'm just smarter. For the last four years, I have succeeded in making everyone in the Fairfield family miserable. You, Rachel, are my professional problem solver, and you come with amazing benefits. I finagled a rent-free house. I've convinced you to borrow money from your dad and then forced you to pay it back. I've suckered you into working for free while building my art reputation. Your slutty mother prepares my meals, and best of all, you've been stupid enough to let people believe you slept with me and now you're going to have my baby."

"You son of a..." Rachel raised her hand to slap him, but he caught her wrist and held it high above her head.

"You are going to help me tomorrow, Rachel. You are going to drive to the studio with me in the morning, I am going to pour myself a big bourbon, and I am going to watch you fix my sculpture. Or I'm going to tell the world how horrible your mother really is, and the whole world will know Rodney is not only a Fairfield but a Scott too." Ian dropped her wrist, walked to the porch door to enter the house, and turned.

"All those years ago, I told you I would never tell the world Rodney is my half-brother only so one day I could hold it over your head. I don't care what promises your mother made to my father. I don't have to keep those promises. She loses my father's monthly stipend as soon as the cat is out of the bag. I'm so glad I have this nugget to hold you accountable.

You're so gullible and easy to manipulate, Rachel. It's been easier than taking candy from a baby, though who'd have thought I could get you to give birth to my fictitious baby while I'm sleeping around town with my own band of slutty women. The sweet, innocent, beautiful Rachel Fairfield sleeping with the town asshole. I'm just surprised you waited so long to sleep with Tony. How many years did you remain celibate? It must be driving Tony crazy that I get to claim fatherhood." Ian let out his cringy guttural laugh, sending a powerful inertia through Rachel's body.

She visualized launching herself at him like an Amazon warrior, squeezing the life out of him with her bare hands. But alas, she stood frozen, feeling the heat from within steam out of her pores.

He took one step in and then turned his head back to her. "He's lucky I only drank five shots, or he would have had more than a bump on his head. You know there was never any deer on the road, right? Rodney's been trying to tell you that for years. I'm leaving bright and early tomorrow morning. You better be ready." He walked back inside, slamming the slider shut.

An invisible knife plunged into her heart. Rachel felt nauseous.

No deer.

Rodney's accident wasn't caused by a deer crossing the road.

Five shots. Ian had been drunk.

That bastard!

She leaned up against the pergola beam and slid down to the concrete patio in utter despair. She felt used. Stupid. How could she be so gullible? So blind? Her whole life had been a tornado of lies, deceit and cover-ups. Ian Scott had ruined her entire life, and she let it happen.

She remembered that day in Mr. Scott's office. Hiding, waiting for Ian to meet her. Ian had promised to hold her hand and kiss her cheek if she stayed put. She was only eight or nine years old. She had no idea what she was doing, but Ian had made her feel special. Made her feel important. So, she went. He had shown her the spot to hide and told her he was going to come back with soda for both of them.

Ten minutes later, she could hear two people talking. Then they were making all sorts of weird noises. Grunts and groans. Rachel's curiosity eventually motivated her to peek. At first, she didn't understand what she was seeing. Two naked people in an embrace. The woman sounded like she was in pain. She began walking toward her to see if she needed help. When she realized it was her mother, all hell broke loose.

Months later, her mother had given birth to her baby brother, and her father had mysteriously moved out. She hadn't understood what she actually witnessed until years later. She had been dealing with so many changes in their life and hadn't thought about the encounter until her mother sat her down when she was about to enter high school.

Lily and her husband had gotten together very young, eager to have children. They spent years without any full-term pregnancies. Lily's struggles to get pregnant were well known in the community, and a local woman, Charlotte Willow, had approached her about adopting her expecting child. Lily convinced her husband adoption was the only way they would ever have children. Rachel became their daughter officially when she was only six-weeks old. The first five years of Rachel's life were blissful, but eventually Lily and Declan's relationship began showing signs of despair.

Lily discovered Declan's infidelities early on in the marriage but stayed together for the sake of her daughter. At some point, Lily, who was working part-time at a local diner, met Mr. Pierce Scott, who was a frequent customer. He had found Lily attractive immediately and began showering her with attention. The lure of compliments, gifts and after-noons together became too much. Initially tentative to start a physical relationship, Peirce masterly manipulated her into believing he would leave his wife, marry Lily, and Rachel and Lily would move into his ma nsion.

Rachel's unexpected discovery put an immediate damper on the re-lationship, and once Lily discovered she was carrying his baby, Scott did the bait and switch. He forced her to sign a legal agreement in which she agreed to never publicly announce his rightful place as Rodney's biological father, and in return, Lily would receive a monthly stipend until Rodney turned twenty-five. Declan agreed to be listed as the father on the birth certificate if Lily asked for nothing in the divorce settlement. Lily knew a divorce was easier to explain than a fatherless child, so she agreed. Lily had to find a way to support herself and her two children, so she opened the café and never looked back.

One day during freshman year in high school, Ian approached Rachel threatening to tell everyone about Lily's secret affair and illegitimate child. Her mother was already stressed trying to raise the two of them alone while managing a restaurant. Rachel couldn't let the secret expose her mother's indiscretions, so she agreed to do whatever Ian asked.

Lily had always had a heart of gold. She was the hardest working woman Rachel knew, and she appreciated everything her mother had sacrificed to ensure they had a great life and a solid foundation. She knew her mother wasn't an angel, but she understood how the events unfolded, and she knew her mother did what she thought was best once she was put in an awkward financial position.

Rachel's adoptive father was a supportive man, who had simply been too young and immature to be a good dad at the time. Over the years, he had grown to love Rodney as much as he loved Rachel, but he was not an emotionally connected father figure. Although she didn't have Lily or Declan's DNA, she had their heart and their love, which was more than Rachel could ever need or want.

Additionally, Lily had decided early on Rachel's birth mother would have full access and a chance to build a relationship with her daughter if she desired. Lily's willingness to share Rachel with Charlotte was an act of unabated generosity, for which Rachel could never explain in words how invaluable the motherly relationship had been to her throughout her life.

Lily and Charlotte formed an unlikely friendship early on, as Lily needed a shoulder to cry on when the stress of the business was too much. Rachel never judged her biological mom's choice to release her motherly obligations, and that monumental gesture allowed their relationship to grow exponentially.

Her biological mom didn't help raise her and missed many of Rachel's significant childhood memories, but once she had gotten her own life back on track, she was relentless about being an emotional sounding board for Rachel, sending her emails and texts reminding Rachel she was there for her every day, all day. Charlotte was level headed, energetic and enthusiastic about exposing Rachel to new ideas and helping her see things Lily didn't. When Lily concentrated on the black and white of life's choices, her mom would show her the gray. How many people are lucky enough to have two mothers to love? She enjoyed the benefit of having been raised in both the yin and the yang way of life.

Now Rachel's gullibility, her stupidity and naivety, had put it all at risk. She had already given so much of her life to protect those secrets. To ensure Lily's name was not tarnished. To allow Rodney to grow up knowing he had a father who loved him. Rodney understood his mother and father didn't live together, but that it didn't mean they didn't love him with all their hearts. Rodney did not need to find out his real dad abandoned him before he was even visible on a sonogram.

Rachel truly believed she had been making the right choice all these years. Protecting her brother. Covering up the secret with stronger truths. Important family ties.

Now, Ian's confession was burning holes in her heart and breaking the protective calcifications around her brain that made life functional.

There was no deer. Ian had put her brother's life at risk by getting behind the wheel drunk. He knew he shouldn't have driven him home and he lied to protect his ass.

There had been no deer.

No deer!

Rachel blinked. Then blinked again.

She ran into the house, hearing music blasting in the garage art studio behind a closed door. She grabbed a piece of paper and began writing down phrases. After a few minutes, she ran up to her brother's room.

"Rodney, I think I understand. I finally understand. I need you to draw me a picture."

"What?" he said as he pulled his AirPods out of his ears.

"Draw me a picture of what happened the night of the accident. Draw me a detailed picture."

"No idea, Rach, no idea." He shook his head and went to grab his Air-Pods, obviously frustrated with his sister's years of not understanding.

"Rodney, have you been trying to tell us all this time the golf cart did not hit a deer?"

He looked at her incredulously. "Bout time, Rach. Tell you fer yers."

Rachel hugged her brother from behind. "Rodney, I am so very sorry. We didn't understand. We are so stupid. I think I finally know what you were trying to communicate." She pointed to the piece of paper where she'd written the phrase "crime to me."

"Yes, Rach. I not like Ian. No idea. Crummey."

"Rodney, draw me a picture so I can show mom. Draw me one of your unbelievably accurate pictures of the night everything changed. I love you so much, Rodney! I am going to make this up to you."

Rodney smiled and shook his head in amusement. "Okay, Rach." He began drawing.

While he was drawing, Rachel sent a text to Tony. When Rodney was finished, she hugged him and left his room to knock on her mother's door. Lily opened her bedroom door, and Rachel spent the next thirty minutes explaining everything.

Next, she sent a text to Charlotte.

In the morning, she met Ian in the kitchen. She watched him pour bourbon in his coffee cup, then drove them to the studio... ready to make amends.

Shower of a Promising Future

Chapter Twenty-One

Present Day

L ife was nothing but a string of assumptions.

As she sat in the conference room at police headquarters after finishing her meeting with Detectives Trenton Oliver and Jenifer Townsend, Trina contemplated a scene from the old tv show *The Odd Couple* when Felix Unger reminded students that when one *assumes* they can make and "ass" out of both "U" and "me."

During the course of her investigation, she believed she had been methodical. She truly thought she had been careful not to jump to conclusions while analyzing blips in daily life and innuendos that caught her attention. In reality, she had been making a bunch of bad assumptions all along. The realization finally hit her hard and unexpectedly, like she had walked into a huge wall of crystal-clear glass.

How many times do we make assumptions in the course of daily life?

We assume cars will stop at a red light.

We assume our servers will not store our credit card account details.

We assume our physicians are not accepting prescription kickbacks.

We assume our children, who we have spent a lifetime showering with love and devotion, will do the same as we age.

How many times do bad assumptions cause innocent people heartache?

Assumptions that spouses will not cheat.

Company employees will not steal.

Friends will not share confidences.

Food manufacturers will not poison.

Houses will be built to withstand natural phenomena.

How many dinners and lunches and friendly chats had she had with Rachel where she assumed all references to her mother, or her mom, meant Lily.

She now realized she had never seen a family resemblance, but she assumed—there was that word again—that Rachel looked like her father. Now looking back, she distinctly remembered certain times Rachel would refer to her *mother* and other times she spoke very specifically about her *mom*. Little interchangeable words that held the weight of the entire investigation.

Upon leaving the Artist Warehouses after her painting class, Trina had pulled up the image she'd captured of the delivery driver. The similarities jumped out at her. The same distinct V-shaped jawline, a nose with a subtle extension like Natalie Portman, and enviously tall and slender legs. The woman driving the truck was most likely Rachel's biological mother.

She could not wait any longer. Trina chewed on the concept while driving directly to Lily's house. She was at risk of coming across as tactless, nosy, and judgmental, but she had to give the Fairfields an opportunity to explain.

She got to their house a little before four p.m. Lily had recently arrived home and was preparing dinner. Rachel was upstairs resting, as the exhaustion of working while eight months pregnant was wearing her down. Trina was unclear how to approach the topic, but she figured the best way to secure a bull's-eye was by driving the dart right through the center. Once all three of them were sitting at the dining room table, Trina took the plunge into the deep end.

"You know I have grown to love each and every one of you as a family, as members of our community, and as individuals who, I believe, would bend over backward for me as much as I would for you." She paused and read the confused yet agreeable expressions on their faces.

"Lily, you are one of the most dynamic and determined business owners on 30A, while simultaneously being one of the most commendable, protective and genuine mothers I have had the joy of being around."

Lily smiled, but with clear apprehension not knowing where Trina was headed.

"You have successfully raised two independent, strong willed, compassionate, and extremely talented children. I have never seen two siblings more supportive of their mother and of each other as Rachel and Rodney."

Rodney reached out and grasped Rachel's hand, while Rachel sat up a little straighter in her chair and rested her other hand on her pregnant belly.

"I have had the pleasure of spending one-on-one time with each of you, and I have to say, I am more impressed today than I was a month ago. Rachel, the parental road ahead of you is the most explosive, life-changing experience you will ever know. I truly hope your child brings you enlightenment and decades of prideful moments. And Rodney, this community has been blown away by your personal commitment to restore your strength and mobility while retaining your light-hearted personality." Trina took a breath and an extra moment to gain her confidence.

"The reason I am sitting in front of you today is because I discovered something that might have long-lasting ripple effects to your family. I could dance around the details, but I prefer to rip the Band-Aid off."

All three of them sat taller and more alert.

"A local vet recently had a bottle of Gabapentin displaced from one of their deliveries. I happened upon the missing container of medication when leaving the Artists Warehouses the day that Ian died. Ian's bloodwork shows he had digested the same medication within 24 hours of his death. Since I discovered the stolen, or shall I say, missing medication, I wanted to give you an opportunity to guide me to the possible source."

All three looked confused, then Lily's and Rachel's light bulbs blinked on. Lily gave a nonchalant answer, distracted the conversation toward offering Trina a drink, and reminded Rodney he needed to study for his mobility assisted driver's license test. Rodney left the room, and once Lily returned with a drink, she sat beside Rachel. Lily quietly asked Trina to continue.

"The individual who stole the medication might be a local delivery driver. Is there anyone you know who might have access to a delivery vehicle and would have any possible link to Ian?"

"Yes," they both said in unison and looked at each other.

Rachel continued. "My biological mother, Charlotte Willow, drives for a local delivery company. What makes you think she would have stolen medication and administered it to Ian? Couldn't he have obtained it and administered it to himself?" Rachel wrung her hands and grabbed a piece of random paper from the table.

"Just to be clear, I cannot say that what I uncovered is surefire proof of any wrongdoing, but certain data points are lining a path toward one person. The day Ian was found; I found a bottle of Gabapentin next to a green delivery shirt from Specialty Express. The shirt, bottle and the delivery box are being tested for DNA and possible links to the crime scene. You both have navigated so many challenges in your life, and with the baby's arrival only weeks away, I wanted to give you a chance to explain it away."

For the next two hours, Rachel and Lily shared their lives. Their hardships, regrets, decisions and remediations. Details about Declan's and Lily's affairs. Pierce Scott's legal contract for Rodney's financial security. Declan's willingness to claim Rodney. Ian's lies about the accident and his arrogant and disrespectful manipulation of Rachel's life. Rachel confirmed she discovered the truth about the golf cart accident two days before deployment. In addition, they confirmed they all knew Ian was stealing Rodney's art concepts, but Rodney chose to take the higher ground and interpret the thefts as compliments.

On the next set of questions, Trina knew she was treading precariously. "The realization that Ian lied and caused Rodney's life-altering injuries most likely generated a swarm of negative energy. What happened the night Ian was killed? Where either of you there? Did Charlotte find out and go see Ian? Did you manipulate the integrity of the sculpture using a MIG welding gun?"

Both women looked at each other for a moment and reached out to grab each other's hands. Rachel exhaled deeply, and Lily gave her a slight nod.

"The night that we discovered the truth, Ian had pleaded with me to help him restore the metal artwork he had damaged earlier that day. I knew his desperate need for help would provide me with some leverage, so I put a plan in motion. The next day, Lily took Rodney to the café, and I arranged to meet Charlotte at the studio around noon after her morning delivery route. A dear friend of mine, Tony, agreed to meet me there to provide additional support.

"That day, which was the day before the deployment, Ian slept in, and I spent the morning drafting a document. When Ian woke up around eleven, I drove him to the studio. Soon after we arrived, he began drinking. He was pacing back and forth ranting and raving about the deadline. He was both verbally abusive and threatening to physically hurt me if I didn't finish his project. I called Charlotte and Tony and let them know I needed reinforcements. By the time they arrived, Ian was heading toward loopy. Their arrival agitated Ian more than I expected, so it took us a while to calm him down. Charlotte eventually convinced him to drink some water instead of alcohol, and Tony and Charlotte managed to sit Ian in a chair. When we felt like he had settled down, we had what you could call an intervention. We confronted Ian with the truth about Rodney's accident and demanded he make restitution for his actions."

"Financial?"

"Yes. Unfortunately, there is no way to change the wheels of time, but we wanted him to own up to what he had done and make an agreement to pay my family back for the thousands of dollars we have invested in

Rodney's recoveries. We also presented him with the document I had crafted, in which he admitted his guilt and agreed to never threaten my family again."

"You said he was under the influence. How did he react? Did you believe a document signed while he was not of sound mind would hold up? Legally, that is."

"He had consumed a lot, but after we settled him down, he seemed to relax pretty quickly. It's possible Charlotte helped the process along by adding Gabapentin to his water, but I'm a little shocked she would do that. And I don't know why she would steal it. I had called her in a frenzy telling Tony and Charlotte that I needed their help sooner than later since Ian's rampage was escalating. Being eight months pregnant, I was worried about the baby's safety." Rachel stood up and began pacing.

"Having two stakeholders with me, I felt confident enough to stand up to him. We weren't sure anything would hold up in a court of law, but it was a step in the right direction. Knowing how desperate he was to lean on me to help him stabilize the metal sculpture, I needed to use the only leverage I had. However, I was cognizant to the fact Ian had proven over and over again to be unpredictable."

"Did he sign it?"

"Yes. After an hour of lies, threats and arguments, he eventually caved, and we filmed him signing it. Then Ian passed out. Charlotte did what she could to help us, but she realized quickly she didn't know enough to add value, so Tony and I spent hours stabilizing the sculpture. We left a little after six p.m. Charlotte left at some point while we were working."

"The detectives will go over all this with you again, but what state was he in when you left?"

"Like I said, he was passed out."

"Did any of you return that evening?"

"No. At least, not that I'm aware." Lily shook her head.

Rachel stood with her hands on the back of a chair. "Do you really think my mom, I mean Charlotte, had something to do with Ian's death?"

"Rachel, I don't know. I have provided the police the information so they can move forward with the investigation, but I really wanted to give you a chance to explain instead of being blindsided. Let the detectives do their job and don't make any assumptions."

Trina sat with them for another hour hashing details and possibilities.

Finally, Trina left their house exhausted and apprehensive. She had learned a very big investigatory lesson—never assume anything. If she planned on continuing to support her local Walton County Sheriff's office, it was up to her to remember clues could be immersed in a bath of stereotypes, myths, and ignorant misconceptions. The path to any courthouse required validation and verification.

***

A few weeks later, Trina was sitting inside Rachel's newly renovated tattoo parlor in Lily's garage watching Rachel open baby shower gifts. The room had been painted dark blue with one wall accentuated with several of Rodney's graphite creations. Bohemian music played in the background enhancing the mind-blowing rotation of Rachel's digital designs on a huge flat screen that covered the opposite wall. A stunning sign hanging from the ceiling blazed DreamInk in neon blue against a black backdrop, welcoming visitors to her new artistic haven.

The room was overflowing with local artists, old co-workers and over a dozen friends. Rachel was beautiful, dressed in a blue-jean overall set with a black tank top. Her hair, which she'd let grow out over the course of her pregnancy, was resting in two long braids that had been intertwined with blue and pink ribbons. Her skin glowed as if she had just come back from the spa, and a smile was permanently affixed to her face

.

Rodney stood proudly nearby, passing her gifts and taking pictures. Lily and Charlotte were sitting on a couch in the back taking in the event in its entirety. Tony, who Trina had learned was Rachel's high school sweetheart, was sitting next to Rachel and beaming with fatherly pride. Trina was so happy they had decided to submit a paternity test and confirm Tony was the father. Although the news was explosive to many who had assumed Ian was the father, Rachel finally felt free of the Scott family bondage.

After opening her gifts and with a little help from Tony, Rachel stood up and addressed her guests. "Thank you all for spending today with Tony and me. Each and every one of you has spoiled us with your generosity and kindness. I want to give special thanks to my mother Lily, who has provided unconditional love and support. She has worked relentlessly to ensure Rodney and I had everything we need and more. If I can become half the mother she is, my baby will have the best life."

Everyone cheered, and Lily nodded in appreciation.

"I have lived a very fortunate life, as I have been embraced by motherly love twice. My biological mom, Charlotte, has been a guiding force, a therapist, and my personal fan club throughout life. You may not have shared my home, but you have always shared my heart. I am so lucky to have both of you. Every day, all day."

Rachel grabbed Tony's hand as they stood together in front of the enthralled crowd.

"Now, we would like to have the gender reveal."

Tony took off his T-shirt and rested his hand on a large bandage adhered over his heart. He slowly pulled it off, revealing a tattoo of a hand planting seeds in a garden. Rachel let down the top of her overalls and pulled up her tank top on the side of her torso. She slowly pulled off her own adhesive, which revealed a tattooed image of two baby flowers sprouting from a patch of grass. One had pink petals, the other blue.

The room erupted in screams of amazement, tears of joy, and endless hugs.

After the excitement died down, Trina saw Rodney engaged in a relatively intense conversation with Mike, who Trina had learned was Ian's best friend. After Rodney showed him something in his leather messenger bag, Mike nodded, shook Rodney's hand, and walked out.

Trina watched Rodney for several minutes. He stood with pride, broad shoulders, and a smile of satisfaction on his face. A few minutes later, Rodney walked out of the garage to the driveway to stand in line at the Sunset Slice and Scoop catering food truck. While he waited for his slice of pizza, Trina walked over to him to congratulate him on becoming an uncle. After a minute or two of generalities, Trina decided to make an inquiry.

"Are you excited to shower your niece and nephew with love and attention?"

"Supr cited."

"Is everything okay with Mike? It looked like you were settling an argument."

"Settling a bet," Rodney said as he took his last bite of pizza.

"Who won?"

"I did, for sure," Rodney said as he bent over and grabbed his messenger bag.

"I'm so glad things ended well for your family, Rodney. Only good times ahead."

"Made sur of that." He smiled, winked, and walked away.

Trina cocked her head as she stared at his back. Rodney walked slowly, with his controlled limp, toward an e-bike parked on the side of the house. There was a decal on the side of the bike, : "The secret of happiness is freedom, the secret of freedom is courage – Carrie Jones" Trina watched him climb on the bike, adjust his bag, and give a thumbs-up to Mike who was sitting in his car.

As Mike drove away, Trina read a sticker on his rear bumper: "Freedom means Choice."

No... don't let your mind go there, Trina.

***

The day before Rachel's babies were due, Detective Trent finished conducting his investigation into Ian's death.

Charlotte had been brought in for questioning, revealing two crucial, though not murderous details. Two days before the sculpture deployment, she had learned about Ian's involvement in Rodney's accident and agreed to meet Rachel the following day at the studio to discuss what Ian could do to make amends. During her delivery route the morning of that meeting, she was in a minor, fender bender that caused some boxes to fall out the back of the delivery van. She had retrieved all the damaged boxes and reloaded them into the van. At some point during the remaining deliveries, a bottle of Gabapentin rolled out of one of the damaged boxes into the back of the vehicle. She made the vet's delivery, unaware the renegade bottle was still in her possession.

When she arrived at the art studio and parked, the missing bottle of Gabapentin rolled to the front of the van. Although she knew she should report her discovery, she saw it as an opportunity to help Rachel in a stressful situation and impulsively removed two tranquilizers in hope of calming Ian down.

During their attempts to physically restrain Ian, she bumped into the metal sculpture, tearing her shirt and cutting her skin. After Ian signed the document and eventually passed out, she left the studio to allow Rachel and Tony time to work on the sculpture. Realizing the significance of her actions, she had driven to the nearby cemetery to dispose of the remaining pills. Before tossing the bottle in the trash can, she had wrapped it in her uniform shirt in hopes of hiding the contents from passersby.

The South Walton investigatory team confirmed it was Charlotte's blood, not Ian's, on the container. In addition, they confirmed Charlotte never returned to the studio. She was on internal security video at a local restaurant until midnight, and her cell phone pinged at her home for the remainder of the evening.

Detectives Trent and Jenifer praised Trina for providing them with the missing link of Charlotte's involvement even though no evidence existed that pointed to her guilt in his death.

Although she was not charged with murder, Charlotte accepted a federal plea deal for mail tampering, was charged with a misdemeanor for the theft of the pills and was fired from her delivery job. The Scott family did not want to press charges for her having slipped Ian the prescription pills, and the local prosecutor was willing to respect the family's wishes all things considered.

Rachel and Tony were also cleared of any wrongdoing, as they were captured on security camera leaving the parking lot together that evening prior to Ian's estimated time of death.

The surveillance camera on the unit that had been blocked was proven to be unrelated. The lens cover was not the result of a killer's premeditation, but rather for a surprise birthday party planned at a neighboring studio for one of the artists.

The South Walton Sheriff's Office final conclusion was that Ian caused his own accidental death. The theory was that upon waking, a groggy Ian stumbled into the sculpture and landed in an unfortunate position whereby the metal ray broke and punctured his artery. Without any clear evidence pointing to a third party, and with the Scott family's desire to move on, the detectives were closing the case.

When Trina learned of the official report, she couldn't help but feel shamefully deflated. The intrigue and mystery of an unexpected death had led her, along with many others, to believe he had been murdered. The mundane revelation that sometimes bad things happen to bad people left a gaping hole in her mind's eye. As a lifetime corporate career woman, she was used to closure, finality, and right and wrong answers. The lack of evidence, Scott family pressure to close the case, and efforts to reinstate the feeling of safety and community were understandable but not satisfactory.

Unfortunately for Trina, she didn't work in the sheriff's office, and although Rodney's parting words haunted her dreams, she would have to accept the reality that Ian's personal demons had not sparked a killer's instinct. It was time for the Fairfields to live a life free of baggage.

A few days later, Trina sat in her bedroom holding the little black box. Twirling the piece of her past in the palm of her gloved hand, she stared at it as if it held her entire life's worth of secrets. The relief that all had ended well for Rachel and Lily left her feeling fulfilled and energized. Vicariously absorbing strength from the Fairfield family for dealing with a life full of adversity, she was ready to unmask the mystery held in a two inch by four inch cube.

She pulled the cover off the box slowly, revealing something small wrapped in an old piece of newspaper. Unwilling to touch it with her bare hands, Trina kept her latex gloves on as she unraveled the dry, crinkled paper. A keychain fell onto her bedspread, along with a restaurant guest check. She picked up the keychain, reading the name of a nearby storage facility. She read a handwritten note on the check: *Found in the wallet prior to disposal. Find Jasmine.*

Trina held the key in hand. Although it weighed mere ounces, it felt as heavy as an iron sculpture. Was she ready to tackle this thirty-year-old mystery? She sat for a while processing all the what-ifs and maybes. Eventually, she put the key back in the box, took off her gloves, and sent Rachel a text.

Three dots appeared almost immediately.

Yes! Definitely. Stop by any time.

Trina was ready to move on to the next chapter in her life, and to help her take the first step across the threshold, she'd scheduled an appointment with Rachel.

She was eager to wear a uniquely crafted piece of Rachel's art on her body; a tattoo of an open book, symbolizing knowledge, understanding, and the pursuit of honest-to-goodness truth.

She could use a little daily reminder... no more assumptions.

30A

Santa Rosa Beach, Florida

Now that you have read *The Panhandle Picasso*, are you ready to explore 30A in Santa Rosa Beach, Florida?

Although this is a work of fiction, several actual businesses, artists, and organizations are fictionally incorporated into the story.

Stop by and let them know you spotted them in the Kendra Hoey's Panhandle Mystery Series.

<u>Dining Establishments</u>

Shunk Gulley Oyster Bar

It's Heavenly Shortcakes & Ice Cream

Johnny McTighes Irish Pub

3 Sons Bar-B-Q

North Beach Social

Farm & Fire South Walton

Old Florida Fish House

Blue Mountain Beach Creamery

The Meltdown on 30A

Stinky's Bait Shack

Hotz Coffee

Vue on 30A

Vin'tij Food & Wine

Cousins Maine Lobster Food Truck

Beach Camp Brewing Co.

The Citizen

Crust Artisan Bakery

AJ's Grayton Beach

For the Health of It

Pickle's Burger and Shake

Coastal Coffee & Café

Sunset Slice & Scoop Food Truck

Local Businesses and Destinations

Mercy Tattoo Studio

Historic Gulf Cemetery

The Pavilion at Watersound Town Center

Beachy Blooms 30A

Seaside Lyceum Lawn

Dive 30A

Grand Boulevard at Sandestin

Studio Thirty A (Yoga)

Draper J Office Building

Western Lake

Kindness Pet Hospital

Cook Family Dentistry

Bastide Home and Garden

Topsail Hill Preserve State Park

Stallworth Lake

Allen Lake

Cessna Landing

Hogtown Bayou

Oyster Lake

Ed Walline Regional Beach Access

Events, Organizations and Programs

Underwater Museum of Art (UMA)

Cultural Arts Alliance of Walton County (CAA)

South Walton Artificial Reef Association

The Artists Warehouse of South Walton

Bayou Arts Center

Prison Art Program

Art for All & Art on Demand

Point Washington Medical Clinic

Panama City Beach News Herald

30A Songwriters Festival

ArtsQuest Fine Arts Festival

Digital Graffiti Festival

Alys Beach

Artists

Jared Herzog, Singer

Jamie Rich, Photographer

Beth Christina Art, Jeweler

Mary Dilley, Jeweler

Mary Ellen DiMauro, Clothing Designer

Bradley Eiland, Artist

Lindsay Tobias, Artist

Ginger Leigh, Artist

Bobby Lowe, Artist

Allison Wickey, Artist

Follow Me

@panhandlemysteryseries

All Authors Appreciate Constructive Feedback

Please consider leaving a review

The Panhandle Patient

(Book Three)

Did you enjoy The Panhandle Picasso?

Keep reading for a sneak peek at Kendra's third novel

The Last Wave

Present Day

She wiped droplets of perspiration off her forehead and chest. That was a workout. She was exhausted and exhilarated.

She rested her hand on the sheets, peered down at his abs, and ran her finger through the glistening perspiration.

Rock hard six-pack. Perfectly symmetrical. Indented at all the right places and highlighted with wisps of sun-dyed blond hair. She glanced up, confirming his eyes were shut. She was going to take advantage of the moment and enjoy the private view.

His brown hair, lightened by hours surfing in the Florida sun, rested playfully in small tight curls on his head. His cleft chin looked like two bumps at the bottom of a Red Delicious apple: slightly elevated but swooping softly like the crest of a hill. She examined his biceps, appreciating the hours he worked in the gym to stay fit.

He wasn't smiling right now, but she could visualize his movie star teeth; so white he blinded her when he grinned. She closed her eyes, thinking about when he'd met her at the restaurant earlier that evening.

She'd walked into the bar scanning the patio seats with perfect views, knowing his buddy hooked him up with only the best. His open button-down, light-green, short-sleeved shirt with tiny white dots accentuated his tan. His brown baggy shorts and flip-flops paired well as his evening's attire, and the dimples on his cheeks when he smiled made him appear as if he had just won a surfing competition. A chorus of happy notes had filled her heart.

He liked her. He really liked her, and she admittedly liked him.

Remembering where she was, she opened her eyes and pushed out a satisfied breath, accepting the new calm that had entered her body. She moved into a crouched position with her legs tucked under her knees, and head bent slightly down over his fantastic form. As her hands rested on the bed sheets, she could feel the dampness reminding her to run a wash later.

She ran her fingertip down his brow to the tip of his nose then let her finger softly braze his lips. She admired his swimmer muscles. His latte-colored skin glistened underneath his own layer of moisture. Suddenly feeling like a voyeur, she pulled the sheet up to cover to his body. He was truly a specimen.

She had to admit; he was the total package.

She originally hadn't been attracted to him. She, along with her brother, had signed up for six weeks of private surfing lessons and had focused on learning. However, the more hours they spent together, she was charmed by his innocent appreciation for the environment, his protection of nature and his vigilance for safety. He also scored points with his keen observation skills, pointing out her brother's aptitude for longevity but weakness for following protocol.

He taught them both proper surf etiquette: don't dive head-first, closet to peak gets priority, wait for your turn, don't get in the way, and most importantly, communicate. He challenged them but never pushed past their limits. He gave them more than what was included in the surfing package, staying late and showing them videos online. He was respectful, polite, and never boastful.

As soon as their six-weeks were up, he asked her out, gaining her respect by having waited until the course was finished. After their first date — fabulous dinner followed by a stroll through the quiet streets of Inlet Beach — she was smitten. He dropped her off, kissing her cheek, tempting her with his sultry lips but remaining 100% a gentleman. Although he earned a meager living, he never asked her to pay, and she knew he was picking up extra shifts at his part-time job to cover the expenses.

When he gave her his precious olivine Shaka sign necklace from his trip to Hawaii, where he had placed in the top three in a national surfing competition, her heart swelled a little larger. He was as proud of the necklace as he was of his surfing reputation.

She officially had a crush. He checked all the boxes. She couldn't find any faults, except maybe his age. But nowadays, it was acceptable for an older woman to date a younger man.

She struggled with her own emotional tug-of-war. Should she unlock the door or keep peering through the screen? Would he prove to be self-centered, arrogant, or even worse, dumb? Over time, would he expect stereotypical female acts of service? Would he demand home-cooked meals and leave his dirty clothes on the floor? Was it really worth it?

She eventually caved and invited him over for a dinner with her brother. Although she knew she was setting expectations too high, she cooked filet mignon paired with seared scallops, hand-rolled gnocchi, and grilled corn on the cob. Dinner was followed by apple crisp and lots of conversation. They talked about their future, his dream for setting up a surf shop, and his penchant for rescuing dogs.

The evening was bolstered with sips of Clase Azul Reposado Tequila. After her brother left, the sipping turned into gulping and honesty began to flow. As the minutes turned into hours, they began diving into each other's past.

He had grown up in Fort Walton Beach and spent most of his free time at the water's edge. He never attended college but still earned enough to travel the coasts. He had two younger brothers and was raised by a single dad who was tough but had a tender heart. His brothers leaned on him for emotional support and an occasional bed to crash on. He said all the right things.

She kept her past wrapped as tight as her grandmother was with her wallet. Tiny, meaningless details with no real wallop. Yes, she grew up in a good home. Yes, she was a cheerleader for the basketball team. Yes, she was the rush chair of her college sorority. Well, that one was a lie.

The night had been going so well....

She remembered the exact words he had said that night. The night that her feelings morphed from this is a possibility to it's never going to happen.

"He's not good enough. He'll never be good enough." He had said it nonchalantly, not realizing the impact of his words.

But tonight was not about then. It was about now.

She stood up, grabbed her iPhone from the night-stand. She peeked out the first-floor window and confirmed the fishing cart was still parked on side of the house, barely visible under the glow of the porch light. She stepped back and pulled the shades in case the neighbors were passing by. She held the phone out in front of her, camera app open, finger poised.

He looked so peaceful.

She wanted to remember how good he looked, right now. She held her finger perfectly still above the button. She wished her phone could capture his smell, the ocean night air, and his sun-kissed skin.

She cherished the moment of silence.

The quiet after the storm.

It's one thing to enjoy the pinnacle, but she relished in the after.

Remembering how he sounded and what he said.

Reliving the feeling of his muscles under her arms.

The appreciation mixed with disbelief at the raw energy exerted.

She lowered her finger from its hovered position. She was tempted. The scene was perfect.

She wanted something tangible. A photo would be great, but she wanted something she could hold. Something she could feel to remember this day. This night. This once-in-a-lifetime memory.

His fingerprints on my skin, the scratches down my back.

The blue and black color forming on his skin.

Those will be seared in my mind forever.

Now? It was time to erase herself from this evening.

Thank goodness she worked out too.

He was going to be heavy.

The Panhandle Predicament

The Panhandle Mystery Series by Kendra Hoey
Book One

One Discovery Changes Everything

Why did Trina Scotsdale fall down the Detective rabbit hole?

Retirement should be a walk in the park, but Trina Scotsdale finds her quaint life turned upside down after she discovers a skeleton in Point Washington State Park soon after moving back to her parents' beach bungalow in the picturesque coastal community of Grayton Beach, Florida. The discovery jars long-buried memories, awakening in Trina a compulsion to assist in the identification of the victim. Inner demons stirred by digging into the past collide with the present-day investigations, turning Trina's quest to solve the mystery into a journey of self-discovery. As the identity of the victim comes into focus, Trina finds herself in a Panhandle predicament.

Author Biography

Kendra Hoey

After raising three kids and juggling a full-time career, I left the corporate world in 2021 and moved to Florida. I quickly developed an immediate connection to the Scenic Highway 30A community, which unconditionally promotes entrepreneurial pursuits and artist creativity. Inspired by local southern authors and my own lifetime of fiction consumption, I was unexpectedly inspired to write using the charm and uniqueness of my small beach town as the backdrop for a mystery series.

I wrote the *Panhandle Mystery Series* to explore one woman's drive to achieve a lifelong dream of solving mysteries, while at the same time struggling with her own inner demons. In the process, I hope I have created stories that both convey the breathtaking beauty and serenity of the Florida Panhandle while providing readers with engaging mysteries.

Those who already love 30A will recognize many restaurants, state parks and community organizations. For those who have not yet ventured to the Panhandle, I hope I sparked your curiosity.